Tour

into

Danger

For Penelope,
good luck in
everything!

Tour Into Danger

Lea Tassie

Lea Tassie

Electric eBook Publishing

Tour Into Danger by Lea Tassie
Copyright © 2003 Lea Tassie

Manufactured in Canada.

National Library of Canada Cataloguing in Publication Data

Tassie, Lea, 1935-
 Tour into danger / Lea Tassie.

ISBN 1-55352-076-9

I. Title.
PS8589.A8732T68 2003   C813'.6   C2003-910800-7

Electric eBook Publishing
6369 Oak Street
Powell River, B.C., Canada V8A 4L8
http://www.electricebookpublishing.com

For Al

Mahalo nui loa!

PROLOGUE

Greg's car was still in the garage.

Angela parked, heart thumping and palms moist. He should have been at the restaurant by now, giving her the whole day to think up a plausible lie. She let herself in and put the change from her pocket into the two foot high glass vase beside the fireplace.

It was stupid putting money on view like that, but Greg seemed fascinated by the coins. He often put his hand in and let them trickle through his fingers. There must be close to five thousand dollars in the vase by now.

"Where have you been?" Greg's voice. Angry. She smiled brightly to hide the way her body shrank from him.

His slap knocked her sideways, burning her cheek and bruising her elbow on the rough stone of the fireplace. He was poised to strike again, his heavy black eyebrows pulled down in a scowl, thick lips taut with fury.

Anger roughened Angela's voice. "Why do you have to know what I do every minute of the day?"

"You're my wife." He moved closer, forcing her to tilt her head back to look at his face. "Answer me!"

His rage brought memories of barely healed bruises, a broken arm. And rising fear. It was hard to believe this was the same man who'd courted her with Caribbean vacations and diamonds little more than four years ago.

If she told him the truth, he'd tear her apart.

"I was shopping."

"This early?" Greg sneered. "You?"

It was true she didn't bother getting up until mid-morning most days. Mrs Hanson, the housekeeper, got nine-year-old Rob ready for school. But she had to convince Greg she wasn't lying or he'd break more of her bones.

She'd have to tell more lies to her sister, too, and Penny was getting suspicious. She'd already wondered out loud why Angela was so clumsy all of a sudden, falling down stairs and banging into doors.

She should tell her sister about the beatings; Penny had fought her battles all through school. But Penny was too impulsive; she'd wade in with feet and fists—and lawyers—and Greg would kill all three of them.

Greg's hand clamped around her throat. "I asked you a question, you little slut! Where were you?"

Fear ballooned into terror. She couldn't think. She was shaking so much she could barely stand.

"I took my diamond necklace to be fixed."

"Why now? Why first thing in the morning?"

"Because of the party tonight. The jeweler said he had to have it early or it wouldn't be ready. I thought you'd want me to wear it."

Greg's hand loosened on her throat.

She relaxed a little. She might have made it as an actress after all. She'd done plenty of acting the last couple of years.

He'd kill her if he found out she'd pawned it. The money, a ridiculously small amount, was in her bag. She had to get more money soon, before he hit Rob again. Just a little more. Then she and Rob would be on their way to Toronto. She had friends there she could trust.

"You never told me the necklace was damaged."

"I thought you'd be angry. It was my fault."

He let go of her and straightened his tie. "Accidents happen." He picked up his briefcase. "I'll be at the restaurant the rest of the day. Give me the claim ticket for the necklace and I'll pick it up this afternoon."

Her knees almost buckled. "He didn't give me one."

Greg put the briefcase down in a deliberate fashion that sent shivers along her spine.

"No claim ticket, Angela? For a necklace worth thousands?" He strode across the room toward her, arms swinging loosely at his sides. She put a hand on the mantel to brace herself.

"Liar! I want the truth. You and that useless sister of yours are up to something, aren't you?"

The crack of his open hand across her face stunned her and she staggered.

He'd hit Rob that way a month ago. She grabbed the poker and swung it at his head. But she was too close. The poker struck his upper arm.

He roared. His fists, closed and iron hard, smashed into her face. She felt her legs collapse, felt the back of her head crack against the hearth.

Greg kicked her in the ribs. "Get up!"

She didn't move. Blood seeped through her blonde hair, spreading over the hearth.

"Angie..." He knelt and took her hand. It was limp.

"Angie!" Her eyes were open, staring.

She was still. Too still.

Carl Fredericks heaved his lanky six-foot-two frame off the sofa and picked up the phone. "Yeah?" He listened, his breath quickening. "Why should I get involved in your personal problems?" He'd always thought Greg was a loser, but what he'd just heard proved his boss was the prize scumbag of all time.

"Yeah, I can see where you going to prison would put the business down the tubes."

He couldn't afford to lose what Greg's drug dealing brought in. The Plan was so close to being a reality that just one more year ought to do it. Then he'd be gone and nobody'd find him where he was going.

"Okay, I'll be right over."

Carl put the phone down and considered the methods of disposing of a body. If they did it right and Greg stayed cool—and kept his mouth shut—it would be okay.

But would Greg stay cool? He'd killed his wife, which wasn't cool at all. Why hadn't he just booted her out?

He ran a comb through his pale blond hair and hid his ice-blue eyes behind aviator sunglasses. His cocker spaniel, Wildwood Butterscotch Candy, bounced around his feet, wriggling with excitement. He picked her up and rubbed her ears while she tried to lick his face.

"I won't be long, girl. Then we'll go to the park."

He put her down. "Gotta find you a boyfriend pretty soon. Some big horny dog with a pedigree to match. No SPCA strays for my Candy girl." Which reminded him he'd been meaning to send some cash to the SPCA. Next week would do; he had to get Greg off his back first.

ONE

The shouting was getting louder. Rob slid out of bed and edged the door open. Didn't matter if it creaked; old Godzilla Greg wouldn't hear it with all that yelling down there in the living room. What were they doing, him and Carl? Watching a video? Having a fight? They wouldn't be doing that if Mom was here.

His stomach hurt. Why didn't she tell him she was going away? Or take him with her? Was she mad at him? She'd been gone two whole weeks and never even talked to him on the phone.

When he was little he'd asked her for a new Dad because his old one had died before he was born. He'd been so happy when she married Greg and he had a Dad like all the other kids. Just showed how dumb he'd been. Greg wasn't a real Dad; he was ugly and mean, just like Godzilla.

Rob crept on hands and knees to the railing that protected the second floor gallery from the open living room below. He lay flat on the floor and peered over the edge, hoping Greg wouldn't look up and catch him out of bed.

Two guys were down there with Greg. He knew Carl, standing with his elbow on the mantel, but not the other guy. Carl came around a lot, but he and Greg always went to the basement to play pool, so it was hard to tell what he was like. Greg was beside the couch, where Rob had dropped his sports bag when he came home from the gym. Greg would be mad at him for leaving his stuff lying around.

The stranger was skinny like Carl, but shorter, with long brown hair in a pony tail. He stood in the center of the room, waving his hands around. "You guys are ripping me off! Screwing around with the stuff."

"Take it easy, Larry!" Greg's voice boomed. It felt like it was right in his ear and Rob shivered. "Relax! We don't cut junk more than anybody else."

They were talking about heroin. Rob knew heroin was really bad. A policeman from the drug section had talked to the whole school about it right before summer break.

The guy called Larry was dancing around like he had a wasp up his pant leg. "Yeah? Talk to my customers!"

"How do we know you haven't been cutting it yourself to make a few more bucks?" Rob didn't like Carl's voice. It was kind of smart-ass.

"Yeah," Greg said, "Carl's right. You want to cheat your customers, that's your problem."

"I'll show you who's cheating!" Larry yelled. He pulled a knife from his boot.

Rob's mouth felt dry; the cop shows he watched on TV had stuff like this and somebody always got killed.

Larry lunged at Carl, the knife held low, point up. Carl just stood there like he was frozen. Why didn't he fight back? Or run?

There was a strange hollow thump. Larry staggered and fell. Then a funny sharp smell.

Greg had a gun in his hand.

Rob gasped, a low keening coming up out of his throat before he could stop it.

Greg looked up, right at him.

Rob wriggled backwards to the wall and ran into his room. He got into bed as Greg's feet thudded on the stairs. Greg came in, snapping the bright ceiling light on.

"You were out of bed, weren't you?" Greg's black eyes glared at him.

"Yeah." He could feel sweat running down his sides.

"Pretty realistic, huh?"

"What?"

Greg yanked the covers up over him. "We watched a movie earlier. They did a lousy job on the killing scene and we decided we could do it better. That's what you saw."

"Oh. It looked awful scary."

"Larry's a good actor. Go back to sleep, Rob. I mean it. Your mother will be upset if you don't do as I say." Greg's eyes were like a freezing black night.

"Okay," he said to the eyes. "Sure looked real, though." Was Larry still on the floor? There weren't any sounds coming from downstairs.

"It was supposed to. And you were supposed to be asleep. Why did you get up?"

"The noise woke me," he said, trying to sound sleepy.

Don't let him get mad. Don't let him hit me.

Greg stood there, staring at him, his shadow dark and heavy across the bed, then went to the door. "Good night."

"G'night," Rob said. The door clicked shut.

He stayed still, listening, but they were being really quiet. Did he dare get up and open the door a crack? What if Greg was waiting for him?

He'd counted off fifteen minutes on the clock by his bed when he heard the door handle turn. He closed his eyes and burrowed deeper under the covers.

Footsteps came across the room and stopped beside the bed. Rob tried to breathe like he was sleeping. There was silence for a long time.

"Rob? You awake?"

He didn't answer.

Another silence. Then the footsteps went away and the door closed again. Softly this time.

What were they doing? He could hear their voices and they seemed to be moving around. He hoped Greg wouldn't look in the garbage and find the football sweater cut up in little pieces. Old Godzilla had made him play hockey all winter and now it was football. He hated chasing the ball and getting tackled. He was going to say he'd lost the sweater, so maybe Greg wouldn't make him play any more.

Rob was out of bed and halfway across the room when the front door slammed. The living room was almost dark; only a night light burned on the gallery.

Thick carpet muffled his footfalls as he ran around to the other side of the gallery and into a spare bedroom. He edged to one side of the window and looked down.

It was hard to see. The outside lights were off and the street lamp didn't help much. Heaving and grunting, Greg and Carl were loading a long bundle into the trunk of Greg's Cadillac. Then they got in the car and eased out onto the side street. They turned left and the headlights came on as the car went up the hill.

Rob ran back to his room and sat on the bed. Had Greg really meant it about doing a movie scene? But why did he have a gun? If he was acting, he'd just point his finger and make out like that was a gun. That's how he and Simon did it when they clowned around pretending they were cops.

There was one way to find out.

He went downstairs to where Larry had fallen. It was too dark to see anything and he didn't dare turn the lights on. He squatted and felt around with his hand until he hit a damp, sticky patch. He wiped his hand on his pajamas and ran upstairs again.

In his room, Rob flipped the bedside light on. The crumpled flannel was smeared with red. He felt like throwing up. Why wasn't his Mom here? She'd know what to do. He scrubbed away tears on the sleeve of his pajama top. Crying was little kid stuff.

He could call 911. But what if Greg got back before the cops came? Or arrived while they were here? He'd be mad. Not just mad, he'd go ballistic.

He could run away. Not to Gramma's, though; she thought Greg was gold. She'd probably even phone Greg to come and get him. His thumb tasted weird and he rubbed it on his pajamas. His Mom said he was too old to suck his thumb. He had to try harder not to do it.

If he ran away, Greg would know he didn't believe that stuff about movie scenes. Maybe Greg knew he didn't believe it anyway. Would Greg shoot him, too? The bad guys in the movies shot anybody that got in their way.

He could go to Simon's. No, Greg knew Simon was his best buddy and that's where he would go first. Maybe Aunt Penny could hide him in that theater where she used to work.

Rob dressed in his favorite jeans with the torn knees, an old T-shirt, sneakers and a windbreaker in case it rained. From behind the books on his shelf, he took the thin leather wallet that held his Mom's rainy-day money. It fit neatly into the zippered pocket of his jacket.

He turned the light out in his room, ran down the stairs to the front door, then stopped. What if his Mom came back? What if she came back tonight?

For a moment he wavered. If he ran away, there'd be nobody to warn her about what Greg had done. If he stayed, Greg might shoot him like he had Larry. Rob opened the door and froze. A tall, dark shadow was hurrying along the walk toward him.

Penny Davis opened the back door of her parents' house and stepped into a kitchen filled with the rich, dark aroma of warm chocolate. She put her box of groceries on the counter beside a rack of cooling chocolate chip cookies.

"I'll put those things away later," her mother said. "Get a plate for the cookies and I'll make tea." The kettle began its muttering whistle and Dora unplugged it before the noise rose to a scream. There was the rush and sizzle of boiling water, then the lid of the teapot clinking home.

Dora laid a cautioning fingertip on Penny's wrist. "Your father's low. Got turned down for another job today."

Her father, an assistant bank manager caught in the crossfire of a holdup eleven years ago, had lived in a wheelchair—and been out of work—ever since.

"I hope this trip of yours to Toronto turns out to be worthwhile," Dora said. "Though I know your father's going to miss you dreadfully."

Penny carried the cookies into the living room. Her father's smile was a poor imitation of the real thing. "I blew it again," he said.

He wants to have a pity party, she thought. How can I deny him? He's trying so hard to be a breadwinner.

She knelt beside him and took his cold, bony hands in hers. "I know it's tough, Dad. Something will break soon."

"For you, too, Penny. Live theater is flourishing in Toronto; there's bound to be a job for you there."

Whatever it was, it had to pay well enough so she could send Dora money every month. In spite of her guilt, she was eager to go. It would be an adventure, flying to another city to live and work.

Penny looked at her father. He was so thin and haggard. If he did get lucky and find a job, could he work an eight-hour day? His doctor had told him the nerve damage caused by the bullet would worsen over the years.

Dora rested her hand on her husband's shoulder. "I made your favorite cookies."

Reg's face brightened. "Darling, you spoil me." He turned to Penny. "The police were here this morning."

"What was it this time?" Penny asked.

"Same old story." His hands lay passive and resigned in his lap. "They want to know where the money's hidden."

Penny slammed her teacup down, splashing tea into the saucer. "Why can't they leave you alone? Why do we have a police force too lazy to track down the real robbers?"

"I ask myself that every time I get into this chair."

The police had interrogated her only a few times. She found it odd that she felt more resentment than her father ever showed.

Perhaps patience grew with age.

"Reg, darling, we'll get by; we always have." Dora sat on the end of the old green couch beside his chair, her hand on his. "We have each other."

Penny turned away, looked at the photo of Angela and Rob on the mantel. Her sister had a delicate, blonde beauty that made people stop and stare. Too bad the serendipity of gene shuffling hadn't done the same for her own looks.

The photo had been taken in May, on Rob's ninth birthday. Her nephew, blue eyes bright, brown hair looking as if it was never combed, leaned forward to blow out the candles. She'd asked him what his wish was.

"If I tell, it won't come true."

Her sister didn't tell her anything either. She hadn't said a word about going to Toronto to visit friends. Penny turned to her parents. "Have you heard from Angela?"

"Not a word," Dora said. "I suppose she's too busy having a good time. Can't be anything else since she didn't take Rob. Greg's a saint for putting up with her."

"I don't think so," Penny said. "When I phoned Rob last night, he said he was all alone in the house."

Try as she might, Penny couldn't warm to Greg. Though he seemed to adore Angela, there was no doubt he thought it was his right to dictate her sister's every thought and movement. He didn't like her either. It was partly her own fault. She'd been far too outspoken in his presence.

"Are you sure Rob was telling the truth?" asked Dora. "Greg said the housekeeper would live in while Angela was away."

"Lying isn't one of Rob's problems," her father said.

They often discussed Rob's problems these days. Until a couple of years ago, he'd been a likeable, exuberant little boy. But lately he'd become destructive. He ripped at his clothing and wrote on everything, including himself. And he didn't smile any more.

The last time Penny had seen him was a month ago, tramping all over the living room carpet in his skates. Angela had been incredibly patient. How did she manage it? The responsibility of raising a child seemed overwhelming and, the older Penny got, the more afraid of it she became.

"I'd better go say goodbye to him," Penny said. "I should have done it before but I was afraid Greg would be there. He always acts like a wounded bull when he sees me."

"Don't be petty," Dora said, her voice sharp. "He's a good father and a good provider. And he was willing to marry Angela in spite of her past."

He obviously had the means to be a good provider, but the only way he could earn a halo in her eyes was to toss some of that money in the direction of her parents.

Her mother's reference to Angela's past life hurt. If Penny had done a better job of bringing up Angela while Dora concentrated on her wheelchair-bound husband, maybe her sister wouldn't have a "past."

"Rob's just going through a phase," her father said. "It seems like Greg can't do enough for him."

Dora rose and gave Penny an awkward hug.

"Penny," her father held out his hand and pulled her close, "I'll miss you. You take care now."

After the goodbyes, she headed west along Marine Drive. It was almost dark, much later than she'd thought; she'd have to hurry. She would miss her father a lot. No more cribbage, no more evenings gossiping about plays and actors. She'd tried to get him a role in a Westport Players' production, but nothing had come of it.

Penny knew Dora wouldn't miss her that much. Her mother had always put Reg first. She envied them—not many people were lucky enough to find their soul mates and a closeness that didn't seem to need a family to complete it.

A soul mate and an ideal marriage would be fine things. But could she handle kids as well? Children deserved unqualified love and acceptance. It would be cruelly unfair to have a child if she couldn't love it properly.

The third traffic light in a row turned red. She hoped Greg wasn't home. In the last two weeks she'd gone to his restaurant half a dozen times for news of her sister. He'd been polite but his tone said Penny should stop bothering him. Too bad. If she weren't flying to Toronto herself, he'd be getting daily visits until Angela came back.

She hated goodbyes. Well, the worst goodbye was over. Now all she had to do was get through the one with Rob.

Jack Kinkaid strode through the noisy, cluttered bull pen of the Vice and Drugs Section into Detective-Sergeant Ian Baker's office. If he could convince his boss that this trip to Toronto was a waste of time, he'd go home and unpack. Maybe varnish the driftwood sculpture he'd been working on. Or plan how to nail Greg Moller.

Ian looked up from the pile of paper on his desk. "Where have you been? I expected you in here by nine."

Ian's paunch was bursting the buttons off his shirt; one hung by a thread. His sandy hair seemed to have receded a whole inch in the last month. Job pressure and too much beer, Jack thought.

"I've got plenty of time. I'm booked on the midnight flight." He pulled a wooden chair away from the wall, swung it around and sat with his arms resting on the back, his long legs stretched under Ian's desk. "Heard the radio call on the Gastown homicide so I went and had a look. Big mistake."

"Yeah, that was ugly." Ian slumped and wearily rubbed his forehead. "Second drug-related death this month."

The first one had been young, too. Were they ever going to make any headway in this war? As soon as one dealer was behind bars, another turned up to take his place.

The murdered girl had had a knife protruding from her chest and blood splattered from her heavily made-up face to her leather mini skirt. The detective on site pointed to the needle tracks on her arms "Probably her pimp. Punishing her for taking drugs instead of cash and went too far. Her ID said she was fifteen."

"So why am I wasting time tailing this Davis woman to Toronto? She could be going on vacation instead of delivering drugs for Moller."

"You know we have to follow every lead." Ian pushed a photograph across the desk. "This is her. Penny Joanne Davis. Jakubowski got a shot of her coming out of Moller's restaurant."

The woman had intelligent blue eyes, an open expression and wore her blonde hair in feathery bangs and a pony tail. "Girl-next-door type except for that stubborn chin." He wondered if she was tall. He had a thing for tall women.

"Girl next door? Yeah, right! Terry Wellburn is still convinced her old man was the mover on that bank heist eleven years ago."

Jack nodded. "I know, I talked to Terry last night. He was celebrating the Adam Lister bust. Bought me a beer at The Swan."

"The credit union robbery on the east side?"

"Yeah. Talk about luck! Patrol car stopped to check the doors and caught Lister with a briefcase full of cash."

"You should be so lucky with this Davis broad."

"I'd feel luckier in Vancouver, chasing Moller."

"Don't push it, Kinkaid!"

"Okay, okay. You're the boss." He should have known better than to argue. "Who's tailing her now?"

"Parker. You can take over from him at..." The telephone rang. "Barbara! What can I do you for?"

Jack mouthed, "I'm not here!"

"He was around awhile ago. You want to leave a message? Okay, I'll tell him." Ian put the phone down. "What's up with you two?"

"Nothing's up. We're history."

Ian looked disappointed. "She dump you?"

He'd planned to have this discussion later, over a beer. "No. She wants me back."

"So you dumped her. Running away again?"

He wasn't keen on admitting he'd been a sucker, but what were friends for? "She told me she was pregnant, so I said let's get married."

"Always figured you for a family man." Ian grumbled about the hassle of a wife and five kids, but he was always buying candy and presents for them. Ian could afford the luxury of a family; he had a safe slot in administration. "Or were you just doing the right thing by a lady?"

"She's not a lady. And she's not pregnant." He fingered his mustache. "Found out after I bought the diamond."

"Too bad, I liked Barbara. Didn't think she'd pull that on you." Ian shoved his chair back and propped his feet on the bottom drawer of his desk. "I've introduced you to lots of nice girls. Sara and Kelly. Oh, yeah, and JoAnne. Then Barbara."

"I appreciate it. You've got good taste when it comes to women."

"But you ducked out on all of them."

"Yeah." Jack aligned the papers on the desk into neat rows. "Too bad they all wanted to get married."

"About time you quit hiding behind that 'line of fire' garbage, isn't it? After we bust Moller, we'll take a few cases of beer out on my boat and drown that theory of yours about street cops staying single." Ian glanced at his watch. "Now, get your butt off that chair or you'll miss your plane."

Penny unlocked her apartment door and Rob scuttled into the room ahead of her, his face still as white as when she'd met him at his front door.

At first she hadn't believed his story about Greg killing a man, afraid that he'd started telling lies as a new way of misbehaving. Then he took her into the house to look at the stain on the carpet. Ketchup, she'd thought, it has to be ketchup. Until she knelt and touched the stain with one finger and raised it to her nose.

The unmistakable smell made her mouth go dry and turned her knees to wet putty. She'd wobbled to her feet, one thought in mind. Get out of here! She'd driven as fast as she dared, Rob silent beside her.

The familiarity of her apartment made her feel a little more in control. She put her arm around Rob's shoulders, unusually muscular for such a skinny kid. "Don't worry, Rob. We'll figure a way out of this." He wriggled away and fastened the door chain.

Two things were clear. Greg had murdered someone. And when he discovered Rob was missing, he'd come looking for him. She couldn't let her nephew go home with a murderer.

What if she'd arrived ten minutes earlier and walked into the middle of the killing? Right now she might be at the bottom of Burrard Inlet with something heavy tied around her ankles. Her mouth felt dry again.

"Where did Greg go?"

Rob swallowed, lower lip trembling. "I don't know. I think he and Carl put that Larry guy in the trunk of his car. Can we go some place he won't find me?"

What could she do with him? He had to be with people he could rely on. She didn't qualify. No job, no money, no time. Plus she didn't have a clue how to handle him. She yanked the elastic off her pony tail and tried to think.

No sense phoning the police. When they heard the name Davis, they'd swoop in like scavenging seagulls and probably arrest her for kidnaping the boy. She could drop him off at her parents' house on the way to the airport. No, that was the first place Greg would look.

A horrible thought struck her.

"Does Greg know you saw him kill that man?"

"Yeah." Rob was at her bookcase, pulling books out to the edge and pushing them back in.

She took a step toward him, the implications all too clear. Greg would come looking for Rob, not because he wanted his stepson home where he belonged, but because Rob had seen him kill.

Penny took two more steps, put her arms around Rob and held him tight. Rob could testify against his stepfather. Could put him in prison for life.

Greg was smooth as oiled glass. He'd find it easy to con the cops into believing that Rob had had a nightmare.

For a moment she wanted to curl up in a ball and pretend none of this was real. But she had to protect Rob. Angela would never forgive her if anything happened to him.

She had to get him away, out of Vancouver. Her own seat to Toronto was booked; shouldn't be any problem getting one for Rob, too. So what was one more charge on her Visa bill? He was her sister's child.

She held him at arm's length. "I'm catching the midnight flight to Toronto. You're coming with me."

"All right!"

It was a relief to see the color coming back into his face. Now that she had a plan, she felt better, too. But what would happen when Greg found out she'd taken Rob?

"Are we going to see my Mom?"

"Yes."

"Far out!"

Once he was off her hands, she'd get back to the original point of her trip. She could use Angela's theater contacts in Toronto in her search for work.

"Do you know how to find her?" Rob asked.

"Her friends will know where she is." Greg had said she was visiting the Wades, people Penny had met before.

Penny hurried into the bedroom. "Come and talk to me, Rob. Do you have any money?" They'd need every cent.

"I took Mom's rainy-day money that she hid in my room. I was going to take a taxi here."

She blinked, surprised by the unexpected warmth of knowing he'd planned to come to her for help.

Penny snapped the locks on her big suitcase. What was Angela really doing in Toronto, anyway? Visiting and shopping trips had never been her style. More like her to go to Vegas with fifty dollars in her bag and hope to finance the stay with her winnings. Four years of marriage to Greg couldn't have changed her that much.

"Rob, what did your Mom say when she phoned? Did she say

when she was coming home?"

Rob's glance fell and his lips quivered. "She never talked to me. She never even said goodbye when she left."

Hadn't said goodbye? Penny had a hard time believing it. Angela had been a doting mother from the minute she knew she was pregnant. She'd seemed restless and unhappy lately but there was no doubt she adored Rob.

"She must have had a good reason not to tell you what she was up to, Rob. We'll find out when we get to Toronto."

"I'll lock all the windows, Aunt Penny."

"Good. Then you can phone for a taxi while I finish packing my other suitcase."

At the last moment she remembered her sister's package. The last time she saw Greg, he'd asked her to pick up a necklace Angela had taken in for repairs. Half the size of a small box of chocolates and wrapped in red and silver gift paper, it fit into the suitcase easily enough. She hoped it was worth a bundle; Angela would need money. Or would she go back to Greg in spite of what had happened?

In the taxi, Rob asked, "Did you tell anybody you were going to Toronto?"

"No. Yes, I did. I told Greg that I might go but I didn't say when."

"So when he finds out you're not home, he'll know where we are."

He'd figured that out a lot faster than she would—proof that he watched more cop shows than was good for him. Right now that was a bonus.

"He won't know for sure. And by the time he finds out, we'll have left Toronto." Rob might feel better if she mentioned calling the police. "The first thing I'll do when we land is phone the Vancouver police. They'll stop him from following us."

The sun might come up in the west tomorrow, too. The cops wouldn't care what a nine-year-old said, especially when he was Reg Davis' grandson. They'd never believed anything her father said. She hoped Angela's rainy-day stash was big enough to hide them for a few weeks.

They crossed the Oak Street bridge, Rob clinging to her hand. "Aunt Penny, didn't you tell Gramps and Gramma?"

"Yes, of course."

"They'll tell Greg where we went."

He was right. "We'll just have to leave Toronto right away, then."

When the taxi arrived at Vancouver International Airport, it was after ten and fully dark. The heat of the July day had dissipated in the salty tang of a sea breeze. Penny glanced at the cars pulling up behind the taxi and her knees went weak again. Suppose Greg had followed them to the apartment? What if he were close behind them now?

Rob was looking at the cars, too. He tugged the smaller suitcase away from her. "Hurry up, Aunt Penny."

The lineup at the check-in counter was short and in a few moments she put the luggage on the scale and showed her ticket to the slim man behind the counter.

"I'd like to buy another ticket," she said, indicating Rob. "For my nephew. Could we have seats together?"

"Sorry, you'll have to arrange that at the sales desk." He glanced at the clock behind him. "You'd better hurry."

"Story of my life, all this red tape." Penny hefted her suitcases. Dodging through milling crowds and piles of luggage, she found the sales desk and repeated her request.

The sales agent had blood-red finger nails and a bored expression. She bent to her computer for a moment. "Sorry, there are no seats available on that flight."

"No seats on a midnight flight?"

"That's what I said."

Penny groaned. "Now what?" She swung away from the counter, banging a suitcase into the knees of a man behind her. He staggered. She dropped the case and reached out to steady him.

"I'm so sorry! Are you all right?"

"I'll live." He adjusted the two cameras that hung like a bulky necklace on his rumpled gray suit.

Probably a tourist. He had a deep voice, the kind she loved to listen to when it belonged to a well-trained actor. She took a closer look. He was well over six feet, with deep-set gray eyes, dark brown hair and full mustache. A faded scar creasing his left temple and the bump on the bridge of his nose made him look like a boxer. Or the captain of a tramp ship. She imagined him with a white peaked cap set at a rakish angle, sailing to exotic ports.

He smiled then, his reserved expression transformed into—what, the lead actor? No, not the lead. More like the boy-next-door who'd fallen out of a tree while trying to rescue a kitten. Charming and vulnerable and altogether too much like a kid needing his mother. She already had one of those; she didn't want another. And he'd probably never been on a ship in his life.

She repeated her apology and added, "I must learn to watch where I'm going."

"It's okay," he said. "Forget it."

Penny led Rob several feet away, out of the jostling flow of traffic.

"What are we gonna do?" Rob asked.

She didn't know, but she couldn't tell him she was floundering. "I can't let you go to Toronto by yourself."

He was sucking his thumb again. "I don't care where we go," Rob said. "Just so we don't have to stay here."

Penny rested one hand on his shoulder for a moment, feeling the fragility of his young bones. The trusting way he looked at her made her even more nervous. What if she failed him?

Penny herded Rob and the suitcases back to the sales desk. The man with the gray eyes had moved a little distance away, his face buried in a newspaper. "Where else can we go?" she asked, trying to control the urgency in her voice. "We're packed and we're here and we want to get on a plane. Together. Tonight. It doesn't have to be Toronto."

The woman clicked away at her keyboard. After a moment, she said, "How about Hawaii? Three o'clock? I can get you two seats on that flight."

It was the wrong direction. They'd be twice as far from Angela. But they couldn't stay here.

"Fine. That'll do just fine." She handed over her Toronto ticket and her Visa card.

The woman completed the tickets. "Flight 457. You can check your luggage through in about half an hour. Have a good vacation."

Yeah, sure. She was supposed to be heading east to find a job and a sister who could be, given her past, in some kind of trouble. Instead she was going west to Hawaii. Running from a murderer and accompanied by a frightened child, who might, if she said or did the wrong thing, poke holes in the fuselage. Sounded like a great vacation.

She sat on the edge of a lounge in the passenger area. Rob kept looking over his shoulder. She found herself doing the same. But Greg couldn't have followed them. He'd have confronted her by now, demanded the boy be returned to his custody.

"You want something to read, Rob?" He needed some distraction; his thin body looked taut and he'd ripped the hole in the knee of his jeans to twice its original size.

"A comic book? And a pop?"

After that it was time to check the luggage in. Back in the lounge, Penny finally put down her magazine. She needed to know everything that had happened at Greg's house tonight so she'd have a better idea what she was up against.

"Rob, let's find a corner where we can talk without anyone hearing us." She searched the concourse until she found a deserted alcove. "Tell me exactly what happened."

He told her in meticulous detail and her imagination provided vivid pictures to go with his words.

Greg had not only killed a man, he was dealing drugs. She had often wondered how he could live so well on the income from Gregoire's. The restaurant was popular but it only minted meals, not gold.

Had Angela found out? Was that why she kept a rainy-day stash in Rob's room? That would explain the Toronto trip; she was planning to leave Greg. She'd be looking for a place to stay and work. Then she'd come back for Rob.

Rob shifted from one foot to the other. "Can we go back to the passenger lounge? It's closer to where we have to get on the plane." He darted away without waiting for an answer and Penny had to jog to keep up with him.

When their flight was announced, Rob was on his feet and running before the message had ended. They were first in line for the security check.

The x-ray beeped loudly at Penny's bag and her face grew warm.

A female security guard took her to one side and made her dump out the bag's contents. The woman's breath smelled of liquor.

"I keep meaning to clean it out, but I never do."

"This is what did it." The guard held up Penny's Swiss Army pocket knife. "Put the bag through again. What do you carry the knife for?"

"To peel apples," Penny said over her shoulder. She'd never get the knife back. Not that it mattered. Turning her head, she found herself staring at a brown mustache barely a foot away and looked up into the gray eyes of the man in the crumpled navy suit.

He backed up a step and grinned. "Hey, don't hit me!" Penny flushed again. If this was boy-next-door humor, she could do without it.

"I won't. I'm sorry." Biting her lip, she put the bag on the conveyor. When it came through, she picked it up and turned, almost stepping on the guard's foot.

The guard held her closed hand just inside Penny's bag and Penny felt the impact of something falling inside it.

"I shouldn't do this," the guard said, "but I like apples myself. Enjoy!"

When they were in their seats, clear of the crush of people clogging the aisle, Penny squeezed Rob's hand. "Feel better now?"

"Uh-huh." His face was still drawn and his eyes were bleak. She wished he were young enough that cuddling would make him feel secure.

As the plane lifted off the runway she felt an incongruous fizz of excitement. Well, why not? She'd always wanted to travel and just because they were on the run didn't mean they couldn't enjoy Hawaii for a day or two. Greg had no idea where they were and it would take him a while to find out. Maybe he never would.

The plane thundered into the dark sky and banked to the left. For a few moments, Vancouver's great sprawl of twinkling lights spread below. How long would it be before she saw it again?

The movie was a love story but it might keep Rob's mind off Greg. Hers, too, she hoped.

When the film ended with the hero and heroine finally in each other's arms, Penny sighed. Fun to watch, but real life wasn't like that. Having the perfect relationship meant finding exactly the right guy. She'd hadn't come anywhere close yet.

Rob was asleep. She eased his headphones off, glad that he was getting a temporary rest from his fears.

Her thoughts kept returning to Greg. His impeccable dress and smooth manner had never rung true. But she'd assumed his urbane mask covered an astute and perhaps ruthless businessman, not a drug-dealing murderer. Why hadn't she let her uneasiness about him prod her into a closer examination? But making assumptions about people usually worked. It saved time, simplified the complex art of living.

The interior of the plane was dim and quiet now. Most of the passengers were trying to sleep. Penny couldn't. She had to tell her baby sister that she'd married a murderer.

TWO

The 747 banked to the right, the windows framing a vignette of Diamond Head, lush and tropical in the dawn light. Most of the passengers were craning for a glimpse of the island paradise. Jack Kinkaid copied them; he was supposed to be a tourist after all.

As the jet made its final approach, he watched the woman and the boy, two rows ahead and across the aisle. The kid's nose was pressed against the window and she must have unbuckled her seat belt because she was almost on top of him. She was putting on a pretty good tourist act herself.

If she hadn't nearly crippled him with her suitcase, he'd have stuck to his plan of being anonymous, part of the usual Hawaiian scenery. But she'd stared at his face with such interest that he knew he had to change his strategy.

He'd pretend she turned him on, so he wouldn't spook her by showing up everywhere she went. Plus his "cute but helpless" act, which always seemed to work well with women. If Ms Davis had normal mothering instincts, she'd soon tuck him under her wing. The scheme wasn't perfect, but there was no time to come up with anything better.

He'd tried to approach her an hour ago, but she'd frozen him out. Funny how she'd clammed up and retreated when he smiled at her in the airport. Probably brushing him off so he wouldn't be in the way when she made the pickup.

Her abrupt change of destination bothered him. No way she could have spotted him as a cop. Maybe she'd been laying a false trail by booking for Toronto, or got new instructions at the last minute.

Forget it for now. He needed a shave and a shower and he had to phone Ian. It would help if Ian had found a lead on Ms Davis' Hawaiian contact. Meanwhile, all he could do was sit on her tail. Had she brought the boy with her as cover? It was an old ploy but still worked sometimes. She certainly looked like an ordinary tourist. Well, not that ordinary. He watched as she moved into the aisle, blonde hair cascading around her shoulders. She was tall, probably five eight or nine. Too bad she was a drug courier; the idea of being tucked under her wing was appealing.

He'd have to play it carefully; he didn't want to scare off her contact and delay the pickup. The sooner they got hard evidence of a link to Moller, the sooner they could get him—and her—out of circulation.

Jack went through Customs ahead of Davis and the boy and drifted off to one side. It was possible her contact might meet them.

Pathetic wailing distracted him. A tiny girl with pale blonde curls howled as though her world had come to an end. Jack knelt beside her.

"What's the trouble, sweetheart? Can't you find your Mommy?"

She howled louder.

"Come on, lovey, tell Uncle Jack what's wrong."

He was reaching to pick her up when something sharp struck him in the ribs, nearly toppling him. A young woman with fierce red hair stood over him, fury in her eyes.

"You pervert! Get away from my daughter!"

"Hey!" Jack got to his feet, wincing at the pain in his side. "She was crying and she was all alone. I was just trying to help."

"I'll bet!" The woman stalked away, the little girl blinking tearfully at him over her mother's shoulder.

Too bad she'd misread his intentions. Oh, well, just because his ID proved he was a cop didn't mean his halo was visible. Jack rubbed his side. He'd probably have a doozy of a bruise.

He checked the Customs line-up. Davis and the boy were walking toward the exit. He fell in a few yards behind and followed them toward the buses.

The air was as balmy and the sky as blue as they had been four years ago, when he'd come here on a package tour with Sara. He'd enjoyed the whole show; palm trees, beaches, and everybody saying "aloha" until Sara ruined it with her marriage ultimatum. He'd liked her a lot, but cops made lousy husbands. Families deserved men who were going to be around to look after them and that was something he couldn't guarantee. Not that he didn't want a family, but there was no way he'd ever change jobs. Too many bad guys roamed the streets; too many innocent citizens got killed.

He followed Davis and the boy onto the airport bus. When they got off in Waikiki at the Pacific Princess Hotel, he strolled behind them up the wide steps into the lobby.

The hotel was old, the lobby small and crowded with racks of postcards, sunglasses, peaked caps, muu-muus and cheap shell jewelry. The carpet was worn and the lobby was open to the street, as if the builder had forgotten to put in the last wall.

He stood behind the newspaper rack while Ms Davis registered and headed for the elevators, the boy close beside her.

The desk clerk was reluctant, but his ID and a little pressure got him a room two doors away from Ms Davis. He dumped his camera bag and overnighter on the bed. Leaving the door partly open so he could hear if Davis opened hers, he phoned Baker in Vancouver.

"Kinkaid! So how's Honolulu?"

"Fantastic, Ian. I'm surrounded by sexy hula dancers and drinking mai-tais."

"Sure you are. Find out anything about this boy she has with her?"

"Give me a chance!"

"Yeah, all right. Might be Moller's kid. I'll check it out. I phoned the local drug squad about the situation so you've got an 'in' there."

"By the way," Jack said, "Davis got a real good look at me, so I'm going to make like I've fallen for her. Gives me an excuse to be on the spot."

"Okay. But don't get so interested in watching her butt that you don't watch your own, Kinkaid."

"You're joking. The way I feel now I'd sooner cuddle up to a salmon than a woman."

Which was the truth, straight up, Jack thought, after he'd given Ian the hotel phone number and said goodbye. Salmon were more predictable and he'd never yet heard one tell a lie.

He walked down the hall and listened at her door. The shower was running. Good, that gave him a chance to clean up, too. He'd probably never know when or how she contacted the supplier but, with a little luck, he intended to be around when she took delivery.

Dressed in chinos, T-shirt and a loose cotton jacket over his shoulder holster, Jack checked the binoculars and 35mm camera in his camera bag. A miniature camera nestled in his pocket. He soft-footed down the hall again. Her shower was still running.

He called the Honolulu police and was put through to Lieutenant Koyama, head of the drug squad.

"I've spoken with your Sergeant Baker," Koyama said. "I'll give you what help I can, but I'm short-staffed."

"So are we. I'm on my own tailing this woman so I don't know when I can meet with you."

"When you have her in sight and it looks like she'll stay put for a while, call me and I'll join you," Koyama said. "The local scene is heating up, particularly in the schools, and we may be able to help each other."

At eight-thirty, he heard a door open and went to his own, which was slightly ajar. The Davis woman and the boy came out and walked away from him toward the elevator. He waited until the doors closed, then ran down the stairs.

By eleven, he'd shadowed them through breakfast and half a dozen stores. She bought clothes for the boy, a swim suit for herself, sunglasses, macadamia nuts and a couple of beach towels. All very innocent and touristy. The red bikini was the most interesting part; if he got a chance to see her in it, that would be more than okay with him.

He caught up with them in the lobby of the Pacific Princess. "Well," he said, putting on his most ingenuous smile, "hello again! Having a good time?"

She didn't look pleased to see him, but she stopped. "Yes, we are. How about you?"

"Great so far. Look, my name is Jack Kinkaid. If you've been here before, maybe you could give me some pointers about where to go and what to see."

She hesitated, then said firmly, "Just follow your nose, Mr Kinkaid. From what I've read, everything in Hawaii is worth seeing."

"That's what I hear. But I've only got a week and I might miss something good if I don't plan. I'd be glad to take you both to lunch in exchange for your help. I was just heading for the hotel dining room."

"Sorry. We have a couple more things to do before we eat. Thanks, anyway."

"That's too bad. Perhaps some other time." Being helpless wasn't working worth a darn. Maybe he wasn't cute enough for her. Or she was too intent on business to think about anything else. She and the boy took the elevator and Jack positioned himself behind the jewelry rack and waited.

Ten minutes later the boy emerged from the elevator by himself and went across the street to the Jolly Roger Restaurant.

Ms Davis might not like it, but she was going to have company at lunch. He was hungry and it was the only way he could get some food without losing sight of her. He strolled into the Jolly Roger and sat across from the kid.

"Okay if I join you? I hate eating by myself."

The boy surveyed him soberly for a moment and seemed to like what he saw. "Aunt Penny told me to come and get a table while she fixed her hair."

So the boy was Moller's kid. Anger made his smile feel as if it was pasted on. The worst of the drug business was the way it preyed on kids. Ms Davis didn't seem like scum, or sound like it, but Ian wasn't usually wrong.

The boy stared at him. "How'd you get that scar on your forehead?"

He fingered the crease, an ever-present reminder of a shoot-out in a cocaine bust three years ago. "An accident. I tripped and hit my head on the corner of a desk."

Penny Davis arrived and Jack stood up, amused by her exasperated glance. If she thought she could avoid him by refusing lunch invitations, she could think again. "I apologize for intruding, but I do hate eating by myself. It's lonesome with nobody to talk to. May I stay?"

"I guess so. Okay, Rob?"

"Yeah, he's okay."

What was that exchange all about? Did the boy monitor her social life?

"Thank you, Penny. May I call you that?"

She studied the menu in cool silence. Jack sighed. Playing Romeo would be difficult if she refused to give him even a smidgen of response. Finally she thawed enough to admit that it was her first time in Hawaii.

"I won my trip," Jack said, "or I'd be at work."

"What kind of work do you do?"

"I'm the accountant for a furniture wholesaler." That might get her talking; she'd done bookkeeping for Westport Players. To his surprise, she looked bored. Odd that she'd worked for them for six years if she hadn't liked her job.

The boy was banging his foot against the table leg in an irritating four-four rhythm. Penny looked at him a couple of times, but said nothing. Jack decided to risk it.

"Rob, you keep time very well, but I wish you'd stop. The noise is bothering me." He thought Penny's intake of breath signaled that he was about to be castigated for interfering, but Rob forestalled her.

"Sorry," he said. He stopped kicking, but didn't respond to Jack's smile. Penny's face relaxed.

Time to change the subject. "I picked up a brochure for the USS Arizona Memorial. I might go there this afternoon and then opt for an early dinner and bed. I'm pretty beat; it's no fun trying to sleep on a plane."

That got a sympathetic smile from her. "I didn't get much sleep, either. Would you like to see the Memorial, Rob? Do you like ships?"

The boy nodded but said nothing. He had dark circles around his eyes and a wary look unusual for someone so young. He'd also ripped his napkin to shreds. Was it lack of sleep? Or something else? If he had a son like this, Jack thought, they'd have a good talk and get it sorted out.

By the time lunch was over Jack knew it would be easy to forget why Penny Davis had come to Oahu. She had a warm contralto voice, intelligence and good looks. She wore no makeup, nor did she need it. Her hair was thick and shiny and smelled like shampoo, not hair spray. She had a lot going for her. Pretending she turned him on wasn't going to require any acting talent at all.

But why the drug business? Was she hooked herself? He hadn't seen any signs of it.

Probably in it for the money. One of the detectives had seen Moller talking to her and decided to check her out. It hadn't taken long to find out who she was, that she'd lost her job six weeks ago and was broke. The clincher had been her picking up half a kilo of smack from a narc fronting as an employee in a small jewelry store.

The narc hadn't busted her because they didn't want to spook Moller or anybody connected with him. It was a long, slow process getting enough evidence for an airtight case and pointless to rush in too soon with too little and have some nitpicking lawyer get him off.

In the hotel lobby, he pointed out the Luana Tours booth. "You can book with them for the Arizona Memorial. It would be great if you and Rob joined me."

"I'll think about it."

He admired her coolness and independence but she was making the job more difficult than he'd hoped. No good pushing her, though.

He waited outside until they got in the elevator. He'd book for the USS Arizona tour in case she decided to do the same. The Memorial was close enough to the city center that Lieutenant Koyama could get there quickly. If she didn't book for the Memorial, he'd adjust his plans accordingly.

Using a public phone in the lobby, he called Baker.

Ian grunted at his lack of news. "We've got a murder now. Larry Wing's body was found in a ditch in West Van early this morning. He'd been shot. Looks like a gangland execution; going to be hard to prove anything."

"I like it. One less dealer we have to worry about. You link him to Moller yet?"

"Could my life ever be that easy?"

"Maybe I should come back. Pinning a murder on Moller would break up his organization faster than me chasing this woman all over Oahu. We know he's orchestrating the big push on selling drugs to kids."

"Stick with it, Jack. If we can nail her, we'll have enough proof to put the heat on Moller. Oh, and Terry Wellburn phoned. Big news on his latest arrest."

"You mean Adam Lister and the credit union job? What's that got to do with us?"

"Lister is plea bargaining. He confessed to that eleven-year-old bank heist we were talking about last night. And he named the other two men involved in exchange for a lesser charge on both robberies."

"Terry always did have the luck of the devil. Who are the other two guys?"

"Chris Mitchell and Reg Davis."

So Ian had been right about Penny Davis. Like father, like daughter.

THREE

You want me to do what?" Fredericks banged his mug down on Greg's kitchen counter, splashing coffee everywhere.

"Something the matter with your hearing? I said, go to Hawaii and get rid of the kid and his interfering aunt."

Fredericks mopped up coffee and tossed the dishrag in the sink. "Sorry, you're looking at the wrong guy."

"What's the problem?" Greg winced as the acidic coffee hit his ulcer. He could tell already it was going to be a bad day.

"No problem. I just don't do killings."

"I don't do killings," Greg mimicked, his temper rising. "Why not? You do everything else."

"I don't, that's all. Never have and never will."

"Listen, Carl, it means fifty grand in your pocket. You're the only guy around here I can trust."

Fredericks gave him a long look, his eyes such a pale blue they seemed almost colorless. "You can hire a good hit man for a lot less. Anyway, why do it?"

"I told you, the brat saw me shoot Larry. He didn't buy the story I gave him, otherwise he wouldn't have run."

"So who's going to believe him? Kids make up stories all the time; they watch too much TV."

"Penny would believe him and she's got a mouth to match her big nose. If I don't shut her up, I'll be in trouble."

He'd set up a scheme to get even with her, but that had to be canceled now. Fredericks could break into her place and get the package back. No point wasting good junk if she was going to die before the cops caught her with it.

"You could be in more trouble if you do. The cops are already buzzing around. Your wife disappears and your kid and your sister-in-law get killed; the first guy the cops look at will be you."

"Not if it happens out of the country when I'm here, and not if it looks like an accident, which it has to. And my wife went on vacation."

"What if they start looking for her?"

"Not my problem, is it? She said she was going to Toronto. So maybe she was lying, maybe she took off with her lover. I'm just going to stand around crying my eyes out, like this morning when I reported Rob as missing." Greg poured himself more coffee. "Carl, most guys would jump at fifty grand."

"I'm not most guys," Fredericks said.

Greg stirred sugar into his mug. Carl was efficient, but when he made up his mind about something you couldn't budge him. Turning down fifty grand was crazy, though. The man had to be hiding something.

"All right, I'll have to find somebody else."

"Call Sam Denton," Fredericks said. "He'll have contacts. You don't want a local mixed up in this, anyway."

Fredericks was right. Greg knew Denton had ordered killings to prevent leaks that might lead back to him. And it was in Denton's best interest to keep the Vancouver franchise running smoothly.

"All right," Greg said, "I'll talk to him. But I still want you in on it."

"What for?"

"To supervise; make sure it's done right. You can identify Penny and Rob for whoever takes the job."

"I don't like it. It's not my line."

"It didn't bother you helping me get rid of Angela."

"That was different," Fredericks said, with a shrug. "She was already dead. Anyway, your source at the airline told you Penny and the kid were using their own names; wouldn't be any trouble for a hit man to track them down."

"Sure, but my way would be quicker. I want them taken out fast, before they talk."

"How much?"

"You're not getting fifty grand just to watch. I'll talk to Denton first, then we'll make a deal."

"If the thing falls apart, I could be fingered. I want enough to cover the risk."

"Yeah, yeah. We get the right guy and nothing will go wrong; don't worry about it."

Fredericks rinsed his mug under hot tap water and left it in the sink. "You want me, I'll be home in about an hour."

When Fredericks had gone, Greg got the Caddy out of the garage and drove to Park Royal Mall. The cops were bound to have a wiretap on his line by now. He shut himself in a phone booth.

The phone was picked up on the second ring.

"It's Moller. I need some help."

"Meet me here in three hours."

Greg took Taylor Way to Lions Gate Bridge and went straight through downtown Vancouver, cursing the traffic until he was across the Oak Street bridge and onto the freeway. He drove fast and US Customs kept him less than three minutes at the border crossing.

With ten minutes to spare, Greg parked across the street from the high rise Seattle office where Denton ran his extensive West Coast drug business behind a respectable facade of investment advice. In the elevator, he tried to estimate how much Denton made. Millions.

The elevator doors whispered open on the twenty-second floor. When the time came, he'd pluck Denton like a ripe plum and crush him. But not yet. He had to build up his reputation, his organization, get a few key men in place.

Denton, sleek and graying, fingers weighted with diamonds, waved him to a maroon calfskin settee. "What's the problem? I know the heat's on, but it'll ease off if they don't find anything. And they'd better not. I've told you before you can be replaced."

"We've got a deal," Greg said. Trust Denton to remind him every chance he got who was boss.

"The deal is only as good as your performance. Now, what's so urgent?"

"One of the street dealers tried to knife Fredericks last night. I had to take him out."

"So?"

"Other than my wife's kid, there's no problem. We dumped the body and there's nothing to connect him to me."

"What about the kid?"

"He saw the shooting."

Denton made a sound of disgust and swiveled his black leather chair to look out the window at Elliot Bay. "I told you not to do business in your home."

"All right, I get the point." He was sweating, his fresh white shirt sticking to his body.

Denton turned back to face him. "I don't think you do. The point is that your stupidity has put the entire operation at risk. If the cops arrest you, order yourself a casket, Moller. I can't afford any leaks."

"I'm telling you, I'm clean." His ulcer chewed at him like a hungry rat. "Okay, the kid's disappeared. I told him the three of us were just clowning around, but he didn't buy it. This morning when I went to get him up, he was gone."

"Where would he go? What would he do? How old is this kid, anyway?"

"Nine, and too smart for his own good. Anyway, I found out he went to my wife's sister and the odds are he told her the whole story. They left the city last night."

"You know where?"

"Yeah, Hawaii. Don't ask me why. She told me a couple days ago she was flying to Toronto."

"Who does she know in Hawaii?"

"As far as I know, nobody."

"Strikes me you don't know much. Well, if she takes her story to the cops there, ten to one they'll ignore her. The thing is, did she tell anybody in Vancouver?"

"The kid left my house after ten and they took a three a.m. plane so she didn't have much time. The cops haven't been around so if she talked, it wasn't to them."

"Obviously she's running scared. You'll have to get rid of her or buy her off."

"Nobody could buy that mouthy broad. I'm sending Fredericks after her. But it's got to look like an accident; the cops are breathing down my neck as it is."

"You'll have to do the kid, too."

"That's okay by me."

Denton clicked his tongue against his teeth. "Can Fredericks handle it?"

"He won't pull the trigger. I don't want to force him; he's the best man I have. I figured you'd have contacts that could give me a name."

"It's in my interest to bail you out this time, Moller. But I'm warning you, one more screw-up like this and you're dead. As in buried. Is that clear?"

Greg nodded, swallowing bile.

Denton leaned forward. "All right. There's a man who does business for me in Honolulu right now; he's the best there is. Phone me when Fredericks has booked a hotel down there and I'll arrange for my man to contact him."

Carl Fredericks looked around his barren apartment. Nothing here he couldn't move out in less than an hour: clothes, a small collection of rare books, cameras. When he got back from Hawaii he'd take the gold bars out of the safety deposit box and give them to his stockbroker for safekeeping. His lawyer already had instructions for disposing of his restaurant supply business.

He snapped Candy's leash onto her collar. She scampered to the front door and waited for him, tail thumping the floor.

Fifty grand. He could update the Plan by six months at least. He let himself think about it for maybe ten seconds, then shook his head. No killing; not for any amount of money.

He locked the apartment door and took the elevator to the lobby eighteen floors below. Outside, Candy strained at her leash, pulling him toward Stanley Park and the gray squirrels she loved to chase.

So Hawaii was his next stop. He'd have to put Candy in the boarding kennel. She hated that but it couldn't be helped. He wouldn't be having any fun either.

FOUR

Inside a small neat house on the outskirts of Honolulu, the telephone rang. Vic Nelson picked up the receiver.

"Yeah?"

"Sam Denton. I've got a rush job for you. Phone Carl Fredericks at the Shady Rest Hotel. He's flying in from Vancouver. Should be there in a couple of hours. He'll give you the details."

"Where's the target?"

"Honolulu."

Vic scowled. He hated working in his home territory.

"How much?"

The figure Denton gave him erased Vic's scowl. Old Denton must want the target dead in a very serious way.

"Aunt Penny, why are we going to Sea Life Park instead of the Arizona Memorial?"

"Because that Kinkaid guy will probably show up at the Arizona Memorial and I don't want to spend time with him."

"Why not?"

How did one explain adult mating games to someone Rob's age? Kinkaid hadn't come on to her, though she could tell that he wanted to. The energy between them was electric. He'd probably make a move next time they met. She'd have to say no. Anybody who had to be led around Oahu by the hand needed a mother, not a lover.

Why was she attracted to him? Accountants were dull and boring; everybody knew that. Not her idea of a dream lover. Besides, something about him didn't ring true. The voice and the way he moved didn't jibe with the 'gee whiz' way he talked.

"It's hard to explain, Rob. If you're disappointed about the Arizona, we can see it tomorrow."

"Yeah, but I don't understand about Mr Kinkaid. I thought he was kinda neat."

Rob, too? Irritated, Penny shooed him into the bathroom.

While he showered she got Tim Wade's number from Information. No answer. She worked out the time difference between Honolulu and Toronto and speculated that Angela and the Wades might have gone out for dinner and a show.

She thought again about phoning the Vancouver police. Even if they listened, and accepted her statement about blood on Greg's living room rug, it was too late. Greg would have cleaned or replaced the carpet by now.

Half an hour later, their small blue and white tour bus, headed for Sea Life Park, eased into the traffic on Kuhio Avenue. The driver called, "Aloha! My name is Kim and 'aloha' means hello and goodbye and good morning and good afternoon and I love you. Everybody say good afternoon to me."

There was a chorus of "Aloha!" and the driver said, "Here in Hawaii we never get fussed about things." He held up his hand with the thumb and little finger extended and the three middle fingers folded into his palm. "We use this sign. It means 'hang loose!'—relax and have a good time. I hope that's what you'll do today."

Penny tried to make the sign, but her little finger wanted to curl into her palm with the other three. "This will take some practice."

"I can do it double!" Rob waved two 'hang loose' hands at her.

The driver continued. "Hawaiian time goes right along with hanging loose. When I make a date to see my friends, I might get there an hour late, or even an hour early. Nobody minds. It's all part of hanging loose."

"I always hang loose," Rob said, "even in school."

He didn't, though. The smudges under his eyes had been there for a long time and his shoulders were tense. She repressed an urge to ruffle his hair. Boys his age usually hated any public show of affection.

The bus driver continued his spiel and Penny shut his voice out of her mind. The idea of hanging loose in Hawaii was at odds with everything she had to think about.

"How long are we going to stay here, Aunt Penny?"

"Until I run out of money, I guess."

After a pause, he said, "Couldn't you get a job?"

"Not legally. I'd have to go back to Canada and apply for a work permit."

"Oh." Another pause. "Okay then, couldn't Gramps lend you

some money?"

"No. He and Gramma have barely enough to live on." Which was why she'd never gone back to drama school after the shooting. Working for Westport Players had given her just enough money to provide the extras her parents needed.

"How about Mr Wilson?"

"Westport Players doesn't have any money, either. That's why I lost my job. Mr Wilson couldn't afford to pay me. He had to find volunteers to do the work."

Rob's expression was grave. "Next time you get a job, you better make sure the company has lots of money. It would be awful if you couldn't pay your rent or buy food."

"Rob, where did you learn all this about jobs and money and being responsible?" This was a side of him she'd never seen before.

"From Mom. She explained about working to get money and how if you don't have any, you could starve."

It sounded like her baby sister was finally growing up and thinking about the future instead of living one day at a time. She'd tried to mother Angela after the tragedy but she hadn't had the patience or skills to handle a rebellious girl of thirteen. But it wasn't until Angela ran away with her newborn son two years later that Penny realized how badly she'd failed at being a mother.

Some people said a person's destiny came from their genes, not their environment. It was a comforting thought but she didn't altogether believe it.

"Would you like to live in Hawaii?" she asked.

"It would be okay if Mom was here. And my friend Simon. I like Vancouver but I wouldn't want to stay there unless Greg was in jail forever and ever."

It must be wrenching for Rob to know that the man he'd loved as a father was a killer. She hoped she could reunite him with his mother soon. After that—what?

When the driver pulled in at the gates to Sea Life Park Rob said, "Look at all the buses! There'll be a ton of people." It was true. The Park was crowded and noisy.

"Let's go see the reef tank aquarium first," Rob said, tugging at her arm. She glanced at her brochure, which told her the aquarium had been designed to display sea life in the Hawaiian coral reefs.

After the heat and bright sunlight outside, the observation passage around the big tank was dark but blessedly cool. Rob pressed his nose against the glass, watching tiny bright-colored fish dart among the coral branches. "I wish I had gills," he said. "I could go in the tank and play with all those guys."

Near the surface, two small sharks swam back and forth, lithe and graceful and looking as deadly as their bigger brethren. "You sure you want to go in there, Rob? Those two would probably have you for breakfast."

Rob bared his teeth and growled at the sharks. "Not me. I'm Superman! No, I'm Superfish."

A large, flat creature with a thin tail glided up from the bottom, then drifted down again. "What's that, Rob? It looks like a little gray blanket with eyes."

"A manta ray."

"I thought manta rays were huge."

"Maybe this is a baby one." He looked up at her. "It would be neat to take it home. I wish I had an aquarium. A big one that would fill the whole house."

A budding naturalist, she thought. Perhaps he wasn't as interested in hockey and football as Greg had said. She remembered Rob stomping around the living room in his ice skates. Had he done that because he wanted his parents to punish him by taking the skates away? So he wouldn't have to play hockey? It was possible.

When they were outside again, she said, "How about the Whaler's Cove show? That's where the dolphins are."

"Cool!"

The signs led them down a tree-lined path to a pale turquoise lagoon framed by the deep blue of the ocean beyond. Rob raced ahead of her. Catching up, she found him hanging over the railing, eager for the show to begin.

Penny stood beside him. "You've got the best view. But don't fall in."

A girl wearing a flower lei rode a dolphin around the lagoon. Another, in the rigging of a whaling ship replica, held out fish for three dolphins swimming in formation. They leapt high out of the water to take the fish. On their last circuit, they slapped their tails in front of the bleachers and Rob yelped as the shower of water sprayed him.

He was drenched but laughing and she couldn't help joining in. It was wonderful to hear him laugh when she hadn't seen him even smile during the past year. She was glad she'd brought him here. Kids shouldn't ever have to look the way Rob had last night.

Had that been only last night? It seemed like weeks.

"What's next?"

She consulted the brochure. "There's a whaling museum and sea lions and a bird sanctuary. And ice cream."

"Ice cream! Then the sea lions."

Rob made short work of his chocolate ripple cone. "Hurry up, Aunt Penny."

She decided not to risk having her half-eaten cone knocked out of her hand in the jostling throngs of people. "You go ahead and I'll follow in five minutes. But stay right by the pen so I can find you."

He darted away like a drop of quicksilver. The sea lion enclosure wasn't far; she could hear them barking. Rob would be easy to spot in his Day-Glo orange shorts.

Jack Kinkaid had ordered vanilla ice cream at lunch and eaten it as though it were the best thing he'd ever tasted. Odd how changeable his face was. When he smiled he looked like the kind of guy who liked to go camping and build fires and toast marshmallows but when he was serious, with those scars, he looked like a TV gangster.

Greg Moller wasn't anything like that. He wore expensive tailored suits and white shirts and looked as if he belonged on the board of directors of some big company. She'd never seen him with dirty hands.

They were dirty now. They had blood on them.

The sea lion pen was farther than she'd thought. On a small rise, she stopped to scan the steel mesh fence. Rob should be there somewhere, with his nose pressed against it.

Then she saw him—almost hidden behind the man who stood leaning over him, his hands on the steel mesh as though trapping the boy against the fence. Rob looked frightened. The man's hand dropped to Rob's shoulder.

Blood thumping, she forced her way through the crowd, yelling, "Rob! I'm coming!" Leaving a trail of protesting tourists, she pushed through the last knot of sightseers and called to him again.

The man straightened and looked at her, then faded into the crowd.

She put her arm around Rob. "Are you all right? Who was that? What did he want?"

"I don't know. He was kind of weird. He asked me a bunch of questions."

"Like what?"

Rob chewed at his thumb. "I couldn't understand what he was talking about."

"Did he want you to go with him?"

"I don't think so."

"Rob, I know your Mom taught you not to go with strangers."

"Oh, yeah, I know all that stuff." He turned away and pressed his face against the fence. "Look at the baby sea lions, Aunt Penny."

A familiar voice spoke her name and she swung around. Jack Kinkaid, the inevitable cameras around his neck.

"Anything wrong?" he asked. "I saw you come racing down the hill and heard you calling."

She was surprised at how glad she was to see him. "I don't know. Some man was talking to Rob and I'm not sure what he was after."

Kinkaid frowned. "What did he look like?"

"Fairly short, slim. Quite dark—Japanese, I think. And he had on a pale pink shirt."

"I'll look for him. Which way did he go?" She pointed and Kinkaid strode away, his head swiveling as he looked to right and left. He was back within a couple of minutes.

"I couldn't see any guy in a pink shirt," he said, "but there are so many people here I could easily have missed him. He's probably out of the Park by now."

Her adrenalin back to normal, Penny said, "I don't suppose he did any harm but I'm not letting Rob out of my sight from now on." She looked around in disgust. "It's incredible that in a place like this, with thousands of people, a child still isn't safe."

"Why don't I find a policeman and you can report it? Just in case this guy goes after some other young boy?"

"I don't want to do that. I didn't see enough to give a proper description." Besides, it would be a frosty day in Hades before she asked a policeman for help. "What are you doing here?"

He smiled, reverting to the boy-next-door. "The same as you, I guess. Following my nose. Well, if you're all right, I'll be on my way."

She felt oddly bereft as he walked away. The danger was gone, but she would have liked company for what was left of their time here. Sea Life Park had lost its charm and, though she knew it was useless, she kept looking for a dark man in a pale pink shirt.

Back on the bus, Rob bounced in his seat like a six year old. Yet earlier he'd been advising her about finances like an adult. She couldn't get a handle on either him or Jack Kinkaid.

She wondered if she'd overreacted at Sea Life Park. Maybe the man in the pink shirt was just being friendly. Or wanted directions. After all, what could he have done in a crowd like that? On the other hand, Rob didn't need any more stress. Neither did she.

Rob was still now. Drawing pictures on his brand-new orange shorts! Where had he found the ballpoint? She was sure she'd hidden all the pens in the hotel room.

Perhaps he was acting up because he felt safe. Or he was overtired. Or it was those mysterious genes. Whichever reason applied, she didn't know how to deal with it. At least she'd be able to hand him over to his mother soon.

It had to be coincidence that Jack Kinkaid had shown up at Sea Life Park. If he did ask her out, would she go? The idea was tempting, but his inconsistencies made her uneasy. His actions and words about the man in the pink shirt had been decisive, not something she'd expected from a man who still needed his mom.

What would have happened if she'd reported the incident to a policeman? Not a darn thing, other than he'd probably have told her it was all her fault for not being with Rob every minute.

"Cops," she muttered, the word like acid on her tongue. The Vancouver police had been responsible for ruining her parents' lives and it didn't look like they'd ever quit.

Penny twisted in her seat and watched the suburbs of Honolulu glide by. Rob was asleep now, thank heaven, his head lolling against the edge of the bus window.

She'd spent a lot of time with her father the last few weeks when she wasn't carrying her résumé around to dozens of places in the city. He looked frail but seemed to be in an optimistic frame of mind. Had he learned to fake optimism so as not to upset her?

Penny closed her eyes to stem the tears that often came when she thought of her father's wrecked life. No matter how hard she tried to be detached, she couldn't help feeling bitter. The police had no evidence that her father gave inside information to the thieves but they judged him guilty just the same. So did the bank that had employed him for twenty-five years, as well as most of his friends.

Where was the justice in having a man under suspicion for

eleven years and never bringing him to trial so the issue could be resolved once and for all? But it was the police who were at fault, not the rest of the justice system. It was the police who'd shot her father and still harassed him, who couldn't be bothered to find the real culprits. It was their fault her father had been exiled by his own community.

"Oh, stop thinking about it!" she muttered. She was overtired and what she needed was to sleep for ten hours. So did Rob, come to that.

At the hotel, she said, "How about we go up to the room and order in a hamburger or something? I'm too beat to go exploring Honolulu tonight."

"Yeah, me too. No french fries, okay?"

"How come? I thought all kids liked french fries."

He grimaced. "They're gross. I hate the smell."

Vic Nelson put on the clean jeans his mother had pressed for him, a T-shirt and jacket. He retrieved his hunting knife from its hiding place, honed it and slipped it into the scabbard inside his leather boot. That done, he chucked several changes of clothing into his bag.

"Your taxi will be here any minute, darling," his mother called.

"Be right there, Mom." Vic slipped a set of false identification documents into an inner compartment of the suitcase and locked it. He probably wouldn't need them, but only idiots took chances.

When he entered the living room, his mother rose from her chair and hugged him.

"Sure you've got everything, darling? Why aren't you wearing a suit?"

"I packed one. Jeans are more comfortable on a plane." Not that she'd know; she'd never been on one.

"But it'll get all wrinkled."

"I'll get it pressed at the hotel."

"That costs money, Vic, dear."

"Listen, Mom, with what the company pays me for these troubleshooting jobs, I could afford to have the suit pressed every five minutes."

"I know, but it seems such a waste of money. Ever since your father left us, I've had to be so careful."

The way she talked, it sounded like his old man had gone six months ago and she was still getting used to the idea. The low-life had walked out when Vic was seven and that was eighteen years ago now.

"Not so careful after I paid the mortgage off."

She brought her hand up to her mouth the way she always did when she knew he was teed off. "Oh, darling, I am grateful, but really, you should have used that money for a house of your own, for when you get married."

She went through that spiel about him getting married every now and then, but he knew she'd never give him up to another woman. Not that he cared; marriage was the last thing on his agenda.

"Why would I get married when I got you, Mom? Now listen, I'll call every day, see how you're doing, pick up any messages. Okay?"

"All right, dear. Where's the company sending you this time? Is there someplace I can phone you?"

"A couple of car dealerships in LA and another one down in San Diego. I'll be moving around a lot."

She sighed. "It bothers me so much not to know where you are. I'd like to phone and say hello."

A couple of swear words slipped out. "Lay off! I'll only be gone a few days."

She drew herself up to her full height of five feet one. "Victor, I will not put up with you taking the Lord's name in vain. There's never any excuse for it."

"Sorry."

"I should think so! I taught you better than that."

A car horn beeped outside. Relieved, Vic picked up his suitcase and headed for the front door.

"Wait, darling." She pulled his head down and kissed him firmly on the mouth. "The Lord bless you and keep you safe. You let me know when you'll be home and I'll make you a pecan pie."

Vic put his arm around her and squeezed gently. "You take care. See you soon."

She stood at the front door until the taxi turned the corner at the end of the block. He wished this job was anywhere but Honolulu. If she happened to see him, he'd have to come up with a good story. Vic reminded himself he'd been coming up with good stories most of his life. He put her out of his mind.

He said to the driver, "Keoki Motel."

The motel, which he'd scoped out after Denton's call, looked even sleazier at night. But the units were all on ground level with separate entrances for each and he knew from the way the redhead behind the counter eyed his cash that she'd mind her own business.

Unit 18 had a couch, TV, a couple of arm chairs, a double bed and some kitchen space. At the back was a bedroom with a second double bed and the bathroom. It would do fine.

Vic brushed the chair to make sure it was clean, sat down and picked up the phone.

An hour later, there was a rap at the door. Vic opened it to a tall, thin man in a pale blue suit and aviator sunglasses.

"Fredericks? The sun went down a while ago, man."

Carl Fredericks took off his sunglasses and eyed Vic. What was Denton up to, sending a boy to do a man's job? This guy didn't look any more than eighteen or nineteen.

"Did Denton tell you the score?" he asked.

"No. Just said there's a rush job on somebody."

Fredericks sat down. He hated this job more with every passing hour. "How old are you, Vic?"

"Older than I look, if it's any of your business, which it isn't." Who was this geek, asking a question like that? Hadn't Denton talked up his reputation?

"Just asking."

"Well, don't ask. You tell me the setup and I'll tell you how we're going to do it."

The kid has a smart mouth, Fredericks thought. I'd like some sign he knows what he's doing. "Okay, there's two people, a woman and a boy. We know they're here but not which hotel they're in."

"No sweat. Take a few phone calls, that's all. Easiest thing is get into the room when they're asleep. A knife is quick and quiet."

Fredericks shook his head. "Can't be that way. It has to look like an accident."

"An accident! That's stupid!" Vic got up and paced around the room. "Your boss wants somebody taken out, I'll take 'em out. Rifle, knife, anything you like."

"You don't want to take the job, we'll find somebody else." He had to make it clear to Nelson right now that he did as he was told or got out.

"You won't find anybody better. You want a freakin' accident, okay, but I'm telling you it's risky, man, and I don't like it. I like to do the job and get out. And get paid." The price Denton had named would buy him a couple of weeks in Acapulco with the best of everything and leave plenty to splash around at home for a few months. It was good timing, too; his bank account was low.

"I don't like it any better than you do," Fredericks said, thinking about the twenty grand he'd talked Greg into and wondering if what he had to go through was worth it. "But that's the way it has to be. Strictly accidental. You can phone Denton and check, if you want."

"Yeah, I might do that later. Okay, Fredericks, let's get on the horn and find out where your people are. Then you tell me what you know about them and I'll work out the strategy."

By eight o'clock, Rob was stretched out in one of the twin beds, sound asleep. Penny turned the television lower and reached for the phone.

There was no answer at Tim's. It must be around two in the morning in Toronto. Where were they? She called Information again to check the number, but that only proved she'd been pushing the correct sequence of buttons.

Suddenly Rob screamed, wrenching her around in her chair.

"No, don't! Don't! Please don't!" he sobbed.

Penny dropped the phone and rushed to Rob's bed. His arms were thrashing, his legs kicking under the covers.

"Rob, wake up." She put her hands on his upper arms, gently at first, then more firmly as he continued to flail. "Rob! Rob, wake up, honey. Everything's all right."

His eyes opened and slowly focused on her face. The thrashing subsided to a shudder and then to stillness.

"What's wrong? Why were you screaming?"

"Was I?" He sat up, blinking. "I had a nightmare."

She held him against her breast. Poor little waif must have been reliving the murder in his sleep. "What about?"

"I don't remember."

She held him away from her. Something in his expression told her he was lying.

FIVE

Penny wakened to the sound of pigeons cooing and Rob murmuring on the lanai, which was called a balcony at home. The small white birds perched on his shoulders and arms and fussed around his feet as he doled out potato chip crumbs. His face was serene, his nightmare apparently forgotten.

Last night, unable to coax him into telling her what it had been about, she lay down beside him until he'd fallen asleep again.

Why wouldn't he tell her? If she didn't know what was wrong, how could she help? Penny sighed. His mother had been just as stubborn at his age.

In the shower she turned the water on full force and tried to decide what to do next. She'd already wasted a day, hoping to talk to Angela.

Greg would have ways of finding them, but she had no idea how long it would take. It would be a good idea to create new identities for Rob and herself, if only she knew how to do it. As it was, she couldn't even use an alias; her charge card couldn't be changed to another name.

She simply had to get hold of Angela. Her sister needed to know that Greg was a murderer and Rob was in serious danger. Her credit might stretch far enough to fly Rob and herself to Toronto, but if Angela was on her way back to Vancouver, what was the point?

She tried Tim's number again. Still no answer. Where could they be? Sight-seeing? Shopping? Gone to Tim and Jane's cabin on the lake? She couldn't even remember the name of the lake. Well, she'd just have to keep trying.

At breakfast, she said, "Want to go to the beach?"

"Sure." Rob downed the last of his orange juice. "I don't swim very good, though."

"I'm a good swimmer. Maybe I can teach you. Your shoulders are well developed and that will make it easier for you."

"My shoulders are strong 'cause I work out," he said.

"Work out? You mean in a gym?"

"Sometimes." He slid out of the booth and headed for the door.

Another secret he wasn't going to tell her, Penny thought, as she followed him. At least there was nothing sinister about working out.

They bought a red and white beach ball in the International Market Place across from the hotel, then angled toward Waikiki beach, wandering along short, quiet streets. The sun was brilliant, the air rapidly warming.

Stepping off the curb to cross Uluniu Avenue, Penny heard the roar of a speeding car. She looked up. And screamed. The car was hurtling directly toward them.

She glimpsed someone scooping Rob off the street. The car swept past, so close she could feel the heat from the engine, and she caught a glimpse of two young men in it. Teenagers. The car, a beat-up, rusty T-bird, fishtailed onto Kalakaua Avenue and sped away.

Hands pulled her gently back onto the sidewalk, voices asked if she was hurt.

"Rob!" she cried. "Where's Rob?"

A tall young man in white shorts and T-shirt, blond hair curling thickly to the nape of his neck, came forward, holding Rob by the hand.

She fell to her knees and hugged him so tightly he protested. "Aunt Penny, I'm okay. Everything happened so fast I didn't even see it." He sounded disappointed.

Penny stood up, clutching the lamp standard to support her jelly knees. The young man was scowling in the direction the T-bird had taken.

"Bunch of young creeps," he said. "They never even looked when they came around the corner. If you'd stepped off that curb a second earlier they'd have got both of you."

A woman beside her said, "He's right. I saw it, too. You were real lucky."

Lucky! Penny stifled the hysterical giggle that rose in her throat. "Thanks for what you did," she said to the man. "That was fast thinking."

He looked embarrassed. "Just happened to be looking at the right time is all."

"I don't suppose you got the licence number?"

"Sorry, I didn't."

The crowd was mostly gone now. The people remaining shook their heads. It had all happened too quickly.

The young man put his hand on her arm. "You okay? You need anything?"

She let go the lamp standard. "I'm okay."

"Too bad about the licence number," he said. "We could have called the cops."

"No way! I hate cops!" The vehemence in her voice startled her. She never talked like that except to her father. The near-miss must have really shaken her.

"How about a coffee? You still look awful pale."

She could do with a hit of caffeine. But not in a coffee shop where she had to look at cars going by.

"Can we get coffee down at the beach?"

"Sure," he said, "Sure, no sweat." He tucked her arm through his, grabbed Rob's hand and led them across Kalakaua and onto Waikiki beach.

Penny stopped and gazed around. The beach stretched away to the north for what seemed like miles. The sand was littered with sunbathers, their beach mats loaded with snacks and toys. Two large catamarans with sails in bright kindergarten colors rested at the edge of the gentle surf and beyond, swimmers bobbed, arms scattering showers of sparkling water droplets.

"Hey, this is awesome!" Rob said.

Penny took one sandal off, put her foot down, and promptly put the sandal back on. Even this early the sand at the top of the sloping beach was too hot for comfort.

They found a space near the water and the blond man helped her spread the beach towels.

"I'll get you that coffee," he said and loped off toward a cluster of concession stands.

Penny peeled down to her new fire-engine-red bikini, enjoying the heat of the sun on her pale skin. An hour of this might soothe her jangling nerves back to normal. Rob was watching the other people on the beach. Too young to know how close he'd been to death, she thought. He was so vulnerable. But she had to look after him, even if it put her life under threat. There was no one else.

The young man came back carrying her coffee, a Coke for Rob and an ice cream cone for himself. He sat beside Penny and said, "My name's Vic. Welcome to Oahu."

"Penny Davis. And this is Rob. How did you know we're strangers to Hawaii?"

His grin was engaging, his green eyes bright. "No tan. Plus I could tell you never saw Waikiki beach before."

Vic wore a heavy gold chain around his neck and a gold ring in his right ear. His boyish face made it hard to tell his age but she'd guess anywhere between eighteen and twenty-five. He had a deep tan and muscles that suggested he spent time working on them.

"Vic, I can't thank you enough for saving Rob, but I'm over the shock now. If you want to leave, it's okay."

He grinned again. "I'm on vacation, too. Can't think of anything I'd rather do than bum around the beach."

"Do you live here?"

He combed his hair back with his fingers, then held her gaze while he licked his ice cream cone. "Yep. If you like, I could show you around. I got nothing to do for the next week except hang loose."

Why not? He was friendly and he'd saved Rob's life. His presence might ward off weirdos like the guy in the pink shirt who had been harassing Rob at Sea Life Park.

"That's very sweet of you, Vic. But there must be things you'd rather do than play tour guide."

"Hey, I'm serious! I like showing people around. Especially beautiful women."

His admiring glances were flattering but she doubted they were sincere; there was too much difference in their ages. He might be a gigolo. If so, he'd used the rescue of Rob as an opportunity to get close to her. He'd be gone fast enough when he found out she had no money.

Rob stood up and reached for the beach ball. "Want to play ball, Aunt Penny?"

Vic jumped to his feet. "I will." He stripped down to skintight green racing trunks. "Guys are better at throwing, anyway." He looked at Penny. "Right?"

"Right," she said and lay back on her elbows as they tossed the ball back and forth. Rob seemed to enjoy himself, but ignored Vic's efforts to coax him into the surf.

Penny sat up. Maybe it was time for a swimming lesson.

"I'm going for a swim, Rob. Want to come along?"

He looked doubtfully at the creaming surf.

"You don't have to. Stay here until you get bored with tossing the ball around. Then I'll take you out a little way and we'll work on your swimming. Okay?"

"Okay."

The water felt cool and alive, swirling around her ankles, then her thighs. The undertow wasn't strong enough to worry about, even for Rob. She plunged in, enjoying the sensuous roll of the water as it buoyed her up. After a couple of minutes she turned toward shore and switched to a breast stroke until she reached shallow water.

"Ready for your lesson, Rob?"

"I guess."

"Okay if I come along?" Vic asked. "I'm real good in the water."

They waded through the surf to calm water, each holding one of Rob's hands. When the water was up to his chest, Penny said, "Remember how to float? Lean back and relax, let the water hold you up."

Rob put his head back and let his feet float up but his body, rigid with tension, began to sink. When he started thrashing, Penny slid an arm under his back.

She showed him how to move his hands. "You can kick your feet, too, but you don't have to do it hard. One or the other will keep you up."

At the end of twenty minutes Rob could float, tread water and do a rudimentary dog paddle.

"Okay!" He stood up. "Can we go further out now? You said deep water holds you up better."

"I'd like that," Penny said. "But stay close to us and yell if anything bothers you."

Gradually they made their way further out, where there were many more swimmers. Penny dove under the surface and the sight of legs moving through the green water reminded her of the fish tank at Sea Life Park. Were there sharks in these waters? Not likely, or there'd be signs posted on the beach.

She watched Rob for several minutes, circling him with slow, powerful strokes. He seemed happy enough, playing in the water as though the ocean was a new toy.

Vic, treading water fifteen feet away, tossed his head to get the hair out of his eyes. "You swim like a pro."

"I was a champion swimmer in my high school."

"Yeah? Why don't you do a few laps? I'll baby-sit the kid for you."

The idea was tempting. She'd let her swimming go the last few months. This was a chance to work on getting back to peak performance.

She couldn't saddle Vic with the responsibility of looking after Rob, though. Rob seemed confident, but he could easily panic. Vic might not know how to handle a frantic and flailing swimmer. He was also a stranger.

Penny gave a longing glance at the blue-green water stretching to the horizon. "Thanks, but I won't. I don't feel like putting out that much energy right now."

"You sure?" Vic said. "I told you, I don't mind keeping an eye on the kid."

"I'm sure."

They swam lazily back toward the beach, stopping now and then to float or tread water. Penny found herself wondering where Jack Kinkaid was this morning. Whether he liked to swim. What he'd look like in racing trunks. And who he really was.

The sun felt marvelous after the salty coolness of the water. Penny flopped down on the beach towel.

"You got sun screen?" Vic asked.

She sat up. "Darn! I forgot."

"You gotta have sun screen in this climate," he advised. "I'll go get you some."

He was back from the concession stands in five minutes.

She lay on her stomach while he stroked sun screen on her back, his touch light and subtly sensuous. She hoped her lack of response wouldn't challenge him to try harder.

"You got the time?" he asked when he'd finished.

She dug her watch out of the souvenir straw beach basket she'd bought the day before. "Nearly eleven."

"Thanks. I'm outta here. Supposed to meet one of my buddies for a bite at noon. You going to be here later?"

"No, I don't want to risk sunburn our first day."

"How about tomorrow?"

"We might go on a tour tomorrow."

"Great, I can help you there! What hotel are you staying at?"

"Pacific Princess."

"I'll be in touch," he promised. "I'm a good guide. I know what places kids like, too."

"Are you sure you want to? I'm not trying to put you off, but wouldn't you rather be with your friends?"

"My buddies are working, my girlfriend's on the mainland and my folks are on a round-the-world trip. I got nobody to play with." He stood up. "You take care now."

He said that the same way her father did. She watched him stride up the beach, impressed by his eagerness to help. Jack Kinkaid hadn't done anything except look for the man in the pink shirt. He had even walked away from her yesterday afternoon at Sea Life Park. Penny lay back, shutting her eyes against the glare that penetrated even her sun glasses, and let the sun saturate her flesh.

Too bad about Kinkaid. She'd prefer his company to Vic's, except for the feeling that Kinkaid wasn't what he seemed to be.

"I'm bored." Rob's voice, muffled by the beach towel.

She rolled over and sat up. "Tell me about Greg and those two men again. I want to be sure I've got it right."

"I already told you all of it."

"Maybe you can remember other things. Had you seen either of those two men before?"

"One of them. A tall, skinny guy. His name's Carl. He comes to the house at night sometimes."

"You said Greg shot Larry. With a pistol?"

"Yeah. It didn't make much noise. I guess it had a silencer on it."

"What did he do when he came up upstairs?"

Rob's lip curled. "He tucked me in."

"Doesn't he usually tuck you in?"

"No way! He says I'm too old for that. And he wants me to throw away my old teddy bear."

"Does he think you'd report him to the police?"

"Yeah."

"Why?"

Rob hesitated. "Because I hate him."

Hate? That was a pretty strong emotion to feel for a man who was supposed to be such a good father.

"Why? Because he's too strict?"

He looked down and fidgeted.

"Rob?"

"I can't tell you. I promised Mom."

What had been going on in that house? Sexual abuse? She was ready to believe anything of Greg now. Was that why Rob seemed scared and embarrassed?

"You'd better tell me, Rob. I know it's wrong to break a promise but your Mom's not here to take charge of things and I have to decide how to keep Greg from finding us."

Still he hesitated. Then, "You know my bad dream last night? I couldn't tell you about it because it was just like in real life." His eyes looked haunted again.

"So what happens in real life?"

He drew his knees up and hugged them as though he was rolling himself into a ball for protection. "Well, Mom and Greg get into fights and they yell at each other. And Greg hits her."

Her temper boiled up, white hot. If she ever got her hands on that slime... She took a deep breath and tried to keep her voice even.

"You mean he knocks her down?"

"Yeah. Last time it was really, really bad. I tried to stop him but I couldn't. The time before that he broke her arm."

And she'd thought Angela was accident-prone! Had swallowed all those lies about Angela falling down stairs and banging into doors. It hurt to think that her baby sister wouldn't come to her for help, wouldn't even admit the abuse was happening. She was sure now that Angela had gone to Toronto to make preparations for leaving Greg.

She'd been so wrong about him. He looked and acted like a successful businessman, whose only failing was being too possessive of his wife and stepson, and that's the way she'd accepted him. She'd pigeonholed him, for convenience. But what difference would it have made if she'd taken the time to look below the surface?

Penny took Rob's hand. "I promise you that he'll never do that again! Why weren't you supposed to tell me?"

"She said you'd lose your cool and rip into Greg. Then he'd get mad and beat her up worse."

Penny bit her lip. Angela was right. If she'd known this last week, she'd have been confronting Greg and hiring a lawyer for Angela. Now that she knew Greg was capable of murder, she was doing the only thing she could do; keeping Rob hidden and trying to find Angela so she could warn her away from Greg.

"She was probably right, Rob. At least she's safe as long as she stays in Toronto." A new and terrifying thought occurred to her. She had only Greg's word that Angela was in Toronto.

The sun's heat couldn't touch the chill that swept over her. Maybe Angela had never left Vancouver, maybe Greg's violence had escalated beyond mere beatings. She must keep that fear hidden from Rob; he didn't need more pain.

"Yeah," Rob said. "I wish we were there, too." He glanced up at Aunt Penny's face and wondered what she was thinking now. Ever since he'd seen Greg shoot that guy Larry, there'd been a voice in the back of his head whispering that Old Godzilla could have shot his Mom, too. It would explain why she hadn't told him she was going away, why she hadn't called. But he wasn't going to listen to the voice anymore. And he wasn't going to tell Aunt Penny about it. Saying it out loud might make it real.

Jack Kinkaid sprawled in a deck chair on a hotel terrace fronting Waikiki beach. Feet propped on the low stone wall separating terrace from sand, he trained his binoculars on the beach. Beside him was a cup of coffee, grown cold. It was his fourth since breakfast and the only interesting thing so far was the way Penny filled out her bikini.

If she was here to do business, she sure didn't act like it. The only person she'd talked to was that beach bum, whose green racing trunks were molded to his body like plastic wrap. He couldn't have found room for a single extra hair inside them, never mind a pound of coke or heroin. Unless that bulge at the front was phony.

She looked after the boy properly, though. Her indignation over the "short, dark man in the pink shirt" had been quite funny. If she'd known the man was Lieutenant Koyama of the drug squad she'd really have freaked.

The sun was getting hotter, reminding him he'd better phone his mother and ask her to water his garden and check his tomato plants. He'd thought of asking her to stay in the house while he was gone but, knowing her, she'd have worn herself out cleaning and tidying and cooking things for his freezer. She was better off in her little apartment where there wasn't so much to do.

Penny and Rob were coming out of the surf, going to their beach towels, packing up. Finally. Jack followed them as far as the Jolly Roger, then went to the phone booth across the street, where he could still keep tabs on them. His call to Ian Baker went through without delay.

"There's a new wrinkle," Ian said, sounding irritable. "Moller's reported his son missing."

"I don't get it. If he sent Penny Davis over here, he must have sent the boy with her. What's going on?"

"You're asking me? Moller says when he went to get the kid up yesterday morning, he was gone."

"I think his story stinks," Jack said.

"So do I. He said he's checked with everybody he can think of and no one knows anything. He also said he thought his sister-in-law had gone to Toronto to join his wife, who's supposed to be vacationing in that area."

Jack rubbed his jaw. "Sounds like he's lying about everything. Do I keep tailing her?"

"Yes, the boy is a side issue. Another odd thing; Carl Fredericks left for Honolulu this morning."

"Why would Moller send Fredericks if he already sent Davis?" Fredericks, who ostensibly ran a restaurant supply business, was a longtime associate of Moller's. He had no record, but any friend of Moller's was suspect.

"I can't figure it," Ian said. "She contact anybody yet?"

"She went swimming with a beach bum this morning, but it looked like a casual pickup."

"Give me a description."

"About twenty, blond curly hair, muscular, tanned. Say five foot eleven and 160 pounds. Oh, yeah, and a gold ring in his right ear."

"Check him out with the Honolulu squad. Phone me if you get anything."

So now what? Stay in the background or barge in on their lunch? He decided on lunch; he wanted to know what plans they had for the afternoon. He molded his expression into that of a shy, dry accountant and barged.

Rob said, "Hi!" and Penny smiled, though her expression seemed strained.

He sat down. "Where did you go this morning?"

"To the beach," Penny said.

"Bet you can't guess what happened to me," Rob said, leaning forward, his elbows on the table.

"You wrestled with a shark?"

"Nah, there aren't any sharks on the beach. A car almost ran over me."

"Really!" It must have happened after he'd seen them buy the beach ball and head for Waikiki beach. What he needed was some backup. He'd missed what had obviously been the most exciting ten minutes of the morning while scouting for a convenient hotel terrace where he could watch them. "What happened?"

"Some kids in an old car came tearing around the corner just as we stepped off the curb," Penny said.

"Yeah, they missed Aunt Penny by only this much," Rob said, holding the tips of two fingers a quarter inch apart. "This guy Vic grabbed me out of the way."

"It was scary," Penny said. "I didn't quit shaking until Vic bought me a coffee at the beach."

Vic? Must be the blond beach bum. Did that eliminate him as her contact?

"I'm glad you're both all right." He was, too. Coming that close to being wiped out by a speeding car would shake anybody up. The boy still had dark circles around his eyes. He waited while the waitress took their orders. "Where are you going after lunch?"

"We haven't decided." Her smile was warm, friendly. "Do you have any suggestions?"

She was leaving the door wide open for him. Obviously she wasn't going to do business this afternoon. Which meant he could quit tailing her and take care of other things.

"You might want to see the aquarium and the zoo. They're a few blocks north on Kalakaua."

"Cool!" Rob said.

Before Penny could ask him to come along, Jack said, "What sort of work do you do?"

"I spent the last six years as administrator for a repertory theater. Don't let the title fool you, though. I did everything from making coffee to selling tickets when they were shorthanded."

"Did you enjoy it?"

"Loved it! Every single minute. Well, almost every minute. Runs in my family, I guess. My father was an amateur actor and my sister and I always wanted to act. Hasn't worked out for either of us, but being behind the scenes is a good second best."

Her face was animated, her eyes sparkling. Jack found it hard to believe that anyone this openly excited about the arts could be involved in drug dealing. Maybe she was a better actor than he was.

"Have you done any acting?" he asked.

"A little. Crowd scenes, mostly. The absolute worst experience I ever had was in *Julius Caesar*. Some of us were walking backward in front of the emperor and I was so intent on being in character that I forgot to watch where I was going and fell off the stage."

Jack laughed. "What did you do?"

"Climbed back up and pretended it never happened."

A vague memory became clearer. "Was that Westport Players? About four years ago?"

She nodded.

"So that was you! I saw that production."

"I didn't know you were interested in theater." She leaned forward, her face eager. Jack found himself wanting to sit beside her and hold her hand. He pulled himself up short. He was supposed to be pretending to fall in love with her, not let it happen.

He rose abruptly. "Sorry to leave you," he said, "but I have to make some calls." He couldn't help being pleased when she looked disappointed.

In his room, Jack called Koyama's department to give them a description of Penny's beach bum. The guy was probably clean, but he had to check. As he hung up, he heard Penny and Rob come out of the elevator. Twenty minutes later, through his open door, he heard them leave again, chattering about the aquarium.

The old credit card trick got him into their room. A quick search of closet and furniture revealed nothing, but in Penny's suitcase was a small parcel with Angela Moller's name printed on it with a black felt pen.

Jack sat back on his heels and contemplated it. Was this the package she'd picked up from the jeweler's? He had to find out. He opened the parcel gently so he could put it back together to look like it hadn't been touched.

Inside the box was a half kilo of heroin.

Now he had proof that she was a courier. Moller must have sent her here to deliver heroin. Jack felt empty and disillusioned, like a kid opening a Christmas package and finding nothing inside.

The heroin couldn't be used as evidence because he didn't have a search warrant. Ian would give him a blast for doing an unauthorized search, so he wouldn't tell Ian. But at least he knew for sure he was on the right track.

Jack reassembled the package, put it back in the suitcase, and made sure everything in the room looked as it had when he came in. Back in his own room, questions began to surface through his black mood.

Why would she bring smack to Hawaii? It didn't make sense, when the major flow of heroin came from the Orient toward the West. Why was it still in her suitcase? If Moller had told her to deliver it, she'd have done that by now. Or was she only hoping to make a sale?

Another question. Why did she hint that she'd welcome his presence this afternoon? Reverse psychology maybe. She could have made him as a cop and figured to get rid of him by making him think her jaunt to the aquarium was innocent.

So why was he hanging around here? If he moved fast, he could pick up their trail. Too late, perhaps, but it was the best he could do.

He put on Bermuda shorts, a lurid Hawaiian shirt and a straw hat and scowled at himself in the mirror. With the cameras around his neck he couldn't look more like the caricature of a tourist if he'd tried.

He didn't have to be out in the field like this, he thought. He could take his promotion any time he wanted and look after the administrative end of things, like Ian. But he'd always liked the rough and tumble of the street.

More important, he wanted to even up the score for the bullet that had taken his father out and wounded his sister nearly twenty years ago. He couldn't do that without being where the action was.

He wondered what clothes Penny had put on for her afternoon jaunt. She had good taste-simple, bright colors, clean lines. He didn't like her taste in bags, though. She could put a kilo of smack into that shoulder bag and nobody'd ever know.

SIX

When they set off for the aquarium after lunch, Rob said, "I wanted Mr Kinkaid to come with us."

"So did I," Penny said. The man was totally inconsistent. He acted like he wanted her but turned down the chance to spend the afternoon with her. Was he immature or just plain weird?

Maybe he thought she was the stereotypical dumb blonde actress after all the babbling she'd done about theater. Well, that was his problem, not hers.

Talking about theater made her homesick for Westport Players. She'd lost more than just a job when Curt Wilson, tears in his eyes, had told her he couldn't afford to pay her wages. She'd lost the fun of prompting at rehearsals and the excitement of opening nights as well as working with a lot of interesting people. She hoped she'd find a similar job in Toronto. But right now she had more important things to think about.

"Rob, what do your Mom and Greg fight about?"

"Oh, he gets mad at her when she doesn't want to go someplace with him. He's always asking her where she's been or what she's done all day or telling her what clothes to wear and then she gets mad."

Her sister had never liked anyone checking up on her. She'd hate Greg acting as if he owned her.

Angela wouldn't go to the police about Greg. She hated them as much as Penny did, though it wasn't something they talked about. Rob, who loved cop shows on TV, thought cops were wonderful. He wanted to be one when he grew up. It wasn't likely he'd go to them on his own for help, though.

Why hadn't her sister come to her? Angela could have insisted on caution. It hurt that Angela felt she had to endure Greg's brutality in silence.

One thing for sure, if she had to run the rest of her life, she'd never let that monster get his hands on Rob again. She hoped he was sweating blood over Rob's disappearance. He deserved to suffer.

A voice shouted her name, jarring her out of her reverie. It was Vic, hurrying to catch up.

"Hi! Where you headed?" His jeans and T-shirt were molded as tightly to his body as his racing trunks had been.

"The aquarium. Rob's hooked on ocean creatures."

Vic looked disappointed. "I was thinking maybe I could take you on a tour somewhere."

"The aquarium and the zoo will be plenty for today."

"How about tomorrow?"

"I've already booked for a tour tomorrow." She dug in her bag for the brochure. "It's called the Little Circle Island Tour and Sea Life Park."

"Well, okay, how about Friday?" Even standing still, with his thumbs hooked into the waistband of his jeans, Vic looked ready to erupt with suppressed energy. "Or like, how about dinner tonight?"

"Not tonight." He could play tour guide if he wanted to; she wasn't interested in anything more than that.

"Okay then, Friday I'll rent a car and take you out. There's hundreds of great beaches."

"I can't afford to rent a car."

"Hey, listen up!" He put his hand on her shoulder. "The car's on me."

"I can't let you spend your money like that, Vic. You've already done so much."

"No sweat. I make good money and my old man's loaded."

"Yes, but..."

He squeezed her shoulder. "No 'buts,' okay? It's only a few bucks; I'll never miss it. And I'm bored out of my skull hanging around. So how about if I pick you up at your hotel Friday morning? Nine o'clock?"

"All right. I appreciate this, Vic."

"No sweat! It'll be fun showing you around. You sure you don't want to go somewhere besides the aquarium today?"

She assured him her plans were firm and he gave her the 'hang loose' sign.

"See you Friday then. Guess I'm going to be stuck with pumping iron this afternoon. You take care now." He strode away.

"Aunt Penny, could you buy me some dumbbells?"

"You want to pump iron, too? What for?"

His expression was a mixture of adult seriousness and childish belligerence. "So I'll be strong when I grow up. I'm gonna get even with Greg."

Should she tell him that wanting revenge wasn't right? But if she had the chance, she'd take revenge on Greg any way she could.

"We'll look for some later."

She couldn't blame Rob for the way he felt about his stepfather. What would Vic be like at forty? He was as smooth as Greg in a puppyish sort of way, but she didn't think twenty years would turn him into a blond version of her brother-in-law.

Why was Vic being so persistent when he knew she wasn't wealthy? Darn, she was beginning to sound paranoid. Plenty of people enjoyed helping others.

The aquarium was wonderfully cool. Rob said, "Phew! Can we have a drink first? I'm thirsty."

"Me, too." In the coffee shop she ordered two Cokes.

She sipped her drink, idly stirring the crushed ice with her straw. In the gift shop, a man with his back to her searched through a rack of post cards. His outfit of pink Bermuda shorts, sloppy multicolored Hawaiian shirt and floppy straw hat made her smile. He'd probably never dream of wearing a getup like that at home.

The man turned slightly toward her and she started. Jack Kinkaid, mustache, scars and the inevitable cameras around his neck. What was he doing here?

Was he following her? But why? He'd had the chance to join them this afternoon and backed away.

Was he so shy that he preferred to worship from a distance? She nearly laughed out loud. Whatever else he might be, Jack Kinkaid wasn't shy. She'd made it obvious she liked him, and though he kept turning up, apparently he wasn't interested. She must have misread the signals.

So why was he hanging around?

She followed Rob as he peered into the small aquariums, only half listening to his comments. When they went outside to the seal pools, she wasn't surprised to see Jack following. What was the stupid man trying to do?

She ignored him while Rob exclaimed over the playful seals that maneuvered through the water with a fluidity of motion she wished she could achieve. At the last pool, Rob said, "Hey, Mr Kinkaid is standing over there."

"Yes, I saw him."

"Don't you want to talk to him?"

"Not right now."

Rob gave her a puzzled look, then darted to the other end of the pool where the seals were playing with a rubber ball, taking turns balancing it on their muzzles.

Jack wasn't being a nuisance. He was merely there. Wherever she went. Why? If any normal man wanted to come on to her, he'd just do it. Jack was playing some kind of game. Or he wasn't as sane as he appeared to be.

She could march over there and tell him to get lost. But that was silly. He had as much right to be here as she did and he was minding his own business. Whatever that might be. Besides, he might go away permanently and, crazy as it seemed, she didn't want that.

"Rob," she called. "Ready for the zoo?"

A bus load of tourists crowded the lobby, forcing them to stop for a moment beside the gift shop. In the window was a leaping dolphin carved from wood, sleek and dynamic, a model of carefree movement. She pulled Rob into the shop.

"It's made from local wood," the clerk said, handing the dolphin to her. "The monkeypod tree. You'll see big ones across the street in the park."

She ran her fingers over the satin finish and flowing lines, and ached to have it, then winced when she saw the price tag. Maybe, if things worked out, she could come back and get it before they left Honolulu.

Kapiolani Park had open stretches of grass shaded by the great spreading branches of the monkeypod trees. Penny strolled toward the zoo, Rob darting ahead of her. Tonight she'd try the Toronto number until she got an answer, even if she had to stay up till dawn. What if Tim and Jane hadn't seen Angela? Penny shivered. If Angela wasn't in Toronto, it was likely she hadn't left Vancouver at all.

"Aunt Penny, look!" Rob's face was pressed against the bars of a monkey cage. "Aren't they silly?"

"Very," she agreed, watching their antics with a minimum of attention.

As she turned away from the cage, she caught a glimpse of bright pink Bermuda shorts and a Hawaiian shirt topped off with a straw hat. Not again! Jack Kinkaid was as silly as the monkeys.

For a moment she stood, irresolute, then hurried to catch up with Rob. If Jack wanted to follow her, there wasn't much she could do about it.

As they walked through the hotel lobby, Rob exclaimed, "Look! There's Gramps in the newspaper!" He squatted by the rack and pointed at the Vancouver Sun.

The headline read "Police persistence gets results." What had happened to her father? She grabbed the paper.

Police tenacity in attempting to solve the eleven-year-old robbery of a downtown branch of the Bank of Montreal paid off today when a man suspected in another robbery confessed to his part in the heist. A police spokesman said some of the stolen money has been recovered and the arrest of two other suspects is expected momentarily.

The cut-line beneath her father's photograph said that he'd been assistant manager of the branch at the time of the robbery and had been shot trying to protect a teller.

Penny fumbled with the keys as she opened the room door. This was wonderful news! Now the whole mess would be cleaned up and her parents could get on with their lives.

"How come Gramps is in the paper?" Rob asked, putting the chain on the door.

"The police arrested those guys who robbed the bank. The paper put his picture in because he's a hero."

"Because he got shot, right?"

"That's right." She knelt to hug Rob and he blinked in surprise. "I'm going to phone home and talk to him."

The phone rang as she reached to pick it up.

"It's Vic. Sure you won't change your mind about dinner?"

He couldn't have got her number, which meant he must be downstairs using the house phone. The last thing she needed right now was Vic and his insistent helpfulness.

"I'm sure," she said, "some other night maybe."

"Oh, well." He sounded disappointed. "Friday then. You won't forget?"

"I'm looking forward to it." Maybe by Friday, she'd have some idea of her next move. If only she could get on a plane right now and go home. That wouldn't work, though; she couldn't take Rob back to Vancouver.

"I'm going to have dinner delivered here," Penny said. "I need to make a few phone calls." Cheeseburgers with onions and mushrooms and french fries, the works-a mini celebration. "See if you can find something good on TV. Keep it down, though."

There was no answer at her parents' house. Strange. They never went out at night.

Still no one home at Tim's either. This was getting beyond frustrating. Where could they be all this time?

When she opened the bag of cheeseburgers, Rob wrinkled his nose and said, "Gross! French fries."

"I'm sorry, Rob. I forgot you don't like them." She dribbled ketchup on her own. "Just leave them, then."

He picked up his bag of fries with the tips of his fingers and dropped it in the bathroom waste basket. He closed the door. "I can't stand the smell."

Was he looking for attention? She couldn't think of anyone she knew, child or adult, who didn't like fries.

They ate their hamburgers on the lanai and fed crumbs to a crowd of cooing pigeons. Penny went back to the phone. After half an hour, she became aware that the toilet was flushing constantly. The bathroom door was closed.

She rapped on it. "Rob? What are you doing?"

"Nothing."

"Can I come in?"

"Yeah."

Rob was sitting on the floor by the toilet, the bag of fries beside him. She watched him carefully take three fries, his fingers protected from them by a tissue, drop them into the toilet and press the lever to flush.

"Rob, is that really necessary?"

"Yeah."

"Couldn't you do them all at once?"

"It might plug the toilet."

Defeated, she closed the door. Arguing with logic was a waste of time. Besides, he'd behaved pretty well so far.

If he was good in her company but bad at home, then it could be Greg's influence that had caused him to become destructive. He said he hated Greg because the man had beaten Angela, but Rob might have reasons of his own.

Penny opened the bathroom door again. "Rob, was it your idea to play sports? Or did Greg make you do it?"

"He made me."

"Ah." On her rare visits to Angela's house, Greg had bragged about buying sports equipment for the boy and giving him the chance to toughen up and become a man.

She'd assumed Greg was being a good father. Making assumptions seemed to be as much a waste of time as arguing with logic.

Another hour of punching numbers and still no one answered either phone. She could understand Tim and Jane not being home; they liked partying and they often went up to the lake in summer. But where was her father?

Her desire for celebration had been replaced by fear. Could the police have arrested her father? After hounding him for so long they wouldn't want to admit they'd been wrong. They might even manufacture evidence to prove they'd been right. She leaned back, suddenly weary.

Vic slammed the phone down. "Stupid broad won't do anything I want."

Fredericks looked up from his science fiction magazine. "She's going with you Friday. That's only the day after tomorrow. What's the problem?"

"Man, you know from nothing!" Vic paced back and forth. "The longer I spend on this job, the bigger chance somebody is gonna remember seeing me around her."

"So what? You got a record?"

Vic stopped in front of Fredericks, fists doubled up. "Shut up! You're about as dumb as they come."

"Cool off, Vic. I just asked a question." The guy seemed to be permanently wired. Didn't matter what he said or did, Vic jumped down his throat. Was the kid on drugs or just crazy?

"I got a reputation for clean kills and clean getaways. I don't like risking that. And getting hauled in to show my face in an ID parade takes time outta my day."

"Okay. So what are you going to do?"

"I'm not waiting for Friday, that's for sure. They're going on a bus tour tomorrow. So are we. There could be a chance to take care of business somewhere along the line."

"Both of them?"

"If I can. But the kid's gotta go first. You'd never figure it out, Fredericks, but if the kid is left on his own, the pigs will glom onto him and ship him back home. Which ain't gonna make anybody happy. If the broad is left on her own, she'll need a shoulder to cry on." Vic grinned. "Come to Uncle Vic, sweetheart."

"You can't go on the bus. She knows you."

"You're gonna be on the bus, Fredericks. I'll drive the rental car."

"That won't work either. Rob knows me."

"So dye your hair and buy some different shades. Do I have to do all your thinking for you?"

Fredericks sighed. The sooner this was all over, the better. He missed Candy and he didn't like the thought of her, all alone, moping in the kennels.

SEVEN

Dolphins arced high out of the water, reminding Jack of the way Penny had yearned over the dolphin in the gift shop yesterday. He'd had a sudden urge to buy the thing for her.

He must be going nuts. Or the heat was affecting him. The woman was a criminal!

This morning he'd made sure he was first onto the tour bus so he could hide behind a newspaper at the back. Penny and the boy were near the front. Glancing at the other passengers, he'd noticed a man a couple of rows ahead of him, on the other side. Fredericks, with his hair dyed black. It looked like the action was about to start.

Sea Life Park seemed as good a place as any for their rendezvous. It wouldn't matter if he was there since Fredericks didn't know him and Penny no doubt had him tagged as weird but harmless.

He had to quit calling her Penny; it was too friendly. The name suited her, though. Bright new penny.

Wrong, Kinkaid. A bad penny, a cold, money-hungry woman who dealt in drugs and used an innocent kid for cover. She and Fredericks were pretending they didn't know each other. Naturally. But why was Fredericks here at all? Had Moller sent him as backup? Something to do with Rob?

Restless, Jack adjusted the cameras around his neck. The morning was half over and nothing had happened. Rob, giggling, ducked under the spray of water from passing dolphins while Penny watched, her face sober.

Had she read the article in the paper about the robbery last night? Maybe that's why she wasn't smiling. She'd know her father had been arrested by now.

Fredericks was at the far end of the bleachers, dark glasses hiding the direction of his gaze. Not likely he was interested in the wildlife.

After the dolphin show, Fredericks followed Penny and Rob through the park. They still hadn't made contact when it was time to get back on the bus. What was going on? Jack ignored Penny's glance as he boarded; he didn't want to draw Fredericks' attention by speaking to her.

Part-way back to Honolulu, the driver turned off the highway and pulled into a large parking lot half filled with tour buses and cars. "This is Pali Lookout," he announced, "an important place in Hawaii's history. It's where King Kamehameha defeated opposition to uniting the islands by pushing the enemy warriors over the cliffs."

The bus doors opened and the driver added, "It's a great view, but the wind is very strong, so watch your step and hang on to the railings. We don't want to lose any of you." He glanced at his watch. "You've got ten minutes."

Rob was off the bus and racing toward the cliffs before Jack even got to his feet. As he stepped out, Penny was hurrying to catch up to Rob and Fredericks wasn't far behind. Was this their meeting place?

At the steel railing guarding the terrace from the cliff edge, Jack looked down the wooded, almost vertical slope to a broad plain a thousand feet below, and beyond the plain to the sea sparkling in the distance. The warm wind blew in violent gusts, whipping his shirt against his body and catching the brim of his cotton hat. It blew off, swirling in the relentless air current, and disappeared into the trees far below.

Already some passengers were retreating, hanging on to skirts and hats, their protests lost in the squalling wind. Rob raced back and forth on the terrace, holding his arms out, letting the gusts play with his body.

The wind died away for a few seconds and Penny's voice, from the far end of the terrace, sounded clear and distinct. "Rob, be careful! Don't fall!"

"I can't fall! The wind's holding me up!" Rob whirled toward the railing. Jack lost sight of Penny as a new throng of tourists swarmed down the steps to the cliff edge, separating her from the boy.

She wouldn't be able to see Rob from where she was. Jack moved closer, hurrying when he saw Rob bend forward between the two horizontal railings to look over the cliff.

A split second before the crowding tourists hid Rob from view, he saw a man with red hair boost the boy through the railings into empty space.

Rob pitched forward, a scream bursting from his throat as he saw the cliff falling away below him. He grazed against a rock projection, which twisted his body around and right side up. His hands scrabbled at the cliff as he slid down. He heard a scream from above as a shrub scuffed his chest. He grabbed it with both hands.

His arms felt like they'd been half jerked out of his shoulders. But he wasn't falling any more.

He raised his head. Aunt Penny was hanging upside down, her legs hooked around one of the railing's metal uprights, and stretching out her arms toward him.

Too far away. She couldn't reach him. He looked down, searching for something to brace his feet on.

There was nothing there. Only the trees far below.

A spasm of terror shook his body. He looked up again, his hands tightening convulsively on the shrub.

"Get a rope! See if the bus driver has a rope! I need some help here!" Mr Kinkaid's voice.

The shrub gave way a little, sending another spasm through him. Rob squeezed his eyes shut. If he was going to fall, he didn't want to look down.

"Move it! That bush is going to give way in a minute." Another man's voice.

Rob clung. Tried not to move. Kept his eyes tight shut. His hands hurt. The muscles in his arms and shoulders were shrieking.

Mr Kinkaid's voice again. "Penny, listen. We're going to grab your ankles and lower you down so you can grab Rob's wrists.

"Do it!" Her tone was harsh, urgent.

Rob opened his eyes. The shrub pulled away from the cliff a little further. He tried to say something, but all he could do was croak. Sweat poured down his body.

He wanted to shut his eyes again, but he had to keep looking so he'd know when she got close enough.

Mr Kinkaid had his legs wrapped around an upright and so did another guy. They had Aunt Penny by the ankles, lowering her down toward him.

The shrub tore away a little more, leaving his right hand with nothing to hang on to. A sob burst from his throat.

Two strong hands grasped his wrists.

"Got him!" His aunt's voice was husky, breathless.

Rob's heart thumped harder. Could she pull him up? She might fall, too. He shut his eyes again.

He felt himself being dragged up, ever so slowly, his skin hurting where it scraped against the rocks.

People were shouting, giving directions. Mr Kinkaid was swearing.

More hands grabbed him, by the arms, then his waist. Then his legs. He was being pulled away from the parapet, his bare knees burning as they scraped the rough concrete.

Aunt Penny hugged him like she'd never let go. He clung to her, the tears coming fast.

Jack got to his feet as people clustered solicitously around Penny and Rob.

Thank God she was safe!

Where had that thought come from? He'd have done anything to save the boy, but if Penny had gone over the cliff, all it meant was one less drug dealer in the world.

Jack pulled his shirt down and brushed his jacket, ignoring the bloody abrasions on his chest and belly from being dragged across concrete.

He scanned the crowd for the redheaded man in big sunglasses and baggy green track suit who'd pushed Rob through the railings. The man was gone. So was Carl Fredericks. Jack couldn't remember seeing him after they'd left the bus. As he started toward the parking lot, the bus driver ran down the steps with a length of rope.

"It's okay," Jack said, "they're safe."

"What a relief!" the driver said, rubbing a hand across his forehead. "I keep telling people to watch out but they don't listen. The winds gust something fierce..."

Jack cut him off. "Have you seen a tall, skinny, black-haired man in sunglasses, pale blue pants and a Hawaiian shirt in the last five minutes?"

"Can't say as I have."

Jack ran toward the parking lot.

Fredericks wasn't there. He must have had a car waiting for him. No sign of the guy with the red hair either.

Penny and Rob came up the steps hand in hand, surrounded by people. The driver helped them onto the bus, then herded the rest of his passengers into their seats.

Jack stopped beside Penny and Rob. "You both okay?" It seemed inadequate but what could he say?

"Yes." She was lying; her hands were still shaking and she was trying to hide it by clasping them together in her lap. "I can't thank you enough for what you did."

"Did you see what happened?"

There was fear in her eyes. "No. It all happened so fast. It's hard to believe he fell."

So she suspected Rob had been pushed over the rail. He knew it. "Is there anything I can do?"

"No. Nothing. We'll be fine."

She didn't sound as if she believed it.

Back in Waikiki, in the hotel lobby, he said again, "You sure there's nothing I can do?"

Her face was pale, her blue eyes wide and still frightened. The boy hadn't said a word since they'd left the Pali Cliffs and he clung to Penny, sucking his thumb.

"There's nothing, thanks. You've already done more than anyone could ask." She turned away and, taking Rob's hand, walked toward the elevator, head high, back stiff.

What was wrong with the woman? She was acting like he'd been the one to shove Rob through the railing. In his room, he phoned the Honolulu drug squad.

"Lieutenant Koyama, it's Jack Kinkaid. I called yesterday about a man I saw with Ms Davis. Your staff come up with anything on it?"

"Maybe. You'd have to confirm it by looking at the mug shots. There's a young hood named Vic Nelson that fits the description, including the gold ring in his right ear."

"So what's his game? Picking up lonely ladies, preferably rich? Or drugs?"

"Neither," Koyama said, "Nelson is a contract killer."

A hit man. And Fredericks had followed Penny and Rob all morning, then disappeared before the attack on Rob. It had been a deliberate attempt at murder. Jack's hand clenched around the receiver.

"I take it you've never made any charges stick."

"We've never had enough evidence to charge him. He's fast and efficient."

"Somebody tried to kill Rob Moller this morning. I saw the man but he didn't look like Nelson." The red hair had been pretty bright; it could have been a wig.

Koyama said. "Perhaps Miss Davis was delivering payment and decided to cut herself in for a share. That would have made her extremely unpopular."

It was possible. Killing the boy would be a way of disciplining her. It was also possible she'd stolen the heroin in her suitcase from Moller and now he was after her. But that didn't compute. Moller wouldn't kill his own son.

Jack told Koyama about the morning's events and described Carl Fredericks. "I'll come over and check those mug shots soon as I can. If the guy she was with on the beach is Vic Nelson, I'll have to rethink this whole scene."

"One thing doesn't fit," Koyama said. "Nelson isn't known for getting friendly with his victims He's a professional."

As Jack hung up, he heard someone knocking on a door down the corridor. Sticking his head out, he saw a boy with a pizza box standing outside Penny's room. He caught a whiff of spicy Italian sausage and fried onions and backed into his room. When he heard the elevator again, he went downstairs and hailed a taxi.

An hour later he was back. After making sure Penny and Rob were still in their room, he phoned Ian in Vancouver.

"It's Jack. There are some strange things going on around here." He gave Ian a quick summary.

There was a moment's silence. "You say Fredericks followed Davis and the boy all morning, but didn't make contact? I don't get it."

"Neither do I. Maybe Moller sent him to get the boy. But he was nowhere around when Rob went over the cliff."

"And you saw a man deliberately push him?"

"Yeah. Would Moller get rid of his own kid? I can't believe it."

Ian was silent again. Then, "I can. For one thing, the kid isn't really Moller's, he's a stepson. And suppose he witnessed Larry Wing's murder?"

Jack thought about Rob's hunted look, his bitten nails. "Yeah, that's a thought. But what about Davis? She looks after that boy like he was her own. Is she a courier or is she trying to hide the boy from Moller?"

Why was he questioning her motives? She had a half kilo of heroin sitting in her suitcase; that proved what her motive was.

Ian grunted. "When you saw them at Vancouver airport, did the boy have any luggage?"

"She was carrying two suitcases. But as soon as they got here, she bought him a bunch of clothes."

"Okay, that sounds like the trip could have been a last-minute decision. But why not Toronto? That's where his mother's supposed to be."

"Maybe the flight to Toronto was sold out."

"So she just grabbed the next available plane, no matter where it was going? Sounds pretty far out to me."

"Listen, Ian, that was late Monday night. Wing's body was found early Tuesday morning, right? So maybe the kid did see the killing and she was getting him out of the way as fast as she could. I can guarantee one thing—that boy is scared of something."

"Okay, let's say you're right. That doesn't mean she's not dealing drugs. She went to see Moller twice last week and we know she picked up heroin for him."

Jack sighed. "Yeah, okay. I still think she's trying to protect the boy, though." Maybe she was a mule; could be that Moller was blackmailing her into carrying drugs.

"You get anything on the guy you saw with her?"

"I just had a look at the mug shots. His name is Vic Nelson and he's a hit man."

Ian's silence was longer this time. "This is getting complicated. It doesn't take two men to get rid of one kid. Maybe there's some kind of turf war going on here."

"Revenge? Like Moller's trespassing on someone else's territory and they're going to kill his kid in retaliation? That could have been done any time after the plane landed. Why try to make it look like an accident?"

"I don't know." Ian said. "Let's go back to the idea that Moller wants to silence the kid because he saw the murder. He gets Davis to take him somewhere far away, like Hawaii, so a convenient accident can happen to him."

"No."

"What do you mean, no?"

"She loves that kid, I'd stake my life on it. I've watched them together. Besides, these guys could be after her, too. Whatever the kid knows, he's bound to have told her about it."

"Don't let a pretty face scramble your brain, Jack. The hit man made a mess of his attempt on the boy and she had to rescue him to make it look good."

Jack swore under his breath. He'd had the same thought himself. Why did he keep wanting to defend Penny? He must be going soft in the head. "I'd like to talk to her, find out what she knows."

"And blow your cover? No. Give it another day. And stick to that kid. I don't want anything happening to him."

Neither do I, Jack thought as he hung up. He liked the boy. He could have had a son like Rob if it hadn't been for what had happened twenty years ago.

The scene he'd walked in on was still vivid in his memory. His father, Keith, dead on the kitchen floor, his sister Connie bleeding from a hip wound, his mother passed out from shock. The house full of cops, most of them friends and all of them grim-faced. They'd got Parker, the ex-con who did it, but that hadn't done Keith any good.

Keith had arrested Parker years before for drug dealing and the man had gone to prison, threatening to kill Keith when he came out. Like most seasoned cops, Keith had ignored the threats. When Parker came out of jail, he picked up a weapon and went straight to the house.

In court, Jack had watched Parker get a life sentence and decided to be a cop like his father. Decided, too, that he wasn't going to have a family.

Connie was lucky; she'd recovered. But not everybody was that lucky.

When Sara had first mentioned marriage, he'd cared enough to question his principles. She was independent and tough and hadn't wanted kids, so he wouldn't have had anybody to worry about except her. But putting even one life in danger was too much.

He hadn't cared enough to marry Barbara until she claimed to be pregnant. Funny how disappointed he'd been when he found out she wasn't. "How dumb can you get?" Jack muttered, cat-footing down the hall to check on Penny and Rob.

EIGHT

Penny closed the door as the delivery boy thanked her enthusi-astically for the second time. She put the chain back on and stared at her still shaking hands. Had she given him five dollars instead of two? Or even ten? She wasn't sure what she'd done.

She wasn't sure of anything. The fluttering pigeons, the palm trees, the heat and sunshine seemed like a dream. The spicy aroma of the pizza was real, though she had no appetite. But it was noon, time for food, and she needed some sense of normality.

Jack Kinkaid carried a gun.

She'd seen the gun when the men had pulled her and Rob onto the terrace and Jack was getting to his feet. That had been real, whatever else wasn't.

All his talk about being an accountant was window dressing. She should have told him to get lost right at the start. But who was he?

A gun. And Rob going over the railing. And she thought some-one had shoved her when she went after him. Kinkaid? It could have been. There'd been no one else on the bus who knew her. But why?

She didn't want to believe he'd pushed her. He'd played a big part in saving her and Rob, and why would he have done that if he intended to kill them? This morning, before the tour, she'd wanted to believe he liked her; had been wishing he'd get up enough nerve to ask her out or explain what game he was playing. Or both.

Now she didn't know what to believe. Jack had acted quickly at the Pali Cliffs, had assumed authority as though he was accus-tomed to it. He was probably none of the things he said he was. Accountants didn't carry guns.

She used her Swiss army knife to cut the pizza into wedges. "Rob, have some lunch." He was sitting in front of the television set, staring at a nature show and sucking his thumb. She wanted to pull the thumb away from his mouth, wanted him to act his age. But how could she lecture him about something so silly when his life was in danger?

He bit into his pizza, eyes still on the television screen. Penny found swallowing difficult, but the second bite went down a little easier. If she could eat a whole piece, it would prove she had control over at least one thing in her life.

Rob put his pizza down. "I don't feel good."

She rested her hand on his shoulder. "Because of this morning? Or something else?"

How she wished Angela was here! Last night's calls to Toronto had produced nothing though she'd tried until it was two in the morning there. There'd been no answer at her father's house either. Maybe they'd gone away to avoid reporters. If she didn't have to look after Rob, she could go home and provide moral support.

The skin around Rob's eyes looked bruised. "Somebody pushed me," he said.

She'd known instinctively it hadn't been an accident. "Did you see who it was?"

"No. I was looking down the cliff. The next thing I was falling."

She had to face facts. Greg had learned where they were. And sent somebody to kill Rob. Her, too, probably.

Penny dropped her pizza in the waste basket. Forget normality! She and Rob were in imminent danger. Greg must have known where they were almost as soon as they'd arrived.

"Rob, was Jack Kinkaid anywhere near you when you went over the rail?"

He looked surprised. "I don't think so. Why?"

"I just wondered, that's all."

"He helped you get me back up the cliff."

"Yes," she said, "Yes, he did."

But why was he wearing a gun? Who was he?

She had to face the possibility that Jack Kinkaid was working for Greg. Maybe he'd been following them even before they got on the plane to Honolulu.

Rob was sprawled in front of the television again, picking at loose threads in the carpet. Better than thumb sucking. There was nothing for him to do except watch TV; they certainly weren't going to leave the safety of the room. But they couldn't stay locked in here forever.

Penny phoned Vancouver again. Even if the police had arrested her father, her mother had to come home sometime.

"Penny! I've been wanting so badly to get in touch with you, but I didn't know how."

"Is it Dad? Has he been arrested?"

"Yes." Dora started to cry.

She'd been right! The cops were determined to carry on their vendetta against her father. She had to find a way to get home and fight them. Some way that didn't put Rob in worse danger.

"Have you hired a lawyer?"

Dora, her voice under control again, said, "I went to Legal Aid. There's something else. Rob's missing. Greg told me and it was in the papers yesterday morning, too."

That was a jolt. It hadn't occurred to her Greg would report Rob as missing. But naturally he would. Window dressing again. It must have been a cruel three days for her parents, fretting over their only grandson.

"He's with me, Mom. He's all right."

"Penny! Why didn't you let anyone know?"

"It's too long a long story to tell over the phone. Did Greg come to you looking for Rob?"

"Of course! What would you expect? His only son is missing. You think he wouldn't move heaven and earth to find him?"

Oh, he'd move heaven and earth all right.

"Penny, Greg told me you were going to Toronto. Is Angela there?"

"No, we're in Hawaii." No reason to keep it secret from anyone now. Greg knew exactly where they were. "I've been trying to get in touch with Angela but no luck. Have you heard from her?"

Please say yes, Penny thought, please tell me she's all right.

"Not a word. I don't know what's the matter with her, going off for so long and leaving Rob behind."

"Don't worry, Mom. Rob's fine." Her mother couldn't do anything to help so there was no point explaining the situation. She'd only get more upset.

"I'll phone Greg; the poor man is beside himself with worry."

Yeah, right.

"I'll come home just as fast as I can. Keep your chin up and give my love to Dad."

There was so much more she wanted to know but she couldn't deal with her father's problems from here. The most important task was getting Rob to a safe place.

Could she fly to Vancouver and put Rob into some kind of protective custody? Phoning the police in Honolulu wouldn't work; it wasn't their problem. It was the Vancouver cops who had to deal with Greg.

And because she was Reg Davis's daughter, it wouldn't do any good to phone the Vancouver cops. They'd called her in twice for questioning in the past year alone, though they had no reason to suspect she was involved in the heist.

But they might look after Rob; surely none of them could be so twisted as to let a little kid be killed.

No. The boys in blue were her last resort.

There was a knock at the door. For a moment she stared at it, frightened. Who could it be?

There was only one way to find out.

Making sure the chain was firmly in place, she called, "Who is it?"

"It's Jack Kinkaid, Penny." His voice sounded deeper, more confident. "I'd like to talk to you."

Anger at his duplicity raised her own voice to a higher pitch. "I'll bet you would! Just forget it!"

"Penny, this is important. Open the door."

"Leave me alone. I won't talk to you. You lied to me!"

She sat at the telephone desk, her elbows on the table, her head in her hands, and willed herself to be calm. Jack called out again, then pounded on the door. Finally the pounding stopped. How had he known what room she had?

Well, of course, he'd asked at the desk. All too easy to think like a criminal—or a policeman—if you put your mind to it. She'd have to learn to think the same way if she was going to get Rob and herself out of this mess.

"Why don't you want to talk to Mr Kinkaid?" Rob asked.

"Because I don't trust him. I think he might be one of Greg's friends."

"He couldn't be. He was the one that got help to pull us back up the cliff."

"I know, but he's wearing a gun. Why would he do that if he isn't a criminal?"

"He might be a policeman. Policemen wear guns, even when they're working undercover."

She hadn't thought of that. But why would a policeman follow her around Hawaii? Surely the Vancouver cops wouldn't push their harassment that far.

"You could be right, Rob, but I'm not willing to take a chance on it." Not on a Vancouver policeman, anyway.

Rob stood beside her. "What are we going to do now, Aunt Penny? Greg's hired some guy to get rid of me, hasn't he?"

She hadn't wanted him to think about his life being in danger. He was only nine; he wouldn't understand. Then she remembered that he liked to watch cop shows on TV. He probably understood better than she did.

"We have to get back to Vancouver. We'll call the police from the airport and ask them to take us to a safe house until Greg has been arrested. And until we go to the airport, we'll have to stay in this room."

Rob's shoulders relaxed a little. "Yeah, okay. I wish I'd seen who pushed me."

"So do I. If you can think of anything else we should do, Rob, I want to know."

"Okay."

He went back to his movie. Penny reached for the phone again.

The result of her call was disheartening. There were no seats on any flight until Saturday and even that was on standby, which meant they'd have to stay in this box of a room all day tomorrow as well. And possibly be penned up in the Honolulu airport for a day or two.

Penny sorted through the contents of her handbag. Anything to keep her hands busy.

She was sure now that Angela's rainy-day money had been meant to finance her escape from Greg. But why had she gone to Toronto without Rob and the money? If, in fact, she actually had gone. Penny shelved the question; all she could cope with was the here and now.

What if camping out in Vancouver airport, waiting for the police to give them protection, didn't work? Changing into her red bikini, she sat on the lanai to think. Reflected sunlight glared from the white walls of the building, intensifying the heat.

Her mind drifted into different scenarios. The worst part, as Rob had realized, was not being able to put a face to the man who was trying to kill them.

If Rob's death had been meant to look like an accident, it could only be because Greg was too deep into drug dealing to risk being investigated. That meant any further attempts would also appear accidental. If she took great care, there was a chance they'd get out of here alive.

"Penny, I have to talk to you."

Jack Kinkaid's voice! Where was he?

He spoke again, his voice tense, urgent. "Penny, do yourself a favor and listen."

There! He was on the next lanai but one.

"How did you get out there?" she demanded.

"This is my room," he said, one hand resting casually on the railing.

She stood up. "You mean you've been here the whole time? You booked in the same time we did?"

"Penny, listen to me."

He'd been there all the time. Next door almost. Panic galvanized her legs. He could get from his lanai to hers if he wanted to. She dove into the room.

Inside, the sliding door locked against human predators and the drapes drawn against sunlight, her panic subsided. Rob hadn't even looked up; he was submerging his fear in the western gunfight blaring from the television screen, his fingers busy pulling strings of elastic out of his socks.

She put on shorts and a blouse, and stretched out on the bed. Jack couldn't get into her room unless he broke down a door. But how was she going to get out of here without him following?

It didn't really matter who he was. If he worked for Greg he was gunning for her and if he was a cop—which she found hard to believe—she had every reason in the world not to trust him.

There was nothing she could do except wait until morning when Vic came to get them. She'd tell him to forget touring the island. Perhaps he'd take them to the airport Saturday morning, though. She wished he was here now, as protection against Jack Kinkaid, but she didn't have his phone number, didn't even know his last name.

Time to try Tim and Jane in Toronto again.

The phone rang only twice before it was picked up and she recognized Tim's boisterous voice.

"It's Penny Davis. I've been trying to reach you for days. Is Angela there?"

"No. Is she supposed to be?"

The receiver grew hot and slippery in her palm. "She told Greg she was going to visit you and Jane. Are you telling me she never arrived?"

"Not that I know of. She hasn't been to see us, anyway." Tim sounded concerned. "We haven't heard from her for a long time."

"But you haven't been answering your phone. You wouldn't know if she was trying to get in touch."

"We've only been away four days, up at the cottage. When did you say Angela left Vancouver?"

"About two and a half weeks ago."

"Well, she hasn't been here. Other than the last four days, we've been home, praying that the air conditioner keeps working. Is Angie in trouble?"

"Yes. If she does show up, would you tell her to phone me? I'll be at this number until early Saturday morning. Tell her it's urgent. No, tell her it's a matter of life and death."

Penny hung up the phone, tears stinging her eyes. Angela had never arrived in Toronto. She'd probably never left Vancouver. That could mean Greg had...

She pressed her palms to her eyes, a searing ache in her chest as memories drifted through her mind—her father coming home in the wheelchair and Angela, upset and resentful of the changes in her life, running to her for comfort. Angela, made-up, jangling with jewelry, defiant, going out on her first date at fourteen. Angela, sitting cross-legged on Penny's bed, talking about love and life. Angela at fifteen, holding newborn Rob in her arms—then the emptiness after she'd run away. Angela, glowing with hope and happiness, walking down the aisle with Greg.

Penny fought the images. She must not cry, or let Rob know how frightened she was. And she must not give in to despair. There had to be some other explanation for Angela's disappearance.

NINE

In the morning Penny stepped onto the lanai, glad to breathe fresh air and feel the soft heat caress her skin. Within seconds a dozen white pigeons fluttered around her, waiting for a handout. She wished she felt as perky as they did, but she'd slept very little.

"You guys like pizza?" she asked them.

She glanced at Jack Kinkaid's lanai. His door was shut, the drapes drawn. She hoped he'd stay there. If he tried pounding on her door again, she'd call hotel security.

He kept insisting he had to talk to her. Why? The man made no sense at all and never had.

Penny went inside and locked the door. The last thing she needed was Kinkaid doing a Superman leap onto her lanai. Her watch said seven. Still two hours before Vic was due and she was ravenous. Should she phone room service? No. Better not open the door if she didn't have to. Breakfast would have to be cold pizza. She cut it into wedges and scrubbed the knife in the bathroom sink. She was half way through her first piece when Rob woke up.

"Are you eating pizza?" he said sleepily.

"Want some?"

"Yeah. I'm starving."

She watched him eat, crumbs and pineapple shreds dropping on the coverlet. He seemed to have slept deeply all night. She'd been prepared for him to wake with nightmares, but he'd never stirred. Perhaps she'd had enough for both of them.

When he was dressed, he said, "Do we have to go back to Vancouver? When Godzilla finds out he'll come after us."

"Godzilla? Is that what you call Greg?" It was the perfect name for him. "He won't know what plane we're on because I didn't make reservations. We're on standby. When we get to Vancouver airport, I'll phone the police and they can send someone to get us. We won't leave the airport until we have a safe place to go. Sound okay?"

His face cleared. "They'll arrest him when they find out about that guy, won't they?"

"I'm sure they will." She wasn't sure but Rob didn't need to know that.

"What'll we do today?"

"Vic's coming at nine. He was going to drive us around to look at the scenery, but I think we'd better stay here. Maybe he can pick up a couple of videos for us instead."

"Okay, but I wish it was Mr Kinkaid who was coming."

"If Mr Kinkaid is one of Greg's buddies, we don't want him around, do we?"

"No, I guess not." He slid off the bed and went to turn on the television.

Penny, picking pizza crumbs off the bed, became aware of an acrid smell. Rob was sitting on the floor with the ashtray between his legs. He had torn off a paper match and was watching it burn in the ash tray.

"Rob, what are you doing?"

He looked up at her. "Pretending I'm burning Greg's restaurant down."

"Oh, Rob!" She knelt beside him. "Please don't do that. Burning the restaurant won't hurt Greg. His fire insurance would pay him whatever the place is worth."

"I never thought of that." He put the matches and ashtray on the desk and went back to the TV, clicking the channel changer until he found a movie.

Penny ached for him, wishing she could ease his pain and make him safe. She'd felt just the same about Angela when she was growing up.

Angela had been thirteen to her twenty when their father was shot. From then on Dora had focused all her attention on him. Penny had taken Angela to buy clothes, helped her with home-work, talked to her.

It hadn't worked. Angela had been dazzled by glamor and money and spent her spare time reading movie magazines and fan-tasizing about the clothes and jewelery she'd wear when she was a famous actress or a millionaire's wife. The fantasies might have been a defense against reality, but nothing Penny said could con-vince her there were more important things in life.

A year later Angela was dating and using drugs. Unimpressed by Penny's warnings, she refused to attend youth programs or go for counseling. By fifteen she was pregnant and announced that she had quit using drugs because it was bad for the baby.

Then she'd taken Rob and run away to Toronto, leaving a note that said there was no future in dull, backward Vancouver. Three years later she came home, poised, lovely and soon in demand as a model.

Angela still ignored her advice. Penny had warned her against Greg, had said he would make her unhappy. Perhaps Angela had repeated her words to Greg and that was why he hated her so much. Lately, in spite of Angela's denials, she'd become sure her sister's marriage was less than ideal.

Would Rob go his own way, too, ignoring her advice? All she could do right now was try to make sure he lived long enough to choose his own path.

It seemed to take forever for her watch to tick away the hour between eight and nine. She paced, filed her nails, paced, picked up her book and put it down, paced again. She even thought of packing, but she had to save something to do for later.

At nine the phone rang. It was Vic. "You guys ready to roll? You want to meet me here or should I come up?"

"I think you'd better come up."

He had on white shorts and T-shirt, an attractive contrast to his warm tan, and a cheerful grin. It was such a relief to see a friendly face she felt like hugging him. Instead, she invited him in. Rob left his post in front of the television long enough to lock and chain the door as soon as Vic was inside.

"There's a problem, Vic. We can't go sightseeing with you. Someone tried to kill Rob yesterday. We'll be safer if we stay in the room."

His eyes widened and the grin vanished. "No kidding?"

"No kidding."

"Who was it, do you know?"

"A hit man hired by Rob's stepfather."

"Wow!" He paused. "Hey! You think maybe the car that nearly hit you was the same guy?"

Penny remembered the heat and the whistle of air as the car had swept by. It hadn't occurred to her that the near miss had been anything but accidental. But it seemed as though everything that happened to them was meant to look like an accident.

"It might have been. If so, that means he's had two tries." The phrase 'third time lucky' flashed into her mind.

Vic sat down. "I can see you're spooked. But what if the guy breaks in here? He has to know where you're staying, right? You'd be better off outta here."

"He'll be watching, Vic. He'll follow us if we leave. Besides, I think he's trying to make it look like an accident and he can't do that if he breaks into the room."

"What a bummer! I bought a real gourmet picnic lunch for us, too."

"That was sweet of you. But we can have a picnic on the lanai."

Vic grinned. "Hey, I got a plan that'll fool the creep. You don't really want to sit in here all day sweating it out, do you?"

She had to admit she didn't. The three hours since she'd wakened seemed more like three days. Three days of being locked into her own mind, going round and round with all the 'what ifs.' Rob needed to burn off some of his nervous energy, too.

"Okay, this place has a service elevator, right? Guy I know used to work here, which is how I found out. It's right at the back of the building. When you get out you're where the food's delivered and laundry and stuff like that. I got a rental car out front so I'll just swing around into the alley and pick you up there. How's that sound?"

"It sounds good." The killer wouldn't pay any attention to Vic, and if he didn't know where they were, he couldn't follow them. She'd have a day's breathing space.

She shook her head. The risk might be small, but she wasn't going to take any chances with Rob's life. Seeing the sights and picnicking sounded enticing, but they didn't dare leave the room.

"I'm sorry, Vic, but I have to say no. Going out is more of a risk than I want to take."

Vic scowled. She didn't blame him. He'd had the day planned and she was ruining it for him.

After a moment, he said, "Haven't been to Diamond Head, have you? Great view from up there. I was figuring on Hanauma Bay for the picnic. It's a conservation area for fish and stuff. Rob would like that."

"I know he would."

"I'd be there to protect you." He flexed his arm and patted the bulging muscle.

"But you could be in danger, too," she said. "What if the hit man shot you or knocked you out?"

"Hey, I never thought of that." Vic held up his hands in an attitude of defeat. "Okay, I give in. How about I go get the picnic stuff? Oh, yeah, and maybe rent a movie?"

"That would be great. Unless you'd rather just forget it and have a picnic with somebody else."

"Nah. Told you before, I got nobody to play with this week. Be back in ten."

After he had gone she wondered what sort of food he'd bought. Hamburgers and french fries? She thought of Rob kneeling in front of the toilet.

"Rob, why do you hate french fries so much?"

"Because of Godzilla," Rob said, still watching the TV screen. "He made me eat them when I didn't want to."

"Why?"

He finally turned his gaze on her. "Mom and I never ate them; she said they were too fatty. Greg said we were wimps. So one time he made hamburgers and fries and said we had to eat them."

"And did you?"

"Yeah. He said he'd hit me if I didn't. He stood behind me and watched till I ate them all."

"No wonder you don't like them."

"I threw up after. He was really mad then."

Rob went to the bathroom and in a few minutes came out carrying her Swiss army pocket knife. "Can I keep this for a while?"

He might do a lot of damage with the knife. On the other hand, she couldn't go out and buy the dumbbells he wanted.

"All right. Just don't carve the hotel into pieces, okay?"

Almost a smile. "Okay."

There was a knock on the door and Vic identified himself. He came in lugging a big cooler in one hand and a video in the other.

"Hope you like horror movies."

"Cool!" Rob said. "I like cops movies, too."

"We can get one after lunch if you're still gung ho on staying here." He walked to the sliding door and opened it. "Let's have a look at your view."

"It isn't much," Penny said, following him onto the lanai. "Just an alley and the backs of other buildings." She stayed well away from the railing.

"You got a thing about heights?" Vic asked, lighting a cigarette.

"Yes, a little." She described what had happened at the Pali Cliffs.

"Hey, no wonder you don't want to go close to the edge." He blew out a stream of smoke. "Well, looks like all we got left is the video."

Half an hour into the movie, with enormous green octopuses clambering out of the sea and threatening to wipe out the cowering millions of Manhattan, Penny's mind drifted to Rob. He seemed to be enjoying the film. Considering how much he liked sea animals, maybe he should think about being a biologist instead of a cop when he grew up.

If he grew up.

Penny shivered involuntarily. It wouldn't do any good to think about that possibility. She forced her eyes back to the screen.

When the movie was over, Vic said, "Time for lunch." He took the cooler to the lanai. "Come on, we can at least sit in the sun while we eat, otherwise it's not a picnic."

"There are only two chairs," Penny said.

"I'm going to sit on the floor," Rob announced. "Better than sitting at a table."

With a flourish, Vic produced a bottle of Dom Perignon and two champagne glasses.

"Champagne! Vic, you must have spent a fortune!" Was he trying to impress her? He must know by now that she wasn't wealthy.

He grinned at her. "I go for top of the line. On everything. Anyway, I told you, my old man's loaded." He popped the cork and poured them each a glass.

The champagne was cool, sparkling and delicious. "This is wonderful, Vic." The hot sun on her back felt good, too.

"Glad I picked something that turns your crank." He took a Coke from the cooler and handed it to Rob.

It was pleasant sitting in the open air, though nothing like the sunny beach she'd turned down. She reminded herself that Greg's hit man was around somewhere. So was Jack Kinkaid.

"You got a boyfriend?" Vic asked.

"Not at the moment," she said.

"No kidding? I figured there'd be a bunch of dudes after you."

One would be enough. She thought of Jack Kinkaid. Weird. She dismissed the thought.

"I broke up six months ago with a guy I was thinking about marrying. I'm in no rush to find anybody else."

"Yeah?" Vic's gaze caressed her slowly from head to toe. "I bet he was ready to slit his wrists when you gave him the heave-ho."

At some other time his open interest might have been flattering. Now it left her uneasy.

"Bruce wouldn't slit his wrists over anybody. Besides, he's already engaged to someone else."

"Guess you're not sorry to be rid of the guy, then."

No, she wasn't sorry to be rid of Bruce. He'd been exciting, his wit outrageous. It had taken her a while to discover that Bruce was in love with Bruce. And with his own virtuoso performances as a courtroom lawyer.

"Have some more of the bubbly stuff." Vic refilled his own glass. "You might as well get happy."

"No, thanks, I've got to keep a clear head."

"Oh, right." He finished the champagne himself while relating snippets of his life as a little boy. He was an only child, he said, and she sensed a hint of loneliness underneath his brash veneer.

"I'll unpack lunch," he said.

If he'd been aiming to impress her, he'd succeeded. There were shrimp, pink and perfect in onion, lime juice and olive oil; a peppery watercress salad, then the perennial picnic favorites; potato salad, hard-boiled eggs, cold chicken and black olives, served on china plates with silver service and linen napkins.

"Eat up," Vic said. "There's more to come."

Penny ate, wondering about him. His taste for gourmet food was in sharp contrast to his gauche youthfulness. Odd that he'd been raised to appreciate expensive food but not taught the sophistication to match. It occurred to her that he might be hanging around because he liked to show off and she was someone new for him to impress. He was immature enough to indulge in that kind of shallow thinking.

The "more" was Camembert and crackers, miniature glazed strawberry tarts and honeydew melon slices packed in ice.

Rob finished off his fourth tart, looked regretfully at those left in the box and wandered back to the television.

"As Rob would say, that was awesome, Vic. Thank you."

He smiled shyly. "You're gonna have dinner with me, too. Okay?"

"I don't think so. It just doesn't make any sense to go out when we're safe here."

"Hey, I told you a good way of getting out of here and I know plenty of places around Honolulu where nobody'd ever think of looking for you." He pulled a second bottle of champagne from the cooler and opened it. "You want to change your mind? We can take our time with this one. We got all afternoon. Right?"

"Why not? But only one." She watched Vic drink, obviously enjoying himself.

"Why don't you have a nap?" he said. "Always goes good after a meal. Then you'll be ready to party tonight."

There was no way she could nap, tired as she was.

"I'm not sleepy," she said.

He got up and made a restless circuit of the room. "Okay, how about another couple videos, then? I can get a chase movie for the kid. What do you want?"

"I like adventure stories."

"Right. I'll see what I can do. I might be a little while. Gotta make a phone call."

Jack Kinkaid paced. He'd decided not to force his way through Penny's door. If she kept herself and the boy locked in they'd be safe enough. Confident that she had enough common sense to know that, he'd gone to Koyama's office this morning to see if he could learn anything new.

"Who does Nelson work for?" Jack had asked.

"He's freelance, as far as we know."

That didn't help much.

"I could arrest Ms Davis for possession of heroin and take her back to Canada," Jack grumbled.

When he'd returned, he could hear the television blaring in her room. Frustration made him irritable. Nothing seemed to be happening, except that someone wanted to kill young Rob.

As he paced, he decided a key piece of the puzzle was missing: Angela Moller. They had to find her. Whether or not she was involved in the drug business, she might be willing to spill whatever she knew about Moller.

Jack sat down and put in a call to Ian.

"You might find out where Angela is by questioning Moller about the information he gave when he reported Rob as missing. Surely he knows where his wife is."

"He said she was vacationing. In Toronto."

"Can you talk to him right now? It's important, Ian. I have a feeling Angela Moller is the key to this case."

"You and your gut feelings! Okay, I'll get back to you."

It was two hours before he called back.

"You were right, Jack. There's something strange going on. Moller gave us a number in Toronto where he said his wife was visiting. The people there hadn't heard from her for months. And they had a call last night from Davis, asking the same question."

So Penny was searching for Rob's mother, too. What did that tell him?

"What did Moller say to that?"

"Now he says she walked out on him and he doesn't know where she is. Says he didn't have the heart to tell the kid so he made up the story about her being on vacation."

"Moller doesn't have a heart."

"Maybe not. Anyway, we're checking the airlines, whatever that will prove. Moller says her car's still in the garage, so she either took public transport or went with a friend. When I asked if she had a boyfriend he looked like he was going to take a swing at me."

"Did he say anything else?"

"Yeah, he came up with the idea that his wife had kidnaped the boy."

"He's squirming, Ian."

"There's more. Then he accused Davis of kidnaping Rob, said both women were flakes. Said Penny was probably going to deliver the boy to Angela. Which I suppose is reasonable if Angela's left him."

"How'd he seem?"

"Twitchy. For once your gut instincts worked, Jack."

"So what next? Can you search his house? Find out if she took any clothes or whatever?"

"I sure can't get a search warrant based on mere suspicion and there's not enough evidence to go after him on drugs or Larry Wing. I don't want him too nervous."

"Any word from Forensics on the murder?"

Ian sighed. "Not for another day or two yet. Let's hope it gives us something to bite into. You had any luck tracing Fredericks?"

"No. He has to be using an alias. The only way I'll find him is by sticking to Rob and Penny. But I don't like using them as bait; I've got no backup. I'd rather send them back to Canada. We'll need a safe place for them until this thing is over."

"For the boy, yes. Davis can take care of herself."

Ian was still convinced that Penny was acting as a courier for Moller, so he didn't care what happened to her. But all along, those gut feelings had been telling Jack she wasn't involved with drugs in spite of the heroin in her suitcase. It was time he listened to them.

Ian scoffed at intuition but Jack couldn't remember it ever failing him, not even in his rookie days. Ian's trouble was he'd been pushing paper too long; he'd lost his feel for the street.

Everything pointed to Rob having witnessed the murder of Larry Wing, who was a known associate of Moller's. Penny had whisked Rob out of the country within hours of the event. Yesterday someone had tried to kill the boy and make it seem accidental. Moller knew he was under suspicion for dealing drugs and if he was trying to kill his stepson, he'd want it to look accidental so he wouldn't be investigated.

As far as he could see now, Penny's only involvement was trying to protect her nephew and return him to his mother. He'd swear she hadn't delivered or picked up any drugs here in Honolulu.

Jack phoned Vancouver again, this time to talk to Terry Wellburn.

"What's happening with the old bank robbery case?"

"I'm gonna win this one!" Terry's voice was exultant. "We arrested Reg Davis and the third guy yesterday. Neither one is talking, but I'll bet you a beer they will when they find out Lister has already confessed."

"Congratulations!"

"I can tell you one thing, old buddy. When this one is wrapped up, I'm going to have one big celebration."

"Count me in."

So Penny's father had been arrested. As much as he wanted to root for Terry, he hoped for Penny's sake that her father wasn't guilty.

Jack felt like smashing his fist through a wall. He wished now that he had forced Penny to listen to him. If he'd done that, she and Rob could be back in Vancouver, somewhere safe.

TEN

When Vic was gone and Rob had locked and chained the door behind him, Penny showered. She came out feeling fresher, though her eyes were heavy from lack of sleep.

"Rob, it's your turn." He had to do something besides sit on the floor and watch the idiot box.

While Rob was showering, she decided to change her clothes and pretend she was going out to dinner. It might prevent her from worrying about Angela, how her father was faring, whether she and Rob would succeed in getting away from Greg's hit man.

The only dressy things she had were brightly flowered silk pants flaring into wide legs and a low-necked full-sleeved red blouse. She put them on and looked in the mirror. The outfit looked elegant, but felt as comfortable as an old pair of pajamas.

There was one more reason to dress up, she thought, as she fastened red hoop earrings. Fugitives wore jeans and dark sweaters and stayed in the shadows. The less she looked like a fugitive, the less she'd feel like one. Maybe.

Penny grinned wryly at her reflection and shook her head. She'd been a fugitive for barely a day and a half, though it felt like weeks, and what she wore wouldn't change that. But it made her feel better to act like a normal person. She swept her hair up and twisted it into a french roll at the back of her head.

Angela's package was still in her suitcase. Perhaps the necklace would go with her blouse. She took the package out of the suitcase, then reconsidered. The necklace could be valuable; she didn't want to risk losing it.

The phone rang and she stared at it. Angela!

She picked up the phone with trembling hands and Jack said, "Penny?" Angry, she slammed the phone down.

When Rob came out of the bathroom, dressed in clean shorts and a polo shirt, she said, "Okay so far?"

"I guess. When's Vic coming back?"

There was a rap at the door and Vic's voice demanding it be opened.

"Speak of the devil," Penny murmured, as she took the chain off.

"What's that mean?" Rob asked.

"Oh, just an old saying my grandmother used. Doesn't mean anything, as far as I remember."

Vic had brought two movies, a Western and one with Clint Eastwood as Dirty Harry for Rob. It was nearly six by the time they'd watched the Western, had a snack from the cooler and cheered for Dirty Harry. If her dream lover had been there instead of Vic, it would have felt like an ordinary evening at home with the family.

"You look good in that outfit," Vic said. "Change your mind about going out to dinner?"

"No. Thanks for asking, but..."

A fire alarm jangled loudly in the corridor. Startled, Penny hesitated, then grabbed her bag.

"Rob! Come on." But he was right beside her.

Vic opened the door and led the way to the staircase. "Better not use the elevator." People were emerging from almost every room, hurrying toward the stairs.

Out on the sidewalk, Penny looked up at the hotel. "I don't see any smoke."

Someone in the crowd said, "Fire might be at the rear. Could be hours before they let us back in."

Vic said, "Look, I'll get a cab. You don't want to stand out here if your hit man is someplace around."

"But..."

"Don't argue. I gotta look after you and the kid, don't I? If we can't get back inside, might as well go get that dinner I promised. If anybody follows us, the cabby won't have any trouble losing him. I know a few tricks myself."

"All right." Anything was better than being exposed like this. She had to trust somebody and Vic had been good to them.

Vic elbowed his way into the crowd. Penny, holding Rob's hand, started to follow. Someone grabbed her by the arm.

Jack Kinkaid!

"You! What do you want?"

His grip tightened. "I have to talk to you. You must know you and the boy are in danger. I can help you."

"I'll bet you can!" She spat the words out. "I know who you are, you're working for Greg Moller."

Out of the corner of her eye, she could see a taxi parked at the curb. Vic was leaning down, talking to the driver. She relaxed in Kinkaid's grip for a second, then tried to yank her arm free and head for the cab.

"Wait!" Kinkaid spun her around to face him and shoved an ID card in front of her face. "I'm a cop. Vancouver police force."

Years of accumulated anger and resentment exploded into a slap across his face that had him almost off his feet. Her hand burned but she'd gladly do it again.

"So what are you here for? To grill me about some crime I had nothing to do with? To arrest me because you can't prove my father is a thief? Don't you guys ever quit?"

She snatched Rob's hand again and fled to the waiting taxi. Vic opened the back door and she dove in. "Let's go! I'm ready to party."

The taxi pulled away. Penny didn't look back. Jack Kinkaid was a Vancouver cop! And she'd actually thought she liked him. Were they going to carry out their vendetta to the end of her father's days? Or even hers?

When she'd caught her breath, she said, "Vic, I don't want to stay out late tonight. Rob and I have to be at the airport by nine in the morning and we still have to pack."

He looked startled. "You're going home? Already?"

"It seems the best thing to do."

"Bummer!" Oddly, he sounded annoyed. What had he been doing, planning a leisurely conquest? Too bad; he'd have been disappointed.

"Sorry if I ruined your plans," she said, "but I'm not going to hang around here like a sitting duck. At home I can get protection for Rob and me until the cops do something about his stepfather."

"It's okay, doll," he said, patting her hand. "I understand what you're up against. I did figure on taking you some more places, but that's the way it goes."

The cab-driver said, "Where to, buddy?"

Vic gave him an address and turned to Penny. "I'll come and get you in the morning, take you to the airport. It's the least I can do."

"You've done a lot already, Vic. I'll always be grateful."

Startled, his cheek smarting from Penny's slap, Jack tried to go after her. His way was blocked by more people coming out of the hotel.

Jack dodged around them and sprinted along the sidewalk, but the few seconds delay had been enough. The taxi was pulling away. The man sitting beside Penny turned his head and looked back.

It was Vic Nelson.

There wasn't another taxi in sight. Cursing, Jack managed to get the cab's licence number before it turned the corner. The woman had mush for brains!

All right, she probably didn't know Vic Nelson was a contract killer. Unless he did something fast she'd soon find out the hard way.

Why had she run from him? He'd told her he was a cop; she'd seen his ID. How could she connect him with Moller? Why the smack across the face?

He considered the 'accident' at the Pali Cliffs. If at first Penny had thought he'd led the hit man to her, she knew now it wasn't true. So what was her problem?

Maybe just as well there hadn't been another taxi around. If Nelson saw him following and smelled cop, he might panic and kill at once.

The wail of fire engine and police sirens pulled his attention back to the hotel. There was still no sign of smoke or flame.

Penny no doubt trusted Nelson because he'd saved Rob from a speeding car. He himself had been openly following her and giving her mixed messages about his intentions. In her place, maybe he'd pick Nelson as a hero, too.

Had Nelson's rescue of Rob been a setup? A ploy to get Penny to trust him? It made sense if the intended murder was meant to look like an accident. Nelson and Fredericks were likely working together. He could think of no other reason for Fredericks being on the tour bus in his ineffectual disguise.

Penny and Rob might have spent the day with Nelson. It would have been difficult for Nelson to arrange an accident in the hotel room. Or was he uninvolved? It was possible his rescue of Rob had been spur of the moment and that he'd fallen for Penny in a big way. But Jack didn't believe it.

The police were herding people away from the hotel entrance so the firemen could get in.

Whatever the answer was, he had to find Penny and Rob. Fast. Even if Nelson had only romance in mind, a hit man sure wasn't somebody Penny should be socializing with.

The boy knew someone had pushed him at the Pali Cliffs and had told her. So she knew the 'accident' had been a murder attempt and was scared of everybody.

He'd blown his cover, but that didn't matter if Penny wasn't a courier. He was sure she wasn't. Her attitude and actions were all wrong. Sure, she had the heroin, but Moller could have set her up. She might not even know what was in the package.

It was a good thing he'd chucked his shoulder holster and Smith and Wesson .38 into his camera bag when the fire alarm had sounded. He looked up and down Kuhio Street. The maze of buildings he could see was only a tiny fraction of the city. Penny and Rob were out there somewhere. With a professional killer.

And he was on his own. Koyama couldn't arrest Nelson without a warrant and couldn't get a warrant without reasonable grounds. Murder was "reasonable grounds." But if he waited for that, it would be too late.

ELEVEN

As the taxi battled through Honolulu's evening traffic, Penny's emotions pulled her every which way. She was angry and disappointed about Jack Kinkaid deceiving her, furious because of the continuing harassment and, finally, curious. Why had he been following her?

"Who was the dude chasing after you?" Vic asked.

"A guy I met in the hotel," Penny said. "Trying to work up enough courage to ask me for a date, I think."

They were in a semi-industrial area, pockmarked with run-down, sagging houses and shops. She was puzzled when the taxi stopped in front of a long, low motel trying to look respectable in a coat of pink paint. A lone palm tree leaned over the driveway.

"Why are we stopping here?"

"Gotta pick something up from a buddy of mine," Vic said. "You might as well come in with me. He's bound to have some good booze and we can hang loose for an hour before we head for the restaurant."

Penny looked at the shabby neon sign. "Keoki" flickered half-heartedly, but "Motel" had died altogether. A half dozen nondescript cars were parked in front of various units. Definitely not inviting.

"I'd rather not, Vic. We'll just wait for you."

He gave her an enigmatic look, got out, and said, "Okay. I'll keep it short."

He rapped at the door of unit 18 and disappeared inside. She hoped he would keep his word. She wanted bright lights and music and people and, eventually, food.

Vic was back in less than five minutes. He stopped beside the driver's door.

"Can you do me a favor?" Vic said to the driver. "I need a pack of smokes but I'm waiting for a phone call that's coming any minute." He pointed to the street corner. "There's a corner grocery right there."

"I drive cab, buddy; I'm not an errand boy."

"Hey, come on! This phone call is important. I'll make it worth your while." Vic waved a ten at the driver, who grumbled under his breath but got out, took the ten and walked off toward the corner.

Vic opened the back door of the cab. "You sure you won't come in for a minute?"

"No, really, Vic, I'd rather stay here."

Vic turned his head to watch the taxi driver. When the man had gone into the convenience store, he said, "Tough. You're coming in anyway."

He grabbed Rob by the arm and hauled him out of the cab. Stunned, Penny saw him pull a knife from his boot and hold it to Rob's throat.

"Get out," Vic said. "Do it slow and don't talk or scream. Or the kid gets his throat slit."

This couldn't be happening.

"Move!" Vic snapped, and pressed the point of the knife harder into Rob's throat. Rob squealed in pain.

Penny moved. She stood beside the taxi, numb with shock. She'd got it all wrong. She'd trusted the wrong man. "Who are you?"

"Shut up. Walk over to number 18 and do it natural. I'll be right behind you. With the knife."

The fear in Rob's eyes and the blade at his throat gave her no option. She walked. Vic opened the door and gave her a rough shove. She stumbled across the threshold.

It was a housekeeping unit with cheap, dilapidated furnishings. An overhead bulb bathed the grimy white walls and dull beige carpet in harsh light.

Vic shoved Rob ahead of him into the room and she heard the lock snap. A tall man, fortyish, in blue slacks and white polo shirt came out of the bedroom. His eyes and skin were almost colorless, but his hair was coal black.

"That's Carl!" Rob's voice was shaky.

Vic's boyish expression was gone, replaced by a look that sent a ripple of despair through her. He was nothing like the Vic she thought she'd known.

"That's right, kid," Vic said. "Carl and me, we work together. Now listen up, both of you. Do as you're told and I'll go easy on you." He said to Carl, "Keep 'em quiet while I go pay off the cab."

Carl placed himself between her and the door and pulled a small snub-nosed gun from his pocket.

As Vic came back in, she thought of Jack Kinkaid urgently pushing his ID at her, telling her he was a policeman. Telling her she was in danger. Why had she been so stupid? She moaned.

Vic slapped her hard across the face. "No hysterics. Just keep your mouth shut."

Her cheek was burning and her eyes watered. "What are you going to do?"

He slapped the other side of her face. "I said keep your mouth shut. Or do you wanta see the kid get sliced?"

"Vic," Carl said, "lay off the rough stuff. Give her a minute to figure the score."

Head ringing from Vic's slaps, she looked around the room, saw a phone. Not likely she'd ever get to use it.

Vic bound her wrists behind her back with thin nylon rope and pushed her into a chair, then gagged her and bound her ankles so tightly that the rope cut into her flesh. Rob, tied the same way, was in the chair opposite, his enormous eyes mirroring her own terror.

She couldn't stop staring at Vic. In an instant, he'd changed from a carefree boy to a vicious brutal man. He could be closer to thirty than the twenty she'd guessed. Carl seemed more civilized; at least he'd made Vic quit slapping her. Not that there was any comfort in that.

They meant to kill both her and Rob. Rob had seen Greg murder a man and they couldn't get at Rob without taking her, too. Now that she could identify them, there was no hope they'd let her go.

What kind of 'accident' would it be?

Vic lit a cigarette, turned his back and walked to the window facing the street.

"We'll have to stay here until dark," Carl said.

"Suits me better than doing my boy scout act." Vic looked at Penny as though she was a piece of meat in a butcher's display. "This job has been a pain from the start. You want somebody iced, then ice 'em. Get it over with and get out; that's my philosophy."

"It makes sense," Carl said, "but Greg is paying the shot and he wants an accident, not a hit."

Vic knocked ash off his cigarette onto the floor. "So I'll do the job. One way or another. And get paid. That's all I care about."

"If it looks like a hit, there'll be trouble."

"From your buddy? Not likely. That's his problem, anyway. I've got my own problems The only way to stay clean in this game is to get in and get out, fast, like I told you before. I got a reputation to think about."

"You think you've got problems? If we get caught on this gig and they bust me for dealing, too, it'll be a long stretch. You better live up to your reputation." Carl sat down and straightened the creases in his trousers. "You decided yet how to handle it?"

"Drowning's the simplest. We'll use your rental car to take them to some out-of-the way beach. Soon as it's dark. Leave their clothes on the beach. Take 'em out and hold their heads under. It'll look like they were having a midnight swim and went too far out."

"You had your chance to drown the kid Wednesday," Carl taunted. "Maybe this time it'll work."

His words hit Penny like an electric shock. She remembered Vic suggesting she go for a power swim and leave Rob with him. He'd been trying to kill them even then! He'd probably paid somebody to drive that old wreck of a T-bird at them, too. She shuddered as she remembered his hand caressing her arm.

Vic stared at Carl for about ten seconds. "You better keep that smart mouth of yours shut, Fredericks."

"Sorry. This kind of job isn't in my line."

"Any moron could figure that out. And I still don't like this 'accident' crap." Vic butted his cigarette. "Let's get some grub."

"You want me to go pick up something?"

"I'll go. Your idea of haute cuisine is the pits."

Despite the stuffy warmth of the room Penny felt freezing cold. How could he worry about food when he was planning to kill just hours from now?

Vic checked her ropes, then Rob's. "Gimme the car keys, Carl. There's nothing around here but a pizza joint. Be about half an hour, maybe more."

Penny watched him leave. He'd been looking for a place to kill today, too. Talking about taking them up Diamond Head and to a beach. She'd sat watching television with him, feeling safe because he'd helped them escape from the hit man. And thought his efforts to please her touching and romantic.

Forget all that now. She had to think—she wasn't going to die without a fight.

Penny moaned as loudly as she could. Carl moved to her side, looked at the tears sliding down her cheeks, muttered something unintelligible and loosened the gag a trifle.

It was a start. Maybe he'd loosen the ropes, too. She raised her ankles but he shook his head and said, "Don't push your luck."

She wriggled, trying to ease the bite of the ropes, but the movement made it worse. She could read nothing in Rob's eyes but fear. She wouldn't blame him if he hated her; she was the one that had got them into this. If only she'd listened to Jack Kinkaid.

Stop it! There was no time to waste on regrets. She had to think of a way to escape and, with Vic gone, this might be the only chance. She stretched and shifted, perspiration trickling down her back.

Carl was watching baseball on television and it took two or three precious minutes to get his attention. When he realized she was trying to talk, he frowned and turned back to the game. She banged her heels on the floor.

He came over and untied the gag. "What do you want?"

"I need to use the bathroom," she whimpered.

"This had better be for real."

"Please. I can't wait."

Carl opened the bathroom door and glanced inside. Probably checking it for things she might use as weapons.

"All right," he said, untying her ropes. "Don't make any mistakes or the kid will get it. You know by now it doesn't pay to get Vic mad."

"I won't," she whispered. She locked the bathroom door behind her. It was good to be free of those ropes.

The bathroom window was tiny. Not even Rob could climb through that. Maybe if she opened it and screamed someone would hear. With trembling fingers she grasped the handle. It stuck, then suddenly released with a loud squeak.

"What are you doing in there?" Carl demanded.

She flushed the toilet and looked out the window. Nothing there but steel mesh fencing and what looked like a deserted factory building. Screaming wasn't worth the risk.

"Come out of there! Right now." From his tone, she knew he'd break the door down if she didn't open it. He was rattling the door handle.

The toilet tank cover! It was awkward and heavy but, handled right, she could knock Carl out for a few minutes, untie Rob and get away. It was worth a try.

She lifted it off and stepped to one side of the door, releasing the lock. Carl started to push the door open and she raised the tank cover over her head.

When he was half-way in Penny lunged, bringing the cover down as hard as she could.

But the door blocked her swing and the cover hit his shoulder, knocking him off balance. He fell to his knees. As he struggled to his feet, cursing, she heaved the lid over her head for a second blow.

The outside door opened and Vic walked in.

Penny froze, the tank cover a dead weight in her hands.

Then Vic was holding his knife to Rob's throat. "Drop it!" His voice was full of fury.

The porcelain slab crashed to the floor. She was trembling from head to foot.

Carl rubbed his shoulder, his face white. "You almost broke my collar bone!" The cold venom in his tone was as frightening as Vic's anger.

Vic handed Carl the knife and nodded at Rob. Then he swung on her, his open hand striking the side of her face, and she went down in a heap, arm scraping against the door jamb. He yanked her to her feet and slapped the other side of her face. This time her head struck something on the way down and she lay half stunned.

Vic flung her in the chair and bound and gagged her again. Her hair was loose and falling around her shoulders. She knew by Carl's face that she'd lost any chance for consideration from him. Now he'd let Vic do anything he wanted.

"How did that happen?" Vic demanded.

"She said she had to go to the can. I never thought she'd try anything."

Vic looked down at her, a cold smile playing about his lips, knife held loosely in his hand. "You want to play games? Maybe I can accommodate you." His eyes moved slowly up and down her body, pausing at her breasts, lingering on her throat. She cringed as he traced the outline of her breasts with one finger, the knife point pricking her throat.

She held her breath. Please, don't let him do anything to her in front of Rob.

Vic laughed, the sound scraping across her nerves, and gripped her jaw with strong fingers, twisting her head from side to side. "Scared, honey? Good. Stay that way. One more stupid move and you'll pay. Think of all the things I might do to you." He glanced at Rob. "And to him."

She'd kill Vic if he hurt Rob! The futility of that thought made her want to cry.

"Good thing you came back when you did," Carl said.

"You got that right. Had a hunch I shouldn't stay away too long. I phoned an order to another place I know of. They'll deliver in half an hour."

"What about these two?"

"We can dump 'em in the bedroom and shut the door. You can stay in there to make sure they're quiet until the delivery guy's gone." Vic smoothed his hair and adjusted the gold chain around his neck. "I don't want them watching while we eat, anyway."

The point of the knife flicked at her throat again. "Remember what I said? No mistakes or I'll work your face over. When they drag you outta the water it'll look like the crabs and fish been having a feast. And maybe they will by that time."

Her bones turned to liquid. He'd enjoy cutting her and use any excuse to do it. Maybe he didn't need an excuse.

Rob struggled with his bonds and gurgled behind the gag. Vic turned to him with the laugh that only this afternoon she'd thought boyish and open.

"That goes for you, too, kid. Behave."

"So let's move them before the delivery guy gets here," Carl said.

They carried Penny into the bedroom first and dumped her on her back on the bed. While Vic carried Rob in, Carl pulled the drapes closed and checked the ropes again. Vic looked at her and smiled. "Hang loose, sweetheart!" He went out, shutting the door. After a moment, she heard the sound on the television being turned up.

She twisted her head to look at Rob. His eyes were closed. Perhaps he was trying to shut out the world. She wished she could shut it out, too, but there was no escaping the bite of the ropes into her flesh, or the knowledge that it would soon be dark.

Would they take the ropes off before they pushed her and Rob under the water? There might be some hope of escape—she was a strong swimmer. Vic would never take that chance, though; he knew how well she could swim.

Penny found herself thinking about home. What would happen to her apartment, to her things? How would her parents feel, losing both a daughter and a grandson? What would Angie do?

She couldn't imagine not being alive. Angry, she railed at herself. 'Stop being negative! Just don't give in. Think, Penny, think!'

She tried to think rationally but couldn't. Her mind insisted on asking the same questions over and over. How could they escape? Who would help?

No one. No one knew where they were.

Jack Kinkaid had wanted to help and she'd walked away from him.

She recognized now the concern in his deep-set grey eyes. She could see the scar on his temple, the broken nose. What would it be like to kiss him, to feel his mustache against her face? He was tall—she'd have to reach up to put her arms around his neck. Did she even want to, now that she knew he was a cop?

But he was a real person, not a faceless, uniformed automaton barking questions like the others she'd hated and distrusted for so long. Or would he have been like them when he had her alone?

Why had he lied to her? Why had he been following her everywhere? He was a lousy actor. She'd thought the first time she met him that he looked like a tough guy, not someone who added up columns of figures for a living. But what did that mean? She'd looked at Vic and seen a gauche but likable kid and she couldn't have been more wrong.

Rob was squirming beside her. He was a real person now, too, not just a nine-year-old, not just her sister's son. She loved him, and with this gag in her mouth she couldn't even say it or comfort him in any way.

The door opened and Carl came in, closing it again behind him. He pulled the drapes open a little and looked down at them.

"Don't make a sound," he said, "or you know what'll happen to you."

Penny stared back at his expressionless face. He was as cool as if he were buying a newspaper or ordering a meal instead of preparing to commit murder. Her eyes moved to the window. The sky was still bright but the sun would set soon.

She tried to breathe calmly, evenly. No, she wouldn't make a sound. Or move. If pain and death had to come, let it come from the sea, not from Vic.

The sound of voices came from the living room, Vic's laughter, then the closing of the front door.

Vic came in. "Everything okay? Let's eat; it'll be dark in an hour and we can get on the road." They went out, closing the door and again there was the muffled noise of a baseball game on television.

Rob wriggled and she turned her head to him. He was trying to convey something with his eyes, his gaze moving from her face down toward the foot of the bed and back again. Then he rolled onto his side with his back to her and she could see his fingers wiggling. Did he want her to hold his hands?

She rolled in the opposite direction, her back to him, and squirmed closer, until she could grasp his fingers with hers. He pulled loose and shoved his hip against her hand.

She felt something hard. Not his hip. Something long and narrow. She explored the shape with her fingers and recognition sent hope surging through her.

His gut grinding with anxiety, Jack Kinkaid strode into the police station. Earlier in the day, Koyama had said he was welcome to use whatever facilities he needed but warned him not to take overt action without approval.

Well, Jack thought, he hadn't really expected to be given command of the squad.

A young policeman in Records traced the licence number of the cab Nelson and Penny and Rob had taken and Jack phoned the cab company. The dispatcher promised to have the driver call in.

Jack called Koyama at his home. "Miss Davis eluded me tonight. She and the boy took off with Nelson in a taxi. She was dressed up so maybe they were going out to dinner. I'm tracing the driver now. Could you give me some backup?"

"I can't justify it. You have no proof Nelson intends to harm her or the boy."

"Only my gut instinct."

"If you want to try convincing my boss on that basis, I wish you luck."

Jack hung up and paced around the room. It was his own fault that Penny had ignored him. He should have forced her to listen to him and then taken her and the boy back to Vancouver. If Ian wouldn't go along with finding a safe house for them, he'd do it himself. If anything happened to her and Rob, he'd be kicking himself the rest of his life.

He phoned Ian Baker in Vancouver.

"Kinkaid, haven't you learned to tell time yet? I just got to bed."

"Sorry." He related the events of the past twenty-four hours. "Anything new on your end?"

"Forensics reported on Larry Wing. He was shot to death between eight and eleven Monday night and the body was moved afterward, but nothing ties it to Greg Moller. One of the uniforms is checking Moller's long-distance calls. Maybe he'll hit the jackpot."

"I hope so. What about Angela Moller?"

"What about her?" Ian said grumpily. "I talked to her mother and she doesn't know anything, not even where her daughter gets her hair done. We need to nail Fredericks so we can use him as a lever."

"You think he'd give us the goods on Moller for a reduced sentence?"

"How should I know what he'd do? But it's beginning to look like our only chance."

Jack rang off and went back to pacing. Where was that taxi driver? He got coffee from a machine in the hall. A save-the-whales poster on the wall reminded him of the carved dolphin Penny had admired in the aquarium gift shop. If she came out of this okay, he would buy it for her.

If he couldn't find out where Vic had taken Penny, he'd have to go back to the hotel and wait, hoping she'd call or show up. He phoned the hotel.

"I'm one of your guests, Jack Kinkaid. Is the fire out? Are we being allowed back into our rooms?"

"The problem has been taken care of, sir. We apologize for any inconvenience it may have caused you."

Something about the clerk's tone raised a question in Jack's mind. Had there actually been a fire?

"Was there much damage?"

"Uh, no, sir. No sign of fire was discovered. Every room has been inspected. The police believe someone maliciously activated the alarm."

Of course! Nelson hadn't been able to talk Penny into leaving the hotel and he'd found the only possible means of getting her out into the street. If he'd been with her in the room he couldn't have done it himself. Did that mean Fredericks was working with him? If that were the case, they obviously meant to act tonight. Jack cursed the cab company. Hadn't they delivered his message?

It was nine-thirty before the taxi driver phoned.

"Pacific Princess? I made a couple calls there tonight."

"This was around six. You picked up a young blond guy, a woman and a boy about ten years old, right?"

"Yeah, that's right."

"Where'd you take them?"

"Keoki Motel, out in the old industrial section."

Jack wrote the address down. He knew what he had to do, but he was taking a big risk if Nelson and Fredericks were working together. Trying to rescue hostages on his own from two men who were probably armed was plainly foolhardy. It was also contrary to all his training.

There was a chance it would work. A long shot—but he had no choice. If he hadn't been careless, Penny and Rob would be safe in the hotel. If he'd been able to prove what Nelson was up to, Koyama would have given him backup. He had to make up for some of the "ifs."

Transport would give him an unmarked squad car, but he didn't want to involve Koyama or his department. Whatever happened, he was on his own. He took a taxi to a car rental agency and rented a small sedan.

He found parking on the street, just beyond the motel, and casually strolled back toward the office. It was empty and Jack pressed the buzzer. A chunky middle-aged woman with dyed red hair and wearing an orange and green muumuu came in through the rear door. He could smell beer on her breath.

"Do you have a Victor Nelson registered here?" He produced his ID and she looked at it with suspicion.

"I'm a Canadian police officer working with the Honolulu police force. You can phone Lieutenant Koyama's office if you want to confirm that."

She shrugged and riffled through her registration cards. She shook her head. "Nobody of that name."

"How about a Carl Fredericks?"

She checked again. "No."

"Nelson might be using another name. He's young, blond hair collar-length, well built, wears a gold ring in his right ear."

"What do you want him for?"

"Murder." Maybe not, but she'd never know one way or the other.

Her face went pasty under her makeup. "Sounds like the guy in number 18." She found the card. "He's registered as Charles Farrow. Gave me a home address in LA. There's another guy with him."

"What's he look like?"

"Real tall and skinny, wears sunglasses all the time."

"Canadian accent?"

She shrugged. "Could be. He ain't American."

So Nelson and Fredericks were a team. And since Fredericks was Moller's man, his guess that Rob had seen the killing of Larry King must be correct.

"You know if they're in the unit or not?"

"Long as they pay their bills, I don't keep track of them."

"Mind if I take a look?"

"I don't want any trouble. Business is bad enough without guys like you breakin' the place up."

He didn't want trouble either. Especially on his own. "There won't be any problem."

She retreated fretfully to her lair and Jack went outside to check the layout. Dusk was thickening to darkness but there was enough light for him to see.

Several cars, two of them rentals, were parked in the forecourt. None in front of unit 18.

Walking softly along the sidewalk to the door, he leaned close and listened. No sound, though light showed behind the drapes covering the window.

He'd check the rear. The first window at the back would be the owner's accommodation; the eighteenth after that should be the rear of unit 18. He went back past the office and around the end of the building. Scrubby shrubs and a couple of palms grew in a narrow strip between the building and a steel mesh fence.

Jack drew his weapon from its holster and silently edged his way toward the nineteenth window.

TWELVE

The long, narrow object was her Swiss army knife! She had forgotten about giving it to Rob, had not even noticed him putting it in his pocket.

There was no play in the ropes around her wrists, and it was hard to move her fingers, numb because she'd been lying on them. She wiggled closer to Rob and began working the knife out of his pocket. His oversize T-shirt covered the pocket slit, hampering her efforts, but finally the knife came free.

It fell out of her fingers. Holding her breath, she strained back, scrabbling around the bedspread. There! She grasped the knife and positioned it in her left hand.

Now she had to get a blade open. Then cut the rope on Rob's wrists so he could free hers. Then the ankle ropes. Then get out. Somehow.

If there was time. Carl had left the drapes open a little and she could see that it was already dusk. How long did they have?

Getting a blade open wouldn't be easy. They'd always been stiff and she'd broken more than one fingernail on them. Easy, easy, she cautioned herself, go carefully. Do it right the first time. She got a firm grip on the knife with her left hand and found a blade slot. Her right thumb nail fitted into the slot and she exerted pressure, gentle at first, then stronger.

Her thumb nail broke.

In her mind she reeled off every swear word she'd ever heard. Sweat trickled down her sides.

The nail had broken off square and close to the flesh, but there might still be enough to pry with. Again she fitted the nail to the slot and pried. The blade snicked open just as she heard the handle of the door turn.

She flipped onto her back and slid over a foot or so, the knife still in her left hand, the sharp blade pressing against her right hand.

Vic snapped on the overhead light and stared at her from the foot of the bed. Was he going to move them now? Had her efforts been for nothing? Or did he have something else in mind? If he checked the ropes and found the knife, there was no telling what he'd do to her.

"You're gonna take your last car ride pretty soon," he said, an unpleasant grin on his face. "Figured you'd like to know. Gives you something to think about, right?" He turned the light off and left, closing the door.

The baseball game still blared from the front room. She hoped the men were both baseball fans. Maybe the game would go into overtime. Anything to give her more time.

She turned on her side and squirmed backwards until she felt Rob, then prodded him until he turned on his side with his back to her. It took another moment to position herself so she could touch his hands and the rope around his wrists, and yet another to fit the blade edge against the rope.

Willing her hands to be steady, she began sawing at the strands. The rope was thin but tough and her own bonds prevented her from applying as much pressure as the job needed. Her fingers were cut from lying on the blade and the handle was slippery with blood.

The knife slipped. Rob jerked and made a sound in his throat. She stopped and took a long slow breath before she began again.

At last the strands parted and the rope gave way. She withdrew the knife and the bed jounced as he rolled back and sat up. He took the knife from her and, a minute later, her own hands were free.

She eased her aching arms up and wrenched the gag from her mouth. Two more minutes and they could be through that window. If it opened. If Vic or Carl didn't come in.

She sat up. Rob had pulled off his gag and was cutting the ropes on his ankles. He handed her the knife and she freed her own ankles. Gingerly she swung her legs over the edge of the bed, praying they weren't too numb to hold her up.

It was okay—she could stand, she could use her arms, she could move.

Rob was on tiptoe at the high window, trying to see out. She found the pull cord, quietly tugged the drapes open and examined the window. It opened horizontally, one sash sliding behind the other. If she had a guardian angel, the thing wouldn't squeak when she pushed it open.

It didn't. The scent of the warm night air was exhilarating. The scent of freedom.

They weren't free yet, though. The window ledge was level with her shoulders. She could boost Rob out but needed something to stand on to get out herself. It looked to be about a seven-foot drop to the ground.

"I'll bring a chair over here," she whispered.

She inched her way around the end of the bed and picked up the only one, a small armchair with an upholstered seat. It wasn't heavy, but her arms still shook from her ordeal.

The chair legs bumped against an electric heating panel under the window with a tinny thud that sounded like thunder in her ears. She held her breath, heart thumping, but there was no change in the TV noise from the other room.

Rob climbed up on the chair and then to the window ledge. She squeezed his shoulder and whispered, "If I don't get out, run for all you're worth and find a policeman."

He slipped over the edge, holding on until he was hanging from it by his fingers, then dropped to the ground. The thud and the cracking of the shrubs he'd landed on sounded ominously loud. This time she didn't wait to listen for sounds of movement from the living room.

She swung one leg over the sill and tried to bring the other leg up and out but the window was too narrow. There was nothing for it except to launch herself out sideways.

She crashed into a low bush and tumbled onto the ground, landing on her left hand. A large branch had snapped under her weight, the jagged end ripping across her back. She staggered to her feet, the pain of the gash bringing tears to her eyes.

"Rob?" she whispered. "Rob?"

"Here!" His answering whisper came from behind a shrub only three or four feet away.

She looked right and left. The long, low building was backed by a narrow strip of ground and a high steel mesh fence. On the other side of the fence were two-story structures that might be factories or warehouses; no cars, no people. They'd have to go right or left, around one end of the motel to the street.

Which way?

The light went on in the window above and Vic's voice, hoarse with fury and disbelief, yelled, "Carl!"

Penny grabbed Rob's hand and ran to the right. Dodging shrubs, she headed for a clump of palms at the end of the building.

If Vic was blinded by the bedroom light, they might get that far without being seen.

From the shelter of the palms, she looked back to see Carl and Vic craning out and peering into the darkness. There was no indication they'd seen her. But in a few seconds one of them would be out that window searching the grounds while the other checked the street in front.

They crept from the palms to the front corner of the building, where the office was located, and looked into the street. It seemed clear—but wouldn't be for long. Maybe one of them was already out there.

She recognized the faint sound of someone dropping into the shrubs at the rear.

"Run!" she hissed.

They raced for the street. Penny glanced back at the front of the motel as she ran.

Carl was just emerging from Unit 18.

Rob yelled, "There's a bus!"

The brightly-lit bus was at a stop to the left, maybe fifty yards away.

"Go for it!" Rob could run faster and had the best chance of making it. If Carl chased them, she might be able to get in his way, delay him somehow.

Winded, she stumbled onto the bus behind Rob and the doors whooshed shut behind her. Clutching the railing, she looked back. Carl was in the middle of the street, pointing at the bus, Vic beside him. Penny felt like collapsing right where she was. They'd follow in the car now.

But, for the moment, they were safe.

Habit made her reach for her bag. But her fingers met empty air. Her bag was in the motel.

"Rob, do you have any money?" It was too much to hope that he carried any in his pockets. Would the bus driver kick them off the bus?

He pulled a thin billfold from a back pocket and handed it to her.

She took out a couple of dollars, put it in the fare box and got transfers to downtown Waikiki. Rob had found a seat close behind the driver and she sat beside him, still breathing hard.

The gash on her back was burning and she could feel blood trickling from it. The slashes on her fingers had stopped bleeding but her left hand felt as if one of the bones had broken. She'd jabbed Rob with the knife, too.

"Let me see your hand."

The knife had sliced into the fleshy part of his thumb but the cut was no longer bleeding.

"I've had lots worse than that," he said, but flinched as he took his wallet from her. His cut must hurt.

"Look at my back, Rob. Is it bleeding much?" She twisted around, wincing.

"Just a bit. Your blouse is ripped and you've got a big scratch."

Rob hadn't made a big deal out of his wounds and neither would she.

It was like being in a dream, Penny thought, sitting calmly on a city bus, while out there in the dark two killers were chasing them. She should be doing something clever but she had no idea what. The sudden shift in circumstances had kicked her brain into neutral.

"Are you okay, Rob?"

"Yeah."

"It should never have happened. It was my fault, Rob. I was sure Vic was a good guy. I'm sorry I was so stupid."

She'd been more than stupid; she'd been blind. How could she have trusted Vic so easily? Why hadn't she seen him for what he was? Because he was a good actor, that was why. A lot better than Kinkaid.

"I guess Mom was stupid about Greg, wasn't she?"

"We all make mistakes about people," Penny said, taking his hand in hers. "You know, we wouldn't have got away if you hadn't put my knife in your pocket."

"Mom won't let me have one. Do you think she will now?" He twisted in his seat and looked back. "Are those guys following us?"

"I'm sure they are." They must be, she thought. This is not a dream, Penny. Open your eyes and do something. Vic and Carl weren't going to go away just because she willed it. Rob had been resourceful but he wouldn't be able to save them twice. It was up to her.

"We have to transfer to another bus to get to Waikiki," she said. "If we can just get to where there are lots of people, we should be okay."

"What'll we do then?"

"Phone Mr Kinkaid. If we can't find him, then I'll call the police." If she couldn't find Jack, she'd have to ask the Honolulu police for help. Whether they'd believe her story or not was another matter.

The driver called out the name of the street that was the transfer point. Penny went to the front. Would the bus driver wait if the other bus wasn't there? She sighed with relief as the bus for central Waikiki pulled up behind.

"Quick!" she said to Rob. "If they're out there, maybe they won't see us." In seconds they were on the other bus.

They got off the second bus on Kalakaua Avenue and joined the milling, noisy crowds in the International Market Place. "Stay close," Penny said, "the last thing we want is to get separated."

The dreamlike feeling was even stronger here among the crowds of people, the cacophony of voices, screeching parrots, waterfalls and hawkers. From somewhere over to the right, she could hear the beat of Hawaiian drums They jostled past tables of jewelry, stacks of T-shirts, bins of fruit, searching for a telephone. They were almost at Kuhio Street, on the other side of the market, when Penny saw the bank of public phones.

"Rob, have you got any change?" What an ironic twist if the only thing that kept them from safety was a quarter.

He took several coins out of his pocket and gave them to her. Strange how he was taking care of her when it was supposed to work the other way around.

Her hands were shaking and she dropped the quarter twice before she got it in the slot. As she punched buttons, she gazed at the Pacific Princess across the street and prayed that Jack Kinkaid was in his room.

"Sorry, he doesn't answer."

Nothing for it but the Honolulu police. She'd ask for Kinkaid. If he was a cop, maybe the Honolulu police would know him.

The desk sergeant said, "Oh, yeah. Kinkaid was here a while ago. Let me check." After what seemed an eternity he came back. "He left half an hour ago. Any message?"

So he really was a policeman.

"My name is Penny Davis. He's looking for me," she said, desperate now. "And my nephew. We just escaped from two hit men but I think they're following us."

"Can you grab a cab down to the station here?"

"I haven't got any money! I had to leave my bag behind when we escaped."

"I'll alert a patrol car. What's your exact location?"

"We're in the International Market Place, at the..."

A large hand yanked the receiver out of her grasp and hung it up.

Carl towered over her, blocking escape. Vic's hand was on the back of Rob's neck, his knife, inconspicuous behind the open flap of his shirt, held to the boy's throat.

"Okay, sweetheart," Vic said softly, his eyes slits of anger. "You're history."

"How'd you find us?" she demanded, trying to cover her fear with a show of anger.

"Easy," Vic said. "You went in one side of the Market, we figured you'd head for the other side. And you did. So now we pick up where we left off."

Once the kid and this aggravating broad were in the car, he thought, they'd have no more trouble. He'd picked a good place to fake their drowning and getting there wouldn't take long.

The kid first. Yeah, that would take the fight out of her. And before he drowned her, he was going to enjoy making her pay for everything she'd done.

Jack crept along the back wall of the motel. His footsteps rustled and crunched among the shrubs and dead twigs. As he counted off the windows, he hoped anyone hearing him would think it was merely a scrounging dog. The nineteenth window was wide open and the room light was on. He stood absolutely still, listening.

Not a sound. He took a small flashlight from his jacket pocket and shone it on the ground, looking for gravel by the foundation. Tossing something into the room might get a reaction. Risky, but it was one way of finding out if anyone was inside.

The beam caught a white, jagged break in the main stem of the shrub under the window. The shrub looked as though something had fallen on it. Recently. He glanced back at the open window. Had a body been dumped on it? Or had someone jumped?

His nerve ends tingled.

Jack tossed a pebble in through the open window and stood flat against the wall, listening. Nothing.

He holstered his weapon and clipped the flashlight back in his pocket. Raising his hands to the window sill, he heaved himself up far enough to see inside for a second. No one was there. But there were pieces of what looked like nylon rope on the bed.

Penny and Rob had been tied up in that room! Where were they now?

Nelson wouldn't take Penny and Rob out the back window; he'd want to get them into his car. If the intended killing was meant to look like an accident, it wouldn't have happened here. So, he'd taken Penny and Rob away.

Or, if his guess about the broken shrub was right, Penny and Rob had escaped.

Whatever had happened, he now had enough evidence to call in Koyama and his men.

Jack went back to the motel office. The sullen redheaded woman, roused again from her back room, started grumbling but stopped when she saw his face.

"I need to use your phone. And I want the key to number 18."

She placed the phone on the counter for him and put the key beside it.

"Lieutenant, it's Jack Kinkaid. I think I've located where Penny and Rob were held captive tonight. Doesn't seem to be anybody in there now, but I'd like some backup. I don't know what we're likely to find."

"Where are you?"

Jack gave him the address.

"A patrol car should be there in five minutes. It'll take me about twenty."

Jack walked back and forth, the key to the unit in his hand. It took all his self-control not to storm into the room. Penny and Rob might still be in there, so might the two men. Alone, he could well blow the whole thing.

Two cops piled out of a patrol car. "Kinkaid?"

He led them to unit 18 and, with guns drawn, they snapped open the lock and burst into the room. Nobody there. Nobody in the bathroom or bedroom.

But on the bed and the floor beside it, lay more than a dozen lengths of blue nylon rope. The ends had been cut. The bed cover was creased as though two people had been lying on it and there were smears of what looked like blood. A chair stood against the wall under the window.

When Koyama arrived, Jack showed him the chair and the window and told him about the broken shrub outside.

"It looks like they got loose somehow and went out the window. But where are they now?"

"More important, are Nelson and Fredericks with them?" Koyama said, watching his men examine the unit in minute detail. "You said Nelson is registered as Charles Farrow? I'll get someone to check the car rental agencies again."

One of the officers came over. "Somebody ate a takeout meal—here's the bill for it."

"Good," Koyama said. "Find out if it was picked up or delivered, and if anybody remembers the face of the guy who bought it, also how it was paid for, in case he was careless enough to use a credit card. Anything else? Any ID?"

The detective shook his head. "There are a couple of jackets and some trousers and shirts in the closet. Two suitcases. No tags in the clothes, no names on the suitcases."

"Okay, keep at it." Koyama looked at Jack. "Have you got Frederick's prints on file in Vancouver?"

"I'll get my office to fax them."

The man who'd been examining the ground under the window came back in. "There's some blood on that shrub, Lieutenant. And I found this." He held out a frayed scrap of red cloth, not much more than a few threads.

"She was wearing a blouse that color when she left the hotel tonight," Jack said.

"Come back to the station," Koyama said. "I've put out an APB on Miss Davis and the boy."

"I'll follow you. I've got a rental car."

Koyama eyed him disapprovingly. "Coming here on your own isn't the brightest thing you ever did."

"I had a lead; I had to follow it up. And you didn't leave me any other choice."

"I made what seemed the right decision at the time. It appears I was wrong."

"If I'd handled things right when I spoke to her tonight, they wouldn't be in this mess."

"So we've both made mistakes," Koyama said. "Let's not make any more."

Jack swung his car in behind Koyama's conservative sedan and followed him through the unfamiliar streets.

They should have the motel watched, though it was unlikely Nelson would come back to the unit if he was as efficient as Koyama said.

He walked with the lieutenant across the parking lot. "We'd better check the Pacific Princess right away, just in case Penny and Rob made it back there."

"Mm." Koyama sounded noncommittal.

He obviously didn't believe Penny and Rob had much chance, but Jack was certain they'd escaped from the motel. They might have made it.

The desk sergeant greeted them with, "Kinkaid, there was a phone call from that woman we've got the APB out on."

His heartbeat quickened, his optimism vindicated.

"She phoned from the International Market Place. The line went dead just as she was about to tell me her exact location." He repeated Penny's message.

Jack slumped into the visitor's chair in Koyama's office. "What do you think happened?"

"I think Nelson and Fredericks caught up to them. It would be easy to subdue Miss Davis; all they'd have to do is threaten the boy."

Jack stared down at his clenched hands. Penny had escaped once, it seemed. She'd never make it a second time.

THIRTEEN

Move," Vic said, his voice a low growl. "Stay right behind me. Keep your hands to yourself and your mouth shut, or I'll slit the kid's throat."

Penny swallowed hard, fighting her terror. So close to freedom, so close—and now this. Surrounded by bright lights, music, and people everywhere—couldn't any of them see that something was wrong?

Supposing she screamed and ran? Vic and Carl would escape before anyone could stop them.

And they'd take Rob.

The street was nearly deserted. Vic led them past bright display windows to a shadowed wall.

Still holding Rob by the neck, he looked down at Penny and hissed, "You're gonna die, whether it looks like an accident or not. I don't like people screwing up my plans."

His words chilled her. There'd be no escape this time.

Carl said, "Vic, calm down. We can still do this job right."

"Shut up! You're only along for the ride, Fredericks." Vic looked at Penny. Even in the dim light of the street lamp, she could read the rage in his eyes.

"You cross me a third time and I'll find you if it takes the rest of my life. So do yourself a favor. Do things my way."

If he were going to kill her anyway, what did it matter whether she did things his way?

Vic smiled. "You're worth bucks to me dead and I intend to collect." He leaned a little closer. "But I'd kill you anyway, money or no money. You got it coming."

How much was Greg paying for her death? And for Rob's?

Carl, muttering, headed toward the bus zone, fifty yards away. A motorcycle policeman had stopped, obviously about to ticket the car illegally parked there.

She could scream now—attract the motorcycle cop and distract Vic enough for Rob to get away. But the men had guns;

they'd probably shoot the cop. Vic still had a grip on Rob's neck. She could see the gleam of his knife.

Penny exhaled. Screaming was too risky. As long as they were both alive, there was a chance.

"Move to the curb," Vic said. "When Carl gets rid of the cop, you're getting in the car."

Penny moved. If she acted like all hope was gone, he might get careless. As they stood at the curb, Vic watched Carl and the policeman, but the knife point was still at Rob's throat.

A battered crew-cab pickup squealed to a stop beside them. The driver heaved himself out the passenger door, leaving the motor running, and headed toward a cigarette machine in front of the drug store.

He was the biggest, ugliest man Penny'd ever seen. At least six foot seven with a gut like a sumo wrestler. He was dark-skinned, with a pockmarked scowling face, a stringy mustache and long black hair pulled back into a pony tail. His jeans hung below his belly and he wore nothing above except a brilliantly embroidered but tattered vest. His arm muscles looked like hams Vic moved back a step so he could see around the truck to where Carl was still talking to the policeman.

The truck driver strode back toward the pickup. As he came level with them, Penny shoved Vic as hard as she could against him.

"Hey!" the big man roared. "Watch where you're goin', honky!" He lifted Vic a foot off the sidewalk and swung him around.

Penny didn't wait. "Rob!" She dove in through the passenger door of the idling truck. Rob, behind her, banged the door shut as she put the truck in gear and slammed her foot down on the accelerator.

The truck leapt forward. She turned right and sped to the next corner, turning left this time. She saw, with dismay, that she was on Kalakaua, a wide, busy avenue. There was no place to hide. If Carl and Vic caught up, she'd never be able to elude them.

The dark side streets, where she could be forced off the road or shot at, were an even worse choice. And where was the police station? She was free, but free to do what? Drive around until they caught her again?

She turned left up another one-way street. Four blocks later she was forced to turn left again. On one side were the hotels of Waikiki, on the other the glimmer of water.

It couldn't be the sea. No, a canal, the one they'd seen from the tour bus, a block or two behind their hotel.

She was going around in a circle. She bit her lip and slowed. Why run if all she did was catch up to the killers? She needed to dump the truck, find a phone. Not on this street; there weren't any people around.

She was about to make another left turn when she saw, half way up the next block, real guardian angels.

Two cops walking toward a squad car at the curb.

She accelerated toward the car. Ten feet behind it was a lamp standard. She braked, swung the wheel, and hit the lamp standard with a satisfying crunch of metal.

The steering wheel had slammed into her midriff and, by the time she got her breath, there was a policeman on either side of the cab.

The one on her side, red-haired and freckle-faced, said, "Let's see your driver's licence, lady."

"Just arrest me," she said, almost giddy with relief. Beside her, Rob giggled. It did sound funny asking to be locked up. "I don't have my licence here."

"You drunk?" demanded the policeman.

"No. I'm scared. Two men are trying to kill us."

His expression changed. "What's your name?"

"Penny Davis." Her midriff still hurt.

He looked across at his partner. "She's the APB we heard an hour ago." To Penny, he said, "This your truck?"

"No. I stole it."

"Well," he said philosophically, "I reckon somebody will be looking for it. See if the registration is in the glove compartment, Mike. I'll take the keys. Come on, lady, next stop is the police station."

"I can't think of any place I'd rather be." She crawled thankfully into the back of the police car with Rob and held his hand.

Fifteen minutes later they walked through the back door of the police station and up some stairs into a large room filled with desks and filing cabinets. The redheaded policeman rapped on a door marked "Lieutenant Koyama," opened it and led them inside.

The first person she saw was Jack Kinkaid, on his feet and striding toward her, arms held out as though he was going to hug her. He stopped two feet away, his face lit up with a wide grin.

The grin changed to a scowl. "Why did you take off when I told you who I was?"

She wished he would hug her. Then she remembered that he was a Vancouver cop.

"Why should I believe anything you tell me?" she said. "I knew you weren't an accountant, so you could have been lying about being a cop, too."

The redheaded policeman moved aside, revealing a slim, Oriental-looking man sitting behind the desk. Penny forgot about Jack and his lies.

"You!" she exclaimed. "You were harassing Rob at Sea Life Park!"

The man rose and smiled warmly. "Miss Davis, I'm delighted to see you safe finally. And I was trying to question your nephew, not harass him. I'm Lieutenant Koyama."

"Question him! Why?"

"We'll get to that later," the lieutenant said. "First we need to know what happened tonight, so we can look for your kidnappers."

"Here," Kinkaid said, shoving a chair at her. "Sit down. You look a little frazzled."

Frazzled! If her nerves weren't twanging like an out of tune guitar, she'd fall asleep right where she sat.

Another chair was brought in for Rob, who slumped down, one hand covering the right side of his neck.

"Miss Davis," Lieutenant Koyama said, "I know that you stole a truck to get away from Nelson and Fredericks. Later I'd like to hear exactly how you did it. Right now, I want to know if you saw their car. Could you identify it?"

"I saw it but I don't know what kind it is. There was a motorcycle policeman giving them a ticket when we got away, though."

"Where, exactly?"

"At the bus stop on Kuhio Street outside the Market."

Koyama said to one of the officers, "Get on to Traffic about that." He turned back to Penny. "Now, second, why did you come to Hawaii with your nephew, when from all the evidence, you were intending to fly to Toronto solo?"

She was perplexed. How did they know?

"Because of something Rob saw, a killing. I had to get him away from Vancouver, but the Toronto flight was full."

Koyama turned to Rob, his voice gentle. "Young man, I'd like you to tell us everything you saw or heard in regard to the killing."

Rob told his story quietly while Koyama listened intently and another officer took notes.

"And you can identify Carl Fredericks?"

"Yeah. He used to come to the house. He was one of the guys that tied us up tonight."

"What about the man your stepfather shot? Had you ever seen him before?"

"No."

"Can you describe him? Tell us what he looked like?"

Rob sagged a little in the chair. "He was just a guy. He had real long hair, kind of brown, in a pony tail. And he was skinny."

"Older or younger than your stepfather?"

"Lots younger."

Koyama looked at Jack Kinkaid. "Does that match the description of the victim?"

"Close enough. Rob, can you tell us anything about your mother going away?"

"Just a minute," Penny interrupted. "Do you have to do all this right now? Can't you see he's almost dead on his feet?" She put her hand on Rob's shoulder. He leaned toward her and his hand came away from his neck.

It was covered in blood.

"He's hurt!" She leapt to her feet. "Rob, let me look at your neck."

There was a long gash where shoulder met neck, the blood welling up now that the pressure of his hand was gone.

Koyama spoke into his phone. "Call an ambulance and send the medics to my office when they arrive. And get a first-aid kit up here."

After Jack had dressed the cut, Penny knelt beside Rob, one arm around his waist. "Rob, I'm sorry. I should have checked that you were all right."

He regarded her with eyes that were overbright. "You didn't have time, Aunt Penny."

"Was it Vic's knife that did that? When I pushed him?"

"It's okay. We got away, didn't we?"

"Yes," she said, "Yes, we got away." She felt like crying. "You were wonderful, Rob. So brave."

When the medics had arrived and put Rob on a stretcher, Penny stood up to follow.

"No," Kinkaid said. "He'll be all right in the hospital. We must get your evidence now."

"He needs me! I'm going with him."

"Miss Davis," Koyama said, "Jack is right. There's nothing you can do for him. I'm sure they'll give him something to make him sleep, anyway."

"But he'll be all alone."

"No, he won't. I'm assigning an officer to guard him." Koyama turned to the redheaded policeman standing beside the door. "Colberg, I believe you just started your shift."

"Yes, sir."

"Well, you can spend the rest of it guarding this boy. Don't let him out of your sight. I'll arrange for an officer to relieve you for the following shift."

From the stretcher Rob said, "Way cool!" He looked up at Colberg's freckled face. "I want to know how you get to be a cop. I want to be one when I grow up."

Penny hated to let him out of her sight. Who knew what might happen?

"Your evidence is important," Jack said.

"But..."

"Aunt Penny!" Rob tried to sit up and was restrained by the medics. "You gotta do what they want so they can catch Carl and Vic. You know what Vic said."

Yes, she knew what Vic had said. She'd never forget.

She looked at Kinkaid and Koyama and the other officers and tried to rationalize the choice they were asking her to make. Rob would be in a hospital, guarded. All right. By Honolulu policemen, not Vancouver cops. Even better. And if she could send Carl and Vic to prison, she'd be around to look after Rob until Angela could take over.

"All right," she said to Jack, "I'll answer all the questions you want. Get on with it."

But she turned her back on him and watched the medics carry Rob out the door and down the stairs. Even with a uniformed officer beside him, her nephew looked small and defenseless.

FOURTEEN

Jack studied Penny. Even with tangled hair, bruised face and torn clothes, she was beautiful. And brave. He wanted nothing more than to take her away from here and hold her close for a long time.

He wasn't falling for her, was he? He gave himself a mental kick in the butt, then noticed there were tears on her cheeks.

"Here." He handed her shoulder bag to her. "I brought this back from the motel." She took some tissues from it and dabbed at her face.

He cleared his throat. "Penny, do you know where your sister Angela is?"

"No. I've been trying to get in touch with her for the last two weeks. Greg said she went to Toronto to visit friends, but I hope she's run away from him. Rob says Greg beats her." Penny straightened her shoulders. "He's selling drugs, isn't he? And Rob saw him kill a man. What are you going to do about it?"

He wanted to ask if she knew what was in her suitcase. Better wait until he had her alone, though.

"I'm going to phone my boss in Vancouver and tell him to arrest your brother-in-law. Right now, if the lieutenant will let me use his telephone."

Koyama pushed the phone across the desk and Jack put in his call. "Ian? Yeah, I know I woke you up twice tonight. But we now have enough evidence to pick up Moller."

He relayed Rob's story and Penny's comments.

"Good," Ian said, "we can hold him on that."

"Can you fax Fredericks' fingerprints and the rest of the data on him right away? He and Vic Nelson held Penny and Rob captive in a motel tonight. We can probably get him on kidnaping and unlawful restraint."

"Will do. What are you doing about finding him?"

"Lieutenant Koyama alerted all the airports. If he and Nelson try to get off the island, we'll pick them up. If they don't, we'll have to smoke them out somehow."

"You mean using Miss Davis and the boy as bait?"

"Mmm."

Ian caught his hesitation. "Are they there with you?"

"Yeah. We haven't discussed it yet."

"Okay, do your best; we've got to have Fredericks. Does he know you've got Davis and the boy?"

"Not unless he saw the patrol car pick them up and we're sure he didn't."

"Good luck. And keep me posted. Any time."

"Any time? You sure about that?"

He hung up on Ian's profanity and said, "Moller will be arrested right away." He'd thought that would make Penny relax, but she still sat with her back straight and stiff.

"How did you know we were in trouble tonight?" she asked.

"I knew someone was trying to kill Rob and then found out that Nelson's a professional hit man."

"Jack went to the motel looking for you," Koyama said. "He found the cut ropes and called us. You know the rest."

"I was too late." Jack grimaced, reliving the frustration he'd felt. "How did you get out of there?"

"It was Rob." Penny told them about the Swiss army pocket knife. "First chance I get, I'll buy him one."

"If you don't, I will," Jack said. "The kid's got guts. So do you."

Koyama smiled at Penny. "Your nephew showed great presence of mind for one so young."

"He's had to grow up fast," Penny said. She hadn't realized that before, but it was true. "He's a great fan of cop shows. You heard him say he wants to be a policeman."

"What happened after you got out of the motel?" Jack asked.

She sighed and rubbed her eyes. "We were lucky." The story didn't take long to tell, although living through it had felt like eons.

"Well," Koyama said, "The owner of the pickup may be unhappy, but I'll take care of that."

Jack looked at Penny's drawn face. She was scared, tired and worried about Rob and the last thing he wanted to do was talk her into acting as bait for a killer, but he had no other choice. "We have to find Nelson and Fredericks. The traffic cop's description of the rental car will be a start, but Fredericks is good at covering his tracks."

"So is Nelson," Koyama said. "He has a twisted brilliance. He may be a sociopath or a psychopath. He's typical of both in that he seems to have no moral sense and no regard for anyone but himself."

Jack saw Penny shudder and knew she'd had ample experience of Nelson's corkscrew personality. If she refused to get involved, he could hardly blame her.

"The problem is," he said, "that we can't keep Moller behind bars without Fredericks' evidence, particularly about the killing of Larry Wing."

"Is Larry Wing the man Greg shot?" Penny asked.

Jack nodded. "He was one of Moller's dealers. We've been sure for a long time that Moller runs a big drug operation in Vancouver, but we've never had enough evidence to charge him."

"That explains Angela's expensive jewelry and the big house," Penny said. "I wondered where his money came from." Her hands clenched into fists. "I'd like to see him go to prison for the rest of his life."

"So would I," Jack said. "Not so much because he killed Larry Wing, but because I have a problem with guys who get kids hooked on drugs. And guys who take out contracts on their own kids."

"He's a rotten human being!" Penny's voice was stormy, full of rage.

Did she think her father was rotten? She must know about his part in the bank robbery. "We can put Moller away for a long time, but only if we arrest Fredericks and get his testimony on the murder and the drug operation."

"I want you to get Vic Nelson, too," Penny said. "He swore he'd kill me."

"We want them both." Koyama tapped his pen on the desk. "Fredericks is essential for Jack's case. And I want Nelson, though what he'll get for kidnaping and intent to murder won't keep him inside forever."

"What good does that do me?" Her voice was jerky. "He said he'd find me and kill me no matter how long it took. Am I going to live in fear the rest of my life?"

"We can probably arrange a change of identity for you, relocate you," Jack said.

"Probably! I should have known it would be like that," she said. "So now what? Am I supposed to go home and wait for Vic to come after me? For Carl to go after Rob again?"

"No," Jack said, "definitely not. We don't consider Fredericks a threat. He's never been involved with violence that we know of. Even in the Larry Wing murder, it was Moller who did the killing."

"That's got nothing to do with Nelson," she said sharply. What was Kinkaid trying to say without saying it? "Just tell me what you intend to do."

Jack took a deep breath. "We want you and Rob to be bait. To draw Nelson and Fredericks out of hiding."

Penny stared at him in disbelief. Did Kinkaid know what he was asking of her? Of course he didn't! He'd never been tied up, helpless, and threatened with Vic's knife. He'd never known the terror of believing that he'd die violently within the hour.

"Is that what you've been getting at all this time?" she asked, anger bringing heat to her face. "Why didn't you just say so?"

"It seemed like a lot to ask. But," Jack added, leaning toward her, "we need those two behind bars and trapping them is the fastest way to do it."

"It's way too much to ask," she snapped. "I'm supposed to put my life, and Rob's, on the line—but you quibble about giving us protection if Vic doesn't go to prison."

What Jack was saying proved how sloppy the Vancouver police were, she thought. They were handling this the same way as the bank robbery. They couldn't figure out how to capture the hit men, so they wanted her and Rob to risk their lives.

"It wouldn't be that way," Koyama said. "You'd be quite safe. We'd have officers watching you every minute, every step of the way."

Penny eyed both men. Jack had lied before and maybe he was doing it again. But Koyama seemed straight and he was the one who'd be running the operation.

"All right," she said. "I'll do it. I'd do anything to put Vic in prison." She'd even kill him if she had to. Because that's what it came down to, wasn't it? Kill or be killed? "But I won't allow Rob to be involved in this. He's just a little kid!"

"I don't want to involve him, Penny," Jack said. "But I think we have to. Rob is a bigger danger to Moller than you are. Rob can testify against him; you can't."

"But they were trying to kill me, too!"

"Because you and Rob were always together. It would be no good getting rid of the boy and leaving you alive to testify against them." Jack got up and stretched. "Look, Rob is their prime target. If we put you out on the street by yourself, they won't be interested, no matter what Nelson said to you."

"So the trap won't work unless Rob is the bait?"

"That's correct," Koyama said.

Koyama was wrong; he hadn't seen the way Vic looked at her when he swore he'd kill her. But if only Vic came after her, that left Carl free. Without Carl's evidence, Greg would soon be out of jail and he'd find some way of killing Rob. So the choice was still between Rob being a chunk of cheese in a rat-trap or not living until his next birthday.

"All right," she said. "I don't like it, but I don't see what else we can do."

Jack sighed with both relief and frustration. It was the best solution but he hated to put her through it. What if something went wrong? Even the most meticulous planning couldn't allow for accidents and unpredictable humans.

"Are you sure?"

"I'm terrified," Penny said, "but if this is the way it has to be, then let's get it over with."

"Before we get into details," Jack said, "do you think that either of the men knows I'm a cop?"

"No," Penny said. "Vic asked who you were when we left in the taxi. I said you were just a tourist on the make."

Koyama was scribbling on a piece of paper. "I'll arrange for an item in the newspaper. We'll say the police chased a speeding truck—and give a good description of it—on Ala Wai Boulevard, but the female driver and the young boy with her escaped on foot."

"Sounds good," Jack said. "Let's go with that."

"Miss Davis should take a sedative and get some sleep," Koyama said, "while we set up the trap. She'll be under considerable stress tomorrow. Jack, I'll leave it up to you to look after her."

"Do I go back to the Pacific Princess?" she asked. "What about the fire?"

"There wasn't any fire," Jack said. "The police think someone deliberately set off the fire alarm. I think it was Carl Fredericks."

Her face went a shade paler. "You mean that was a setup, too? To get Rob and me out of the room?"

"We're pretty sure that's what it was."

"Won't it seem odd to them if I go back to the hotel?"

"It's natural that you should," Jack said. "Your belongings are there and Nelson may believe you're naive enough to think a locked door can keep him out."

"Not anymore I'm not."

"I'll have plainclothes men on surveillance in and around the hotel," Lieutenant Koyama said.

"And I'll be with you," Jack said.

"I don't want you in my room."

"I don't care what you want. My job is to protect you and that's what I'm going to do."

Penny was silent during the drive to the hotel and in the service elevator, but Jack had no illusions about her being resigned to his presence. She had it in for him for some reason.

"What's the setup?" he asked the officer who met them.

"There's a man posted at each entrance to the building, at both elevators and in the room across the hall. Also a couple of guys in your room. Radios for communication. Your kidnappers won't get past us."

"What about disguises?" Penny's voice betrayed her nervousness.

"I've dealt with Nelson before," said the officer. "Even if he gets by the men downstairs, he won't get past me, disguised or not."

The policeman left and Jack locked the door. When he turned around, Penny had her back to him and he saw the rip in her blouse and the blood on it. Now he knew why she'd sat so stiffly in her chair.

"You're injured, Penny. Let me take a look at it."

"It's nothing. I fell into a shrub when I went out the motel window," she said. "Really, it doesn't hurt now."

"Don't argue with an officer of the law." He took her by the shoulders and turned her so that the overhead light shone on the wound. Her blouse was crusted with blood. He pulled it gently away from her skin and she winced.

"I'll dress it," he said. "It's nastier than you think. We don't want you getting an infection, do we?"

"I guess it would be more exciting for you if somebody shot me."

He let that pass. She was overwrought and an argument would only keep her adrenalin pumped up. He used the radio to request a first aid kit. When it came, he said, "Come on, into the bathroom."

Her stiffness made it plain that she didn't want him touching her. Was it personal or did she hate all cops?

He draped the bottom of her blouse up over her shoulders, then washed the blood away from the gash. Her skin was smooth and lightly tanned except for the pale strip her bikini had covered. The image of her in his binoculars, playing in the surf, came back to him. With it came desire.

"The cut isn't deep," he said. "Should be okay if you're careful with it."

"Thanks." When he'd finished, she pushed past him, took a fresh blouse from the closet and went back into the bathroom. When she came out, she tossed the bloodstained blouse in the waste basket and went to the phone. "I have to find out how Rob is doing."

After she'd hung up, he asked, "What's the score?"

"He's asleep. The nurse said that slash was a near thing. A bit deeper and it would have hit an artery."

"I'm glad the little guy's okay. He's a nice kid. So how about getting some sleep?"

"Who do you think you are, telling me what to do?" She glared at him, fists on hips, long blonde hair tumbling around her shoulders. "You're not interested in Rob! All you cops care about is your exclusive little club and your little cop games. You use the rest of us like pawns on a chess board!"

He walked to the door and turned off the overhead light, leaving the room softly lit by the bedside lamp.

"Penny, what's your problem? I'm a human being first, a cop second. And you agreed to go along with this plan."

"You're the problem! You and the rest of your cozy group in Vancouver. I'm being forced to put my life and Rob's into your hands and that goes against everything I've ever learned about cops. There's no way I can trust you and yet I'm being forced to."

At least it was cops in general she didn't like, not him in particular.

"Why don't you trust us? We're the good guys."

"Other people may think so, but I know better. You and your buddies have made my father's life a nightmare for the last eleven years. There's no proof he was involved in that bank robbery but you've condemned him anyway."

So that's what it was. Looking at it from her point of view he could see why she was bitter.

"Eleven years," she said, her voice breaking. "All that time he's been in a wheelchair with no job and no money. He can't get another job because he hasn't been cleared. And now you've actually arrested him and...and..." She put her hands over her face as sobs shook her body.

Two strides and his arms were around her, holding her against his body, one hand under her hair, soothing her neck. As her sobs subsided, he murmured over and over, "It's all right. I'll look after you."

Her hair smelled like apple blossoms and her body was molded against his as though they'd been specially made for each other. His hand moved up to caress her scalp with his finger tips. He couldn't believe how right it felt to hold her; nothing else seemed to matter.

This was playing with fire! He was here to protect her—not make love with her. But before he could pull away, she put her arms around him and lifted her face to his. He kissed her forehead, then her cheeks, tasting the salt of her tears, the texture of her skin. She tilted her head so that his lips met hers and his body responded instantly, intensely.

He had to stop. She was vulnerable, her emotions scrambled by what she'd lived through tonight.

Her lips opened under his, her arms clung tighter and, before he could stop himself, his tongue sought the sweetness of her mouth.

Jack pulled away from her, held her at arm's length.

"Don't do this to me," he said, sucking in a deep draft of air. "I'm not made of iron. This isn't the time or the place and I'm not the guy."

He wanted to be, though. He wanted to take her clothes off and caress the curves and warmth of her body, explore and taste her skin, love her the way she wanted and deserved to be loved.

Her face was tight with anger and he knew he'd handled it all wrong.

"One minute you like me, the next you don't! If Vic kills me tomorrow, will that make life easy enough for you? Then you'll never have to make up your mind!"

FIFTEEN

Penny turned away from Jack, fighting back angry tears. She went to the sliding door and gazed out at the lights of Honolulu, willing herself to act cool and in control.

Jack was leaning against the far wall, beside the door. She hoped he was as uncomfortable as he looked.

"Penny, I'm sorry. I do like you. But now isn't the time to deal with it."

He sat on the floor at her feet, leaned against the end of the bed, and drew his knees up. She noticed the lines of exhaustion around his mouth and the concern in his eyes and her anger switched to its true target: herself.

She'd never in her life come on to a man the way she had with Jack. Even when she'd believed he was a dull momma's boy, she'd wanted him. That wasn't the worst of it. He was a policeman! What was wrong with her?

"Why don't your people leave my father alone?"

"The only possible reason is that they believe he's guilty. You know he's been arrested."

She tried to compare Jack with the cops who'd come to the house over the years, with the ones at the station who'd interrogated her. There was no way he fitted the picture she'd carried in her mind all these years. He seemed like an ordinary human being, not a humorless inquisitor.

"But I don't understand why. If you couldn't prove he was guilty eleven years ago, how can you do it now?"

"There's new evidence."

"How can there be? What new evidence?"

"A man recently arrested on another charge confessed to his part in the robbery. He named your father and another man as his partners."

Tears stung her eyes. It wasn't true. She would not believe that. Ever. "Then where's the money? What did he do with the money? He and my mother have been darn near starving to death."

"Penny, I don't have any answers. I'm on the drug squad, not in Robbery." Jack stretched his arms above his head, then tucked his hands behind his head.

"Then how do you know about this man who was arrested?"

"A friend of mine works in Robbery. He told me."

Were all cops vindictive? She had to admit that wasn't possible, though the belief had sustained her anger for a long time. Some, maybe, but not all.

Jack regarded her from beneath half-closed lids for a moment. "We're only human, you know. Some of us," he added wryly, "are more human than others."

Was he reading her mind? Spooky. Or maybe he actually understood how she felt.

"I'm glad you're not pretending to be an accountant anymore. You make more sense when you're being yourself."

"Sometimes. Sometimes I do stupid things, like just now. But I couldn't let what was happening between us go any further. It would have been a mistake for both of us."

"How can you know it would be a mistake for me? Don't I get to make up my own mind?"

"Not when you're scared and hurt and under siege by a killer. I'm not taking advantage of you when you're in emotional turmoil."

Maybe he was right, but she wanted him more than ever. How could she be so stupid as to want a cop?

"Besides," he added, "you might find I'm as bad at making love as I am at adding columns of figures."

"That almost sounds like a challenge."

"Not really."

Did she want him to prove he was a good lover? Yes. Her body ached for him. Why was he holding back? Because he thought he knew better than her what it was she needed. Typical arrogant cop. But her condemnation was half-hearted, a habit of thought.

"How about getting some sleep now?" he asked.

"I can't; I'm too jumpy. I wish I'd never brought Rob to this place."

"Too late for that. Besides, think what could have happened if you hadn't taken him out of Vancouver." He rose and took her hand. "Why don't you stretch out on the bed, at least? Talk if you want, that might relax you."

It felt good to lie down with her head on a pillow and, strange as it seemed, to see him on the other bed, turned toward her with his chin propped on one hand.

"You're a beautiful woman, Penny. I thought so from the first moment I saw you." His voice sounded husky and caressing.

"When was that?"

"In Vancouver airport."

"When I bumped you with my suitcase?"

"I was watching you before that."

"Because you thought I was beautiful?"

"No, because that was my job."

"Your job! Why on earth would you watch me?"

"Because we thought you were acting as a courier for Moller. Drugs or money. Or both."

She sat up abruptly. "Me? Working for that bottom-feeder? That's the most ridiculous thing I ever heard!"

"Is it? Then why do you have a half-kilo of heroin in your suitcase?"

"What?" She couldn't have heard him right.

"Take a look," he said. "I didn't intend to get into this right now, but we might as well."

Furious, Penny flung herself off the bed, stalked over to her suitcase and opened it.

"There's nothing in here but my sister's necklace! Unless this suitcase has some secret compartment I've never found." She held out the package. "Look for yourself."

"Are you sure that's a necklace, Penny? Have you opened it?"

"No." Somebody, somewhere, must have put a hex on the Davis family. First her father being falsely accused, now her. She stared at the parcel, thinking back. "Greg asked me to pick it up and give it to Angela when I saw her."

"Uh-huh."

"What's the matter with you? Don't you believe me?" Then it hit her. "Greg! Greg asked me to pick it up." She ripped the paper off and opened the box. It was full of white powder.

Jack took the box from her and rewrapped it. "Better let me take care of this. I'll put it in the hotel safe tomorrow morning."

This time her fury was directed at Greg. "That evil piece of trash was setting me up!"

"It didn't look that way last week," Jack said. "You went to see him often enough that we checked you out. You were unemployed, broke and related to him by marriage. Then you picked up this heroin. We were convinced you were working for him."

"So that's why you were following me! How did you know what was in the box?"

"The jeweler is a middleman, one of Moller's contacts. And the clerk working for him is a narc we planted."

Penny shook her head at the innocent-looking box sitting on the dresser. If she'd opened it earlier, she might have guessed what the stuff was, but wouldn't have had any idea what to do with it. Maybe flush it down the toilet, like Rob's french fries.

Jack led her back to the bed and spread a blanket over her. "Why would Moller set you up like that?"

"He hates me. He always has. He's possessive and jealous because Angela and I are close. I guess it didn't help that I encouraged her to be independent." She sighed. "I didn't think he hated me that much, though."

"Obviously he does. Can you imagine what would have happened to you if Customs had opened that?"

"I didn't even know he was dealing drugs until Rob told me about the murder." Jack's somber expression brought home the full implications of the box. "You don't believe I'm a dealer, do you?"

"No, I don't, but my boss will take some convincing."

She could feel the blood drain from her face.

"Don't worry about it, Penny. I'll convince him."

"I guess this is one more reason why I should be bait for Carl and Vic, isn't it? I have to do something to prove I'm one of the good guys."

Jack was holding her hand again, smoothing her hair back from her forehead. "You don't have to prove it to me."

Suddenly he stood up, surprising her. "Move over." He lay down on top of the blanket and turned on his side to face her. He tucked her hand under his. "Go to sleep."

She wanted to, but she couldn't. Everything that had happened in the last few days kept replaying on her internal movie screen. Then an old movie came on. Not what she'd call a golden oldie, though.

"When my father was shot," she murmured, "it seemed the whole world was against us."

His breath was warm against her ear and his hand gave hers a comforting squeeze. "I know, Penny. When mine died, I felt exactly that way."

So he'd lost his father, she thought. At least I still have mine, even if he is in trouble. "Did you get over feeling that way?"

"Yes. I knew who killed him and why. Once I decided to do something about it, I was okay."

"What happened?"

He rolled onto his back, still holding her hand. She moved her head so she could see his face.

"My father was a cop. He was shot by an ex-con, another drug dealer, looking for revenge."

"Is that why you became a policeman?"

He turned his face to her, his hair haloed by the soft light of the bedside lamp, the hollows of his eyes dark. "Partly. I probably would have anyway."

"Did you get the ex-con?"

"Not personally; I was only fifteen. The cops my father worked with got him. He was found hanging in his cell three days after they arrested him."

She didn't miss the irony in that. "It must have been a rough time for you," she said.

"It was for all of us. We knew, even as kids, that Dad risked his life every time he went to work. The guy just walked into our house and let loose. And to make it worse, my sister Connie was shot and wounded."

"Oh, Jack!" She wanted to hug and comfort him.

He rolled toward her again, tucked the blanket around her shoulders, and let his arm lie loosely across her waist. "It's all right, Penny. She's married and has a couple of kids now. But she'll never walk right again."

"What an awful thing to live with."

"You've had to live with your own demons. I guess we all have some. Go to sleep now. It's late."

Penny closed her eyes. There was much more to Jack Kinkaid than she'd thought. Did he like her or was she just another case to him? He'd revealed more of himself than he knew by the way he decided what was best for her, as if she couldn't do it for herself.

Dawn backlit the cream drapes on the lanai door when Penny wakened. Jack's body was pressed against her back, his breath warm in her ear, mustache nuzzling her neck. She turned and slid her arm around him.

He kissed her gently on the lips. "Feel better?"

"Yes. What time is it, anyway?"

"Six-thirty. I'm supposed to phone Koyama in half an hour." He sat up and rubbed his face.

She looked at the tousled hair falling over his broad forehead, the sprinkling of grey in his mustache, the grey eyes puffy from lack of sleep, the bump on his long nose—how had he broken it?—the faded scar on his left temple. She knew so little about him, yet lying here beside him seemed as natural as breathing.

"Like what you see?" He was smiling at her.

"Very much."

"Me, too." He bent down and kissed her again. "I sure don't want to get off this bed. I'd be happy to spend at least the next week in it. With you."

"Why don't you?"

"I told you last night. Besides, duty calls."

She knew what that meant. She dreaded it, but reality wasn't going to go away. She sighed and sat up, too.

"Stay there," he said. "Go back to sleep if you can. I'm going to have a shower, then talk to Koyama."

As she listened to the rush of water a few feet away, she played with the idea of joining Jack in the shower, her body tingling, half aroused. She was conscious of the healing itch of the gash on her back, the faint sounds from the street below, the sunlight creeping across the floor.

Did Jack want her the way she wanted him? His reaction last night seemed proof enough.

Penny sat up again. She was being stalked and Jack was here to protect her, to catch the stalkers. Plain and simple. And that would probably be the end of it.

Jack came out of the bathroom and she went in.

When she came out, showered and dressed, a half hour later, he was hanging up the phone.

She went to the desk. "I'm going to call my mother and see how Dad is."

"Do you think that's wise? If things aren't going well, you'll be upset and distracted. You need to focus completely on what's happening today."

Her immediate reaction was to argue. He was right, though. There was nothing she could do to help her father until she was home again.

"I guess the most important thing is to make sure Rob stays alive."

"And you," he said, dropping a quick kiss on her cheek.

Her thoughts returned to Vancouver. What were the days like for her father? Well, at least the legal machinery had begun the process of dispensing justice. One way or the other, the situation was about to be resolved.

The implication startled her. What had she just told herself? That the case against her father could go either way? But he was innocent. Wasn't he?

The doubts were disturbing. Distracting. Definitely not something she wanted to think about. Not today.

"Are we going to have breakfast?" she asked.

Jack shook his head. He was wearing his official face now. "You'll have to play a part today. We want you to act nervous, but confident that you can avoid capture."

She couldn't help smiling. "That's a large order for somebody who's worse at acting than you are."

"Doesn't it reflect the truth? You're scared of Nelson, but confident because you have police protection?"

"I suppose it does." The idea of the police protecting her no longer seemed strange.

"First, you'll pack up your things, check out and move to another hotel. There's a room reserved for you at the Waikiki Princess and two men already in position there. You'll go by taxi, driven by one of Koyama's men."

"So I'm too naive to think they might follow?"

"After the stunts you pulled off last night, we hope they'll believe you're overconfident."

"Like I'm a cautious Superwoman, right?"

He nodded, his features softening as he took her hands in his. "Penny, don't drop your guard, not for a second."

He moved to the desk and glanced at his notes. "Rob's guard reported in. Rob feels fine and he's okay to be discharged, so you can go by taxi and pick him up after you've settled into the other hotel."

"Driven by the same policeman? If they're following me, wouldn't they notice that?"

"No, different man." He smiled at her. "If your brain keeps working like that, you'll do fine."

"Do you think they'll come to the hotel room?"

"I doubt it. They'd want to get you into a car and take you to some secluded spot. Nelson may hate you enough to kill you, but he's not going to take unnecessary risks."

"So. Rob and I are in the hotel room. Then what?"

"Then you can have breakfast."

"I thought we'd never get to the best scene!" If she pretended this was a play she might not feel so afraid.

"There'll be plainclothes men all around, so enjoy your eggs and bacon or whatever." He paused. "What do you like for breakfast, by the way?"

"Hash browns, two fried eggs over easy, two strips of crisp bacon and coffee. Lots of coffee."

"Sounds great. I'd join you, but Nelson did get a look at me and we want him to go on believing I'm just a guy on the make. You'd hardly tell me you were moving to another hotel."

"Nor invite you for breakfast. Couldn't you wear one of your weird getups? As a disguise?"

"I will when I meet you later. It should be enough to prevent him recognizing me. He only got a glimpse last night." Jack glanced at his notes again. "After breakfast, go to the lobby and book for the Polynesian Cultural Center Royal Night Tour. The pickup time is one o'clock."

"What if there aren't any seats left?"

"There will be. But we want you to reserve the seats yourself, so if you're being watched, they can find out where you're going."

"Would I really go on a tour when I know those two hoods are lurking?"

He nodded. "Don't forget you're overconfident. And being surrounded by people will make you feel safe. You've also reserved seats on a plane for Vancouver Monday morning so they'll know they've only got two days."

"Wear different clothes, too, something Nelson and Fredericks haven't seen you in. And change your hair style. You might feel fairly confident in a crowd of people, but you're practical enough to try disguising your appearance."

"Where will you be while all this is going on?"

"Doing what I usually do. Having breakfast in the dining room downstairs. Wandering the streets with two cameras around my neck and a stunned look on my face. I'm going on the Polynesian Center tour, too, and I'll see you on the bus—they pick up people from this hotel after the Waikiki Princess."

"How do I behave toward you?"

He grinned. "Be polite, but keep me at a distance. Just like you did before."

"I couldn't figure you out. I was sure you were playing a role and that bugged me. People who pretend to be something they're not annoy me. A lot."

He looked at her for a long moment, something in his eyes that she couldn't interpret. "Yes, I thought you'd feel that way. Think you can handle the part?"

"I shouldn't have any problem. I've always wanted to be an actress."

"You can do it, Penny. I know you can."

She was pleased by his faith in her. How she'd feel when they were finally on the bus, out in the open, she didn't know. One step at a time, and don't think about a bullet coming out of nowhere.

Jack sat beside her on the bed. "Sure you're all right? I don't like putting you in the line of fire."

"I'm already in it. And will be until Vic is in prison. But do we really have to have Rob in on this?"

"Believe me, I don't want to expose him to more danger, but I can't see any way around it. Rob's the primary target. If you're alone, Fredericks might talk Nelson into backing off."

She saw Vic's face, heard his voice, and a chill ran through her. "I don't think anyone could talk Vic out of something he wanted to do."

He paced to the window and back. "This is the part I hate. I'm used to the risk; it's my job. But it's not yours and you shouldn't have to..."

"Shouldn't have to what?"

He stared at her for a second. "You shouldn't have to take this kind of risk—your life, Rob's life—all because your brother-in-law committed murder. It's as unfair as Connie being disabled because she was a cop's daughter."

"You can't keep the whole world safe, Jack. Everybody takes risks." She'd taken a risk in trying to protect Rob. Angela had taken risks in giving birth, in marrying Greg. "If something happened to my sister, I'd be very sad, but I wouldn't give up the years we shared for anything. Some things are worth the risk."

He frowned, apparently unconvinced, and looked at his watch. "You'd better start packing."

"When do I check out?" she asked.

"Nine o'clock. Gives them a chance to pick up on that item in the paper. It's on the front page of the local section, by the way, so I doubt they'll miss it."

She looked at her watch. Seven-thirty. It was going to be a long hour and a half. Or a short life.

SIXTEEN

Carl Fredericks stirred his coffee, thinking of Candy in the kennel back home and silently cursing Greg Moller. At the far end of the café, two truck drivers were downing an early breakfast. Vic had gone to buy a newspaper.

Vic slid into the booth and tossed the paper on the table, scattering toast crumbs and balled-up sugar wrappers. "It'll be in the local section, if there's anything at all."

"Look at this! The bimbo wrecked that pickup only two blocks from the Market Place." He shoved the paper at Carl.

"Disappeared on foot, it says," Carl said. "And we drove all over Honolulu looking for her." Not that he cared. All he wanted was to get off this cruddy piece of real estate and go home. If Nelson didn't make his hit today, he'd go home anyway. He'd had his fill of the arrogant little swine. Greg would be teed off, but he could live with that.

"Come on, Fredericks, we got work to do."

"Like what? You think we're going to find her again?"

"I'll find her. I'll smell the stinking broad if I get within a mile of her." Vic flung some change down on the table and strode out.

Carl followed, wishing he'd taken something for his headache. It had been a long night, chasing around the city, getting another rental car, finding a new motel. And Vic's continual grouching was beginning to get to him.

Trouble with Vic was he took everything personally. What did he think the woman was going to do—meekly let herself be killed? If Vic was such a hotshot, he'd better start proving it.

Vic tossed the car keys to Carl. "Sit tight for five minutes, will you? I gotta make a phone call." His mother would be up by now, fussing around the house in her pink quilted dressing gown, watering plants and tidying before she went to work.

"Hi, Mom. How are you?"

"Oh, darling, I'm so glad you called! I miss you dreadfully when you're away on these trips. Is everything going well?"

"Couldn't be better. I might be home in a day or two. You better get that pecan pie put together."

"That's wonderful news, Victor. You won't forget church tomorrow, will you? I know that sometimes you let your work get in the way of more important things."

"I won't forget. See you soon." He blew her a kiss down the telephone line and hung up.

Jack watched Penny pack. He liked the way she moved, the way she used her hands. He liked everything about her. It would be great if they could spend some real time together, just relaxing and not having to think about anything serious.

He hoped she wasn't the marrying kind. Maybe she'd be willing to have an affair with him. He was sure she'd be as up front about what she wanted as he was. They could have a good relationship without either of them risking their principles.

Jack stood up and shrugged into his shoulder holster, trying to figure out what was wrong with his shirt. Cripes, all the buttons were in the wrong holes!

"Need some help, detective?"

He looked up to see Penny's teasing smile.

"Uh, I think I can figure this one out by myself." He rebuttoned the shirt, feeling like a clumsy teenager. He'd better start thinking about work instead of play.

The problem was the stage fright that went with waiting for a major operation to start. He hated waiting and he had to sit around here for another hour, wanting Penny with every cell in his body. Just in his bed, though, not sharing a checking account.

He walked over to the lanai door and looked out. Why couldn't life be simple? He didn't need a permanent relationship, didn't want one.

"Do you like this?" She held up a dress—blue and white striped cotton, sleeveless, with a full skirt.

"I like it fine." He added flippantly, "I didn't know you owned a dress."

"I don't. This is Angela's." Her eyes filled with tears. "I wish I knew..."

He took her in his arms, angry at himself for dwelling on his own confused emotions instead of her problems. For the moment he had only one goal: to make sure she and Rob came through this ordeal safely. "We'll find her, Penny." He rubbed his cheek against her wet one. "Don't think about her now."

"I know, but..."

"No buts. Worrying won't help find her." He kissed her and held her away from him. "All right?"

"Sorry." She rubbed her arm across her eyes, went into the bathroom and came back with the dress on.

"You look terrific in that."

His comment brought a smile to her face and she rummaged in the closet again.

"I even have shoes to go with it," she said, holding up white pumps with narrow, pointed heels.

"How in blazes do you walk on those spiky little heels? Don't you tip over?"

She chuckled. "They're very comfortable. Secret weapons, too."

"What?"

She gave him a playful jab in the ribs with the heel of a shoe and he winced.

"Okay, okay, I believe you."

The next time Penny came out of the bathroom, she'd done her hair in two long braids and put on large flat earrings covered in the same material as the dress. She took a pair of blue-tinted sunglasses from the desk, put them on and stood, hands on hips, waiting.

"Very good. You do look different."

She put the sunglasses down. "When I finish packing, do I go down to the lobby with my suitcases?"

"There's a guy in the corridor vacuuming the carpet. He's a cop. Go to the elevator and he'll ride down to the lobby with you. Koyama has other men staked out there."

She looked worried and he couldn't help putting his arms around her again. "There'll be somebody with you every step of the way." He felt her yield against him. "I wish I could stay with you, but you know I can't."

She took a deep breath, then pushed him away. "Okay, go. I'll be fine."

Jack went to his room. One of Koyama's men was on the lanai, surveying the buildings opposite with binoculars. The man turned and said, "Did you tell Ms Davis to stay away from the sliding doors and the lanai?"

"Yes, I did." That had been last night. He hoped she hadn't forgotten. "Any sign of anything?"

The man shook his head and went back to his survey.

Jack called Ian Baker. "We've got Penny and Rob set up as decoys. Lieutenant Koyama is going all out on this."

"Good." Ian sounded tired. "We're getting nowhere with Moller. He's just an innocent, hardworking, upright citizen being harassed by evil police. About what I expected from him."

"Any luck finding his wife?"

"No. I'm beginning to doubt that we will find her. Alive, that is."

"Why?" He hoped Ian was wrong. Angela's death would hit both Penny and Rob hard.

"I took Mrs Davis over to Moller's house to look through Angela's clothes. She doesn't think anything's missing. And the housekeeper is sure Angela wouldn't have gone away without telling her. Both of them said she never went anywhere without the boy."

"And no luck with airlines?"

"Nope. We've been grilling Moller on the Larry Wing murder so far, but I'm going to switch to Angela this afternoon and see if he'll break."

"Good luck."

"You, too. Watch your back, Kinkaid. I don't have time to break in new detectives."

Downstairs in the dining room, Jack sat facing the glass door to the lobby so he could watch Penny when she left the hotel. He ordered breakfast, poured a little ketchup on his eggs and ignored them.

He hadn't felt like this about Sara or Barbara. Just infatuation mixed with sex, that's all it was. A few weekends together and he'd have her out of his system.

She walked past the restaurant door toward the street, head up, shoulders back, looking wary but confident. Doing just great, he thought. Let's hope she can keep it up.

As he paid the bill, he winced at his image in the mirror behind the cash register. He wore a baseball cap with a giant bill as well as outsized sunglasses to hide his face. His cotton trousers were a revolting shade of lime. The Hawaiian style jacket, meant to hide his holster, was a riot of garish patterns and colors.

He hung a camera around his neck and headed for the International Market Place. After half an hour, he emerged on Kalakaua Avenue. What was Penny doing now? Probably on her way to the hospital to pick up Rob. There was no reason why he couldn't act as unofficial backup and make sure they got to the Waikiki Princess okay.

From his cab, he watched them come down the steps of the hospital and get into their taxi. Rob was chattering, face animated, the white bandage on his neck almost concealed by the collar of his polo shirt.

Soon they'd be live bait for a professional killer. Why had he ever gone along with the idea? Come on, Kinkaid, it was your idea in the first place!

He roamed the streets through the endless morning, staring in shop windows, seeing only Penny's smile and Rob's haunted face. After a tasteless lunch he found himself waiting for the Luana tour bus long before it was necessary.

When it arrived, he was relieved to see Penny and Rob sitting on the bench seat at the back of the bus. He strode down the aisle, camera bouncing against his chest, and sat beside them.

"Hi! Great to see you two again." It was hard to stay in character when he felt like hugging both of them.

Rob gave him a wide grin and Penny's smile warmed him right to his toes. He said softly, "Turn down the wattage. Keep your distance."

Her expression changed to cool politeness. "Have you been to the Cultural Center before?

"Yes, I have. Like to hear about it?"

She managed a glazed expression. "Why not?"

"It's like a town, sort of, enclosed by high fences and with a tram line going around the perimeter. And you can travel through the center by canoe."

"Sounds interesting." Her tone was flat.

He nodded. "There are replicas of native villages from places like Samoa and Fiji and Tonga. The natives sing and dance and demonstrate their crafts."

Penny glanced sideways at Jack, smiling.

"What's so funny?" he muttered.

"Your costume," she said. "It's a little early for Halloween."

The bus driver started his spiel and Jack pretended to listen while he thought about the Center. The place was too big and complex to be ideal, but it had to be better than the streets of Honolulu. At least the players in the drama could be contained within a limited area. According to Koyama, the only entrance and exit was through the box office building.

The bus driver broke off in the middle of his story and hit the brakes hard.

"Sorry about that," he called. "Accident up ahead."

The bus slowed to a crawl. Another small tour bus lay on its side off the road, and a car with a crumpled fender blocked the right-hand lane. Tow trucks were moving into position to get the bus back on its wheels.

He'd been on the point of telling the driver to stop so he could get off and help. But today he was a tourist, not a cop. So far.

At the Polynesian Cultural Center, the crowded parking lot seemed to stretch forever. So many people could pose a problem. When the bus stopped, he asked Penny, "Would you like company? I could guide you."

"We'll be fine on our own," she said, with a bright, false smile. "We don't want to hold you up. And thanks for the information."

Jack let them move ahead about thirty feet. He was glad Rob wasn't showing any signs of nerves other than sticking to Penny's side as if he'd been glued there.

He followed them through the gates, the lobby of the big entrance building, and into the grounds. Penny turned right past the restaurant, then left, following the flow of traffic toward the tram depot and canoe landing.

Near an arcade of small shops, several dozen high school kids, led by only two adults, swarmed around him. He tried to force his way through but the kids were laughing, shouting and shoving one another, totally oblivious to everyone else.

Jack swore under his breath. Penny and Rob were getting further and further away. This hadn't been one of Koyama's better ideas—too crowded, too little room to maneuver.

He saw Penny turn her head as they neared the foot bridge across the canal and the terror in her face as she looked at something, or someone, to her left.

He caught a glimpse of Fredericks moving toward the bridge. Fast. Nelson would be close by.

He spoke rapidly into the radio that had been concealed in his camera bag. "Kinkaid. Just sighted Fredericks nearing the canal bridge closest to the entrance. Penny and Rob crossing bridge."

Jack fought harder to get through the crowd but the students, seeing this lone figure in his ridiculous clothes as someone to tease, closed ranks.

SEVENTEEN

When she and Rob reached the footbridge, Penny stopped and turned to look for Jack. He'd promised to stay close behind but she wanted the comfort of seeing him.

He wasn't there.

Uneasy, she scanned the crowd. Where could he be?

She caught a glimpse of a familiar figure pushing through the throngs toward her. The tension she'd been suppressing all morning ballooned to terror.

"Carl's right behind us!" she gasped, clutching at Rob's shoulder.

A few minutes ago Jack had been a few steps behind her. Now he'd disappeared—just when she needed him.

Rob thumped her with his fist. "Come on!" He shot away and, at the center of the bridge, leapt up on the parapet and launched himself off feet first.

Penny, gasping as she caught up, put both hands on the rough stone and vaulted over. Anything was better than being captured again. She heard someone yell—it sounded like Carl—as the water closed over her head.

Her feet touched bottom almost at once. She propelled herself back to the surface and looked for Rob. The canal was shallow, but he was an inexperienced swimmer. He could easily get into trouble.

There he was, hair flattened against his skull, dog-paddling toward a flat-bottomed catamaran style canoe that had just pushed off from a landing dock below the bridge. She struck out after him. They reached the canoe at the same time and hung on to the side while the dozen or so passengers stared at them.

Poling the canoe through the water was a brown-skinned, black-haired, bare-chested young man in an ankle-length red and orange sarong. He grinned at Penny.

"Some people will do anything to get out of paying," he said. "Couldn't you wait for the next canoe or am I too irresistible?"

Penny looked back at the receding bridge but she couldn't see Carl or Vic. Her gaze dropped to the canoe landing. They were there, talking to the attendant and gesturing toward the canoe. Jack was nowhere to be seen. She steadied herself against the freeboard, swallowed and smiled up at the young man.

"Could we come aboard? There are two men after us. We've got to get away from them."

"What do you think, folks?" he said to his passengers. "You like this little show we put on for you? Some visitors want a little adventure while they float through the peaceful villages of Polynesia, right?"

A man laughed. "Sure, let 'em have a free ride. We'll keep the bad guys away." Someone else murmured, "Is this really part of the show?"

The young man leaned down and hauled Rob into the canoe. "My name is Danny. I am a brave Samoan warrior. You will be safe with me."

Rob landed head first, rocking the canoe, and two or three grinning passengers helped him sit up. They obviously thought the whole thing was a joke. Maybe Danny did, too.

"You all like the storms at sea, right?" Danny said. He balanced on the stern, feet apart, and rocked the canoe back and forth. Passengers gasped and clung to their seats.

Danny laughed, black eyes merry. "Now the princess," he said. "We must rescue the princess. Or should we? Any more weight in here and we're liable to sink."

During the byplay, Danny had propelled the canoe a further hundred yards along the canal, far enough from the landing for Penny to wonder if there was a chance of escape after all. Did Danny believe her? He could be making a joke of the episode so as not to alarm his passengers.

Several passengers on the other side leaned outboard to balance the canoe while Penny clambered in. She sat in the bottom, pulling her clinging wet dress down around her legs while her braids streamed water onto the floorboards. A good thing she'd left her shoulder bag at the hotel, or it would now be at the bottom of the canal.

Well, on with the show. She smiled up at Danny. "I'm grateful to be saved by a brave warrior. You're wonderful."

With a practised thrust of the long pole, Danny sent the canoe skimming past one coming in the opposite direction. "All the girls say that; you'll have to wait your turn."

Rob, who had squeezed between a young couple that didn't seem to mind getting damp, looked at Danny wide-eyed. "Are you really from Samoa?"

"You bet! In Samoa I am a famous warrior." Danny pounded his bare chest with one fist, then took up the pole again. "Over here I'm just a humble student at Brigham Young, but when I get home again, watch out!"

They were now too far from the landing for Penny to recognize anyone standing on it. Where were Vic and Carl? She had to know. Jack Kinkaid and his colleagues had lost her somehow—she and Rob were on their own. Where could they hide? She frantically scanned the wide paths along both sides of the canal. There was too much open space.

Carl's lanky form strode along the path on the left, Vic a few yards behind. She hunched down in the bottom of the canoe.

They'd follow the canoe until it landed. And grab Rob the moment he set foot on shore. Once they had him, they had her as well.

The canoe rounded the curve of a small island and her pursuers were hidden from view. If she could find a way to get back to the box office, there'd at least be security guards there.

The glassy water reflected clear blue sky and branches of overhanging trees. The hot sun was already drying her dress. Danny's mellow voice, recounting a Samoan legend, rolled rhythmically over her head and the fronds of tall palms hung limp in the windless air. A peaceful scene, for someone who wasn't measuring the remainder of her life in minutes.

When he'd finished his story, she said, "Could you let us off before we get to the next landing? Somewhere out of sight of that path?" She pointed to the left side of the canal.

He pressed his palm to his forehead in mock despair. "We've only just found each other and already she wants to leave me!"

The young couple sitting with Rob giggled.

The canoe slid out from behind the island and as the left-hand path came in sight, so did Carl and Vic. They weren't having any trouble keeping up; the only hope was to get off and run. Or hide.

"How about Fiji? It's a big place," Danny said. "I could land you next to Fiji for the same as it cost you to get aboard. Heck, I might even go with you. I always wanted to honeymoon on Fiji with a beautiful princess."

"This is your big chance then," she said. "Is it all right if I bring someone else along on our honeymoon?" She sensed, beneath his flippant act, a concern for her. He must have taken her plea for help seriously.

"The more the better, princess. Blonde, brunette or redhead?"

"He's got brown hair."

Danny feigned outrage. "You've got it all wrong. I want wives, many wives, not competition."

"He's only nine."

"That's not competition, princess; that's family." He sighed loudly. "So you've already got a family. You sure know how to take the fun out of things."

When the canoe swung into the right-hand channel around another island, Penny said, "Is this the one?"

"This is it," Danny said. "The fabled honeymoon island of Fiji. I can't come with you now, but wait for me. I'll be back as soon as I get rid of these people."

He dismissed his passengers with a nonchalant wave of his arm. They laughed and looked at him expectantly, waiting for the rest of the story. Out of sight of the left bank, he brought the canoe to rest below a footbridge which presumably connected the island of Fiji with the main part of the Center. Penny scrambled ashore, Rob behind her.

"Parting is such sweet sorrow," Danny crooned. "Good luck, princess. Watch out for the natives."

In a low voice, she said, "Please call security in the entrance building and ask for Lieutenant Koyama. Tell him what's happened; he'll know what you're talking about."

He nodded and pushed off. As the canoe glided away toward the bend, Penny and Rob hurried up the slope to the path and crossed the footbridge to the main area of the Center. A sign post indicated they were entering a Hawaiian village. She walked swiftly, Rob trotting to keep up, and ducked into a grove of palm trees fringing the huts. Maybe she'd made a mistake landing here—this part of the Center seemed deserted. Glancing back at the bridge they'd just landed under, she froze.

Carl was by the railing, looking down at the canal.

When he turned his back and waved at someone—Vic, no doubt—she grabbed Rob's hand and ran. They'd hide in the thatched hut a few yards away until Carl moved on.

The interior of the hut was dark after the glaring sunlight. Penny edged along the wall away from the door. When her eyes had adjusted to the gloom, she saw that the hut was empty except for a loosely piled heap of woven mats in one corner and cooking gear in another. Shafts of light shone through small chinks in the walls and she peered out through the nearest one.

Carl was fifty feet away, looking around. He must have seen that she and Rob were no longer in the canoe and started to search for them.

"Rob," she whispered, "we'll hide under those mats. Be quiet; he's very close."

She pulled the mats away from the wall, spreading them out a little, and Rob crawled underneath. When he was completely hidden, she wriggled underneath on the other side, against the wall.

Dust filtered out of the woven reeds, irritating her nose. She pinched her nostrils together and hoped Rob was doing the same—one sneeze and it would be game over. And she didn't dare caution Rob now, even in a whisper.

Why had they left the canoe? Being with people and listening to Danny's banter now seemed a far better haven than this hut.

Where were her protectors—the policemen who were supposed to be looking after them? Hadn't any of them seen what happened? And where was Jack? The guy who'd sworn nothing would prevent him from staying close to her.

The old bitterness flooded back into her mind. Maybe one of the Honolulu cops had been hurt and Jack had gone to his aid, abandoning her in favor of his buddy. Penny bit her lip hard, trying to control her clashing emotions.

Had Jack been hurt? But what could have happened to him in such a crowd? And wouldn't she have heard some sort of commotion behind her?

Right now she had more important things to do than worry about Jack. How long should they stay hidden here? If nothing had happened at the end of ten minutes, she might risk poking her head out. She began counting, slowly, to sixty. And again.

At the end of the fourth minute, she heard footsteps crunching on gravel outside, closer and closer, then silence. Carl or Vic must be looking inside, waiting until his eyes adjusted to the dim interior. She held her breath, muscles tensed.

Jack stumbled, almost falling, over a sneakered foot. Frantic, he rammed his way out of the group, to a chorus of noisy protests, and ran toward the bridge.

Penny and Rob had disappeared.

Carl Fredericks was standing in the middle of the bridge, looking down into the canal.

Jack drew his weapon. He shouted, "Fredericks!" and ran toward him, dodging people. Startled, Fredericks turned, saw the gun, and yelled something unintelligible as he leapt away from the rail.

Somebody bumped into Jack from the left, knocking him off stride. A searing pain flashed along his left ribs.

He fell to his knees as agony ripped through his upper body. A small crowd gathered but stayed well back, staring at the gun clutched in his hand.

A man was over him, speaking into a radio. "Makua. Kinkaid's down. Get a medic to the footbridge that leads to the tram depot. "

Another man, fat, balding, festooned with photographic equipment, edged forward. "Sorry I banged into you, Mac. You hurt?"

Jack struggled to his feet, one hand pressed against his ribs, and looked across the footbridge. Fredericks was gone. When he lifted his hand from his side, it was red with blood.

The tourist backed away. "Hey, I never did that!"

"What happened?" Makua asked.

"I got trapped in a crowd and lost Penny and Rob. Fredericks was on the bridge and I went after him. Then this. What's the backup doing? Did you see anything?"

"Stay right here," Makua said. "Somebody's coming to patch you up. I'm on my way." And he, too, was gone.

The fat tourist was still there. "All I did was bump into you, Mac. I never meant no harm."

Jack eased his gun back into its holster. He was starting to shake.

"No hard feelings," he said. "You probably saved my life." Nelson must have been following and come after him with a knife when he was alerted by Fredericks. The knife would be in the middle of his back now if this wonderful fat slob had paid attention to where he was walking.

Koyama ran up with another man who looked at the wound underneath Jack's blood-soaked jacket. "Grab his other arm, Lieutenant," he said. "We'll get him to the first aid room. He may need to go to hospital."

"I'm not going to hospital now!"

"No arguments," Koyama said, hustling him forward. "You're bleeding like a stuck pig."

Ten minutes later, his wound dressed and taped, Jack stood up and walked experimentally around the room. He felt a little light-headed and his side hurt like blazes but he'd stopped shaking.

"I still think you should get to a hospital," Koyama said.

"Later. After those two bozos are in the bag. Listen, what happened to the backup? I thought there were supposed to be a dozen guys out there."

"They had an accident on the way here," Koyama said wearily. "The tour bus they were in was sideswiped by another vehicle and it flipped on its side."

Jack stared at him in disbelief. "Tour bus? They were on a tour bus?"

"What did you expect, a copter? Hardly an inconspicuous way to arrive. However, they're here now, spreading out through the Center."

"They're an hour late!" He rammed his fist against the wall, jarring his body and sending a sharp pain through his side. "It could make the difference between Penny and Rob getting out safe or being killed."

"You're quite right," Koyama said, "but the unexpected does happen and I don't have second sight. We're doing the best we can."

"Was anybody hurt?" Jack was in control of his temper again. "I remember now we saw a bus turned over near Chinaman's Hat."

"No. Shaken up a little, that's all. It's not a complete fiasco, Kinkaid. I brought four men with me and three were at the entrance before you arrived. Makua, as you know, was close behind you."

Jack checked his weapon and reholstered it. "I'm going out there. I promised Penny I'd look after her and so far all I've done is screw things up."

"Are you sure you're fit enough?"

"It doesn't matter. I can walk and I can shoot. Maybe I can even run. And I know what's going to happen if we don't pick up Nelson and Fredericks fast."

"What?"

"They know we're after them now. It could be a hostage situation—them bargaining with some handy tourist's life to get out of here."

But it wouldn't be a tourist, Jack thought, striding toward the footbridge, catching his breath as pain hit him at each step. It would be Penny and Rob.

He gazed down into the canal. Had Fredericks pushed Penny and Rob off the bridge? Not likely. He and Nelson would force their victims to walk out of the grounds to the parking lot. Besides, Penny had told him she was a good swimmer and Nelson, having spent time on the beach with her, must know that, too. Anyway, the canal didn't look deep enough to be dangerous.

On the other hand, jumping in would have been the quickest way to escape. Jack looked toward the dock on the left side of the canal and saw a canoe being poled away toward center stream.

Down on the dock, he asked the attendant, "Have you seen a tall woman with blonde braids and a little boy in the last half hour?"

The attendant grinned. "I've seen people do weird things, but nothing like that before. They jumped off that bridge there—right into the canal."

"Where did they go?" Jack demanded.

"Hey, man, is this something serious? I thought they were just doing it on a dare."

Jack snapped open his identity badge.

"Oh. Sorry. One of the canoes picked them up."

"Where would they be now?"

"Could be anywhere. It was Danny picked them up, but they didn't come back with him on the return trip." He pointed at the canoe gliding away around a curve. "That's him there. They must have got off at the other end. You want to talk to Danny when he comes back from this trip?"

"How long will he be?"

"Half hour or so."

"Too long." Jack strode off down the path beside the canal. Too much could happen in half an hour.

EIGHTEEN

Footsteps crunched on gravel again. Penny strained to hear. Going away? Or coming closer? How many people? Then came the heart-stopping answer.

Vic's voice at the door of the hut. "See anything?"

"They're not in here." Carl's voice was even closer. "They must have run to get out of the area so fast."

"She's panicking. Should make it easier."

If they thought that she and Rob were far away, she might have a little more time to find an escape.

"Easier!" The anger in Carl's voice was laced with fear. "Are you crazy, Nelson? That boyfriend of hers is packing heat and he knows my name. There are probably cops all over the place. How do we get out of here?"

Vic's voice was venomous. "We get the kid. Then she'll come along nice and quiet. The four of us walk out of here. If anybody tries to stop us, we can trade her for a ticket out."

"I don't like it."

"Tough."

"Listen, Nelson, I came here to i.d. the kid and make sure the job was done. Not get involved in your war games."

"I don't care what you came for. You're in too deep to get out now. They'll charge you with kidnaping."

"I'll deal with that if I have to. But I'm not facing a murder charge! Let's get out of here."

"You're on my turf," Vic snapped, "and you'll do it my way. We'll get out okay. *After* the job is done. Then you can go screw yourself for all I care."

"It won't work."

"Fredericks, nobody's going to risk the kid's life or hers to get us. And nobody's taking that kid away from me. This is the dumbest job I ever took and I want my dough for it. Anyway, what's your choice? You go back to Canada and tell your boss you blew it, you could be very unpopular."

Silence. Then Carl said, "So where do you think they'd head? The box office?" There was no fear in his voice now, only what could have been resignation.

The crunch of gravel didn't quite muffle Vic's reply. "Makes sense. She'll be looking for a telephone, security guards. That guy with the gun. And I don't think you're right about the cops being here. If they were, we'd know about it by now."

"The kid must have seen me on the tour bus and told her boyfriend who I am."

The voices and footsteps faded away. Penny drew a cautious breath, afraid to give full vent to her relief. A short-lived relief, probably, but any reprieve was welcome. For a few seconds, listening to the men, she'd hoped they would fight and go their separate ways. And known it was a vain hope, born of desperation.

She tried to count off the seconds, but her mind was full of conflicting thoughts. What did Carl mean about her "boyfriend"? Jack Kinkaid? And how did he know about Jack's gun? What had happened at the bridge after she and Rob had jumped?

Where was Jack? He'd promised to stay close but hadn't—he'd let Vic and Carl get at her. She'd trusted him. Had she been wrong? Was he one of Greg's men after all? A bent cop playing both sides?

Rob stirred and broke her stream of racing thoughts. Probably five or six minutes had passed since Vic and Carl left. It might be safe to leave the hut now, but where could they go? Some place crowded with people would be best. Better than being trapped here waiting. And waiting for what? Jack had deserted her and the policemen Koyama had promised probably weren't here either. Had they been playing a cruel game with her?

Penny swallowed. She was being paranoid. It hadn't been a game. But where was everybody?

"Rob?" she whispered.

"Yeah?"

"Stay there for another minute. I'm going to look outside." She squirmed out from under the mats and went to the wall that faced the path. There was nothing to be seen through the cracks except some tourists on the footbridge to Fiji. Cautiously looking out the door, she saw no one near the Hawaiian village. No Vic, no Carl.

"Okay, you can come out. They've gone."

The mats rustled as a grimy Rob wriggled out and stood beside her. She looked down at her dress, still damp and now stained with dust. Her face and hair must be as messy as Rob's, but who cared? They were still alive.

"It was stuffy under there. I almost sneezed," Rob said. "Aunt Penny, I thought the policemen were going to catch those two guys."

"So did I," she said bitterly. "So did I." She put an arm across his shoulders. "Never mind, Rob. I'm sure they will. Right now we have to decide where to go."

"I don't want to stay in here."

"Neither do I. And I think there's supposed to be some sort of show going on around here soon. So we'll have to leave whether we like it or not."

Vic and Carl thought she'd head for the box office. So she'd go in the opposite direction.

"Let's look for the canoe landing at this end," she said. "If Danny's there, he might help us."

Rob followed her into the glare and heat of the afternoon sun. They were facing the footbridge to Fiji, so a right turn should bring them to the landing. She led Rob across the Hawaiian village, stopping in the shadow of a hut on the far side to look for Vic and Carl again. There were more people about now, but no sign of the two men.

A few hundred yards along the path, another footbridge crossed the canal. Take that or go straight on? Penny decided on the footbridge. Half way across, she noticed a canoe disappearing around the bend.

A few moments later they stood on the canoe landing. Her luck was holding; Danny was there, helping his last tourist out of the craft and still cracking jokes.

He grinned. "You been mud-wrestling?"

"Do I look that bad?"

"You're as gorgeous as ever, princess. Want to ride back with me?" He moved closer and lowered his voice. "Did you get rid of those guys?"

"No, they're still around. Did you phone?"

"Yes, but the guy I talked to had never heard of your Lieutenant Koyama."

Perhaps her paranoia was justified. "I guess you'll have to be my knight in shining armor then."

"Okay, I'll bring my spear." He leaned closer, black eyes probing hers. "What kind of trouble are you in, or should I know?"

"If you're going to help, you'd better know what you're up against." She took a deep breath. "Back home Rob was witness to a murder. The guy who did it hired two hit man to kill Rob so he can't testify."

Danny's black eyes widened. "This on the level?" He gave her an intent look. "Okay, I can see it is. What do you want me to do?"

"Tell me where we can hide. I think those two men headed to the box office building. There are supposed to be plainclothes policemen looking for them, but..." She shrugged, at a loss for what to say.

"But nothing's happening, huh?" Danny rubbed his jaw and flashed an automatic smile at the tourists lining up for his canoe. "Okay, you know the Gateway Restaurant?"

"No."

"It's by the first canoe landing, on the other side of the footbridge. Close to the box office, but I can take you in on the opposite side. Friends of mine work in the kitchen. They'll let you stay in there." Danny grinned. "Especially if you offer to wash dishes."

She didn't like the idea of being so close to Vic and Carl, but they'd never look in a restaurant kitchen. "I'll wash dishes forever if I have to."

"Okay, princess, climb in. Keep an eye peeled for your villains and I'll sharpen my spear."

They boarded the canoe, a much easier feat from the dock than it had been from the water. Penny fished a soggy tissue out of her pocket and mopped at her face. She smiled at the incongruity of worrying about how she looked when death was stalking her so closely.

This trip seemed much shorter than their first. Danny entertained his passengers with nonstop stories, puns and comments on the passing scenery.

Penny stared intently at the dock as they approached. But she saw only tourists waiting for a canoe ride, enjoying the sunshine and festive atmosphere.

They got off the canoe last, Danny holding out his hand for Penny. "Follow me, princess. I have to go square it with my boss to take off for ten minutes."

A moment later they were crossing the footbridge that she and Rob had jumped from. It seemed a lifetime ago.

"You'll have to imagine the spear," Danny said. "They wouldn't let me bring it to the university."

The walkway was still crowded and their progress was slow. Near the end of the bridge, Danny pointed right. "See that path? It leads to the back kitchen door."

As Penny turned onto the path and saw the latticework screening the kitchen door, she heard pounding feet on the main thoroughfare and indignant shouts.

She turned toward the noise, terrified.

Carl and Vic were running toward them.

Vic shoved Danny violently off the path and seized Penny by the arm. She knew that the hand tucked inside his loose shirt held a knife or a gun.

"Walk along nice and easy," Vic said. The sneering smile on his lips matched the hate in his eyes. "You know what's going to happen to the kid if you don't."

She knew what was going to happen whether she went quietly or not. It wasn't if, but when.

He forced her toward the main path. Carl, a few feet in front, held Rob by the nape of his neck.

Danny struggled out of the shrubs he'd fallen into and started to follow. Vic snarled, "Get lost, kid. If you want to stay alive. Or I can take you along, too. It's all the same to me."

Danny stood still, a helpless look on his face. His quick tongue was silent now. There was nothing he could do, nothing Penny could say to him.

She looked ahead. They were being taken to the box office building. Then they'd be walked out through the gate, put in a car and taken away to some quiet place. And then...

Penny straightened her shoulders. There was still a chance. There might be policemen guarding the entrance.

They were moving quickly, dodging around knots of tourists, no doubt appearing to be nothing more than a small group in a hurry.

It was cool in the big airy building and relatively quiet, with only a dozen or so tourists scattered around the postcard stands. They'd gone barely thirty feet when Lieutenant Koyama stepped from behind a pillar.

"Stop!" Koyama widened his stance into firing position, his weapon aimed at Vic and Penny.

Three other men appeared, weapons aimed.

Vic yanked Penny to a halt and locked his left arm around her neck, tight under her chin, forcing her head back. She felt the sharp point of his knife at her throat.

"Drop your weapon!" Koyama shouted.

"Screw you!" Vic's voice was loud and harsh in her ear, his breath smelling of stale garlic. "You drop yours or you got two dead pigeons here."

Penny watched Koyama slowly lower his weapon. Was he actually going to let Vic and Carl get away with this?

Vic spoke again, voice harsh with violence barely under control. "We want a clear road out of here. No pursuit. No interference. Twenty-four hours clear. Or the woman and the kid die right now."

"Don't be a fool," Koyama said. "Surrender and you could get off with light terms"

"Tell that to somebody might believe it," Vic rasped.

"And if you get off Oahu?" Koyama asked. "Do I get a guarantee you'll release them unharmed?" From his tone of voice he might have been attending a boardroom meeting instead of being involved in a Mexican standoff with two hit men, bargaining with lives.

"Sure," Vic said. "No sweat. You can have all the guarantees you want. Just so you agree to our terms"

Surely Koyama didn't believe him!

"We can negotiate something," Koyama said.

"Forget negotiation," Vic said. "I told you the terms Give us what we want or you get two dead bodies."

Blind fury overrode Penny's terror. These men saw her as just an object to be bartered with—a disposable pawn in their chess game! Not one of them cared what happened to her and Rob. As for her great protector, Jack Kinkaid—where was he?

Koyama was standing there like a useless wimp. He meant to let Vic walk away! She and Rob would end up in a ditch, their throats cut.

If she was going to die anyway, why not now?

She raised her right arm and speared her elbow deep into Vic's solar plexus.

NINETEEN

Vic gagged, gulping for air. His hold on Penny's throat loosened. She raised her knee and stabbed the sharp end of her heel onto his instep. The cold blade of his knife scraped across her throat as his arm jerked away.

She threw herself to the floor.

The crack of a revolver shot echoed overhead, and something clattered to the floor beside her.

Another shot—a heavy weight dropped on her back, knocking the breath out of her.

Carl shouting, "Don't shoot! Don't shoot!" The thud of running feet. Koyama giving commands. She tried to move but was pinned down by whoever lay across her.

Then the weight was lifted away and she sucked in a long breath. A hand grasped her shoulder and rolled her onto her back. Lieutenant Koyama knelt beside her. He helped her sit up and supported her while she drew in another ragged gasp of breath.

"Are you all right?"

She managed to nod.

When he stood up, she saw what had pinned her to the floor. Three feet away, utterly still, his chest covered in blood. A knife lay beside him.

She looked up at Koyama and he nodded. "Yes, Nelson is dead. It's all over."

A tremor went through her body, then another and another, until she was shaking from head to foot.

A small hand on her shoulder. "Aunt Penny, you were great! Just like Buffy the Vampire Slayer!" Rob looked as cheerful and normal as if he were asking for a cookie.

Thank God he was safe! She pulled him down into her lap, buried her face in his hair and wrapped her arms around him, rocking back and forth.

"You've got more guts than brains, Penny Davis, but I love you anyway." Jack knelt beside her, took his jacket off and draped it tenderly over her shoulders.

She started to giggle. He looked so idiotic in those ill-matched neon-bright clothes, that stupid baseball cap. She laughed until she was gasping for breath and hiccuping.

Jack grasped her shoulders and gave her a little shake. "Stop it! You're getting hysterical."

She dragged in a deep breath and fought for control.

"And where have *you* been all this time?"

He stood up. "Looking for you. I got back just in time to see you being taken into the building."

Rob wriggled off her lap. "Come on, Aunt Penny. You should see what the cops are doing. It's just like on TV."

She rose shakily to a kneeling position. Jack held out his hand and she took it, stumbling to her feet.

"Who shot Vic?" she asked.

"Koyama. He was the only one with a clear shot when you did your nosedive."

"I must thank him." She'd misjudged Koyama, mistaking his quiet formality for weakness. "I thought he'd deserted us. I thought you all had." Her knees went rubbery and Jack seized her as she slumped.

He yelled, "First aid over here!"

A medic sat her down against a wall, examined her and wrapped a blanket around her. "You have mild shock. It will pass. Just sit quietly for a little while."

Shock. Such a tiny little problem. She resisted the urge to start giggling again. So much nicer than a death sentence. Almost pleasant, even. She leaned back against the wall, clutching the blanket, numbly aware of the activity going on around her. Rob sat beside her.

Vic's body on a stretcher, his blood spattered on the floor; Carl, chalk-faced, handcuffed—she looked at them and felt nothing. Shouldn't there be elation, triumph? Others might dance in the streets; she only wanted to sleep.

Rob waved at someone. For the first time she noticed that a crowd had gathered, held back by security guards.

"Princess!"

She turned her head. Danny stood at the edge of the crowd, fifteen feet away, brilliant as a peacock in his orange and red sarong. She managed a smile.

"You put on a great show, princess. You okay?"

"I'm okay, Danny. Just got the shakes, that's all. Thanks for your help."

"I didn't do a thing. Those villains of yours are sure mean suckers."

She nodded.

He was grinning. "You can ride in my canoe any time, princess. You can even bring the kid on our honeymoon."

"That's a deal."

He gave her a jaunty salute and she watched as he disappeared into the crowd. Going back to work. And his university education. And the rest of his life. It hit her suddenly that she too had a future to think about. At the moment, it didn't seem very important.

Rob was watching the police work as intently as he watched his television shows. Would he become a policeman? It didn't matter. At least he now had the chance to grow up and become whatever he wanted to be.

"Rob, are you all right? Did Carl hurt you?"

He turned away from the activity. "Nah. I was pretty scared, but not anymore."

"You had plenty to be scared about."

"Yeah, I guess. But I knew you'd fix those guys." He turned to watch the scene again.

Penny blinked back tears. His faith in her was almost as touching as it was frightening. She'd come close to failing him so many times.

She realized that she was no longer shaking, that she could probably stand up and walk. That what she wanted more than anything was a long, hot shower and twenty-four hours of sleep. That she wanted to go home.

As she got to her feet, Lieutenant Koyama approached.

"I need statements from you and the young man here, but tomorrow morning will be fine. Can you be at the station, say around ten tomorrow?"

"Yes, of course." Tomorrow was Sunday, though, wasn't it? "You don't work tomorrow, do you?"

A rare smile creased the smooth olive planes of his face. "When necessary, Miss Davis. It's the criminals who dictate when we work, not the calendar."

She'd never thought of that. A scene popped into her mind: a half-dozen cops in a major hostage stand-off. No, they couldn't very well knock off at five o'clock and go home. "I guess. Anyway, I want to thank you for—for doing what you did. You saved my life."

His smile vanished. "We do what we have to do."

Jack Kinkaid joined them and she noticed that his face was pale. Why? He'd managed to stay as far from the action as possible all afternoon. Did the sight of blood make him ill? Maybe he should have been an accountant after all.

Koyama spoke to Jack. "See that Miss Davis and the boy get back to the hotel and have everything they need. Then come down to the station." He walked away.

"The lieutenant doesn't seem too happy," Penny said.

"Most cops don't like killing, even when it's filth like Nelson," Jack said. "If you'd been in his place, could you have pulled the trigger?"

"Of course I could! I was terrified of him. And he would have killed Rob."

She saw herself aiming a gun at Vic, pulling the trigger, watching his body jerk as the bullets hit and the blood spurt as he fell. Looking down at his dead body on the ground, knowing she'd been the one to end his life.

"I don't know," she said hesitantly. "I think I could have done it, though. To protect Rob."

"Thank your lucky stars you'll never have to find out. Come on, let's get you home."

He tucked her arm through his, took Rob's hand and walked them across the lobby and out into the parking area. The sky was blue and the sun's heat warmed her face, but it felt distant, as though a thick pane of glass kept her from touching the reality.

"How are we getting back to Honolulu?"

"On the bus that brought the backup team," Jack said and pointed to a small bus parked a few yards away.

She stared at the dents in the side of the vehicle, at the fresh scrapes in the paintwork. "Is that the bus we saw in the accident?"

"Yes. They arrived ten minutes after you and I walked into the Center, an hour later than scheduled."

What if the accident had been worse and they hadn't arrived at all? Supposing only Jack was protecting her? Except that he hadn't been—he hadn't been anywhere around. She felt her knees tremble and clutched his arm.

Jack looked at her and frowned. "You're still shaky. They should have sent you by ambulance."

He helped her down the aisle of the bus, insisted she lie on the bench seat at the back and covered her with the blanket. "You were a real Superwoman in there, but you don't have to be now. Relax. I'm here to look after you."

She'd heard that one before. Last night. Again this morning. It hadn't meant a thing.

Rob slumped down heavily on the seat in front. Jack held her hand. She didn't want him doing that. Or did she? She couldn't seem to make up her mind about anything. She turned her head away and closed her eyes as the bus eased onto the highway. The gentle, rhythmic vibrations of the vehicle were remarkably soothing.

Penny awoke from a frightening dream of men shouting and threatening her with revolvers while she ran and ran and ran but couldn't escape. She opened her eyes to see the tops of buildings sliding by the window. She sat up, the horror of the day flooding back into her mind, and tried to reorient herself.

She was on a bus. In Honolulu, in the heavy traffic of late afternoon. Jack had moved to the seat in front of her and the top of Rob's head was visible beside him. Most of the other seats were occupied by men she supposed were policemen. A low buzz of conversation.

She sat back and rubbed her face. It really was over. They could go back to Vancouver, back to their own lives. Surely the police had found Angela by now and arrested Greg.

But would they keep him in jail? Could they prove anything against him? If not, he'd be released and, as Rob's legal guardian, he'd demand Rob be returned to him.

She wouldn't let that happen. If Angela didn't have the guts to leave Greg, she'd take Rob away somewhere and hide him. It wasn't over yet. Not for Rob.

Penny folded the blanket into a tidy small rectangle. She felt in desperate need of a shower. After that, perhaps they'd go out for a little while, look at things, buy some food, bask in the freedom of doing whatever they wanted without constantly looking over their shoulders.

The bus stopped in front of the Waikiki Princess and she stood up.

Jack rose and turned around. He looked surprised. "You're awake! How do you feel?"

She brushed past him and started down the aisle. "I'm fine now. Truly." Maybe he'd take the hint and go back to the station with the others, leave her alone.

When she stepped onto the sidewalk and reached for Rob's hand, Jack was right beside her.

"I'll go up with you," he said, "just to make sure everything's all right."

"What could be wrong?" she demanded. "The bad guys are taken care of; there's nothing left for you to do."

"I'll see you safely to your room," he said.

"If you insist," she said coldly, and walked into the hotel. She had only one more thing to say to Jack Kinkaid, the last thing she'd ever say to him. It could wait another five minutes.

In the room, her suitcases were still on one of the beds. The other was littered with clothes. Everything was exactly as she'd left it.

Jack stood awkwardly inside the door. He looked puzzled. "You sure you feel okay? Not shaky or cold?"

She turned on him, her pent-up fury erupting.

"Yes, I feel fine. No, I'm not shaky or cold. No thanks to you, of course. Go away. I don't ever want to see you again."

He took a step forward. "But..."

"You fool! You don't even know what you did!"

"Yes, I do, but..."

"Yes, you do," she mimicked. "I'll just bet you do. You promised you'd stay with me. But at the first sign of trouble, you were gone! What happened, Kinkaid? What happened to all your big talk, all your promises?"

"What happened was that..."

"Forget it! I know what happened. You can't keep a promise to someone like me because all your loyalty is for your cop friends. You walked out on me when the going got rough and left me to deal with two killers on my own!"

She felt like crying. Why had she let her guard down with him last night? Why had she let him lull her with sympathetic words, con her into telling him about her father, how she felt about all the harassment? He'd probably tell his buddies and have a good laugh about it.

He stared at her, his face a pale mask. Then he turned to Rob, who looked a little frightened.

"Your aunt seems to be in a bad mood. Since she won't listen to me, I'll tell you what I have to say." He put his hand on the door knob. "Keep an eye on her and if she doesn't seem to have it together, phone the hotel desk and ask them to get a doctor to look at her. Okay? I'll see you at the station tomorrow."

As he opened the door, Penny yanked his jacket off her shoulders and flung it at him. "Take this with you!"

He looked at the crumpled heap by his feet. "Keep it for a souvenir." The door slammed behind him.

Penny snatched up the jacket, ready to fling it into the hall after him. It felt damp in places and crusted in others. She carried it to the window and looked at it in the bright light.

It was soaked in blood.

She dropped it on the floor, feeling nauseated. Vic's blood—from when Jack had helped put him on the stretcher.

Rob said, "Why are you mad at Mr Kinkaid?"

"You wouldn't understand. We'll talk about it later." One more word about Jack Kinkaid and she'd cry.

"I'm going to have a shower. Then it's your turn. Afterwards we're going out, just you and me, and have dinner and maybe go to a movie."

The world seemed brighter and more real when Penny came out of the shower. Twelve hours in bed should get her back to normal, then a visit to the police station and she'd be free to go home. The first thing she'd do there was work on helping her father clear his name.

"Rob, have you still got your mother's rainy-day wallet? I need to borrow some money from it so we can pay for dinner."

He found his jacket in the litter on the bed, unzipped the pocket and handed the wallet to her.

"Into the shower, Rob. It'll make you feel better."

Penny opened the wallet and took the money out. Some hundred dollar bills and a couple of twenties. She put a hundred on the dresser. As she started to tuck the rest of the money back inside, she saw the compartment had a flap that could be lifted up. A little hiding place, she thought, the sort of thing Angela had always liked.

Curiosity won; she lifted the flap. Underneath was a receipt, creased and faded but still legible. She took it over to the lanai door to read it in bright light.

The receipt from Argyle & Henderson Investments in Georgetown, Grand Cayman Island, was made out to Angela Davis. Why not Moller? This must be something to do with Greg. The amount was for $325,000.

Then she saw the date. June. June eleven years ago. When Angela was only thirteen. June, when the bank robbery had taken place.

Penny swayed, put her hand out to brace herself on the door. The receipt could mean only one thing. Her father had been in on the bank robbery. There was no other place he could have got the money. He'd sent his share of it offshore, put it in Angela's name. Maybe her own, too.

She stepped onto the lanai, clutching the receipt in nerveless fingers. Her eyes looked at the surf on Waikiki beach, the green fronds of palm trees lazily responding to the soft breeze. All she could see was her father's face.

She went inside, made her way shakily to the armchair in the corner. He'd come home from the hospital in the wheelchair, had quickly learned to maneuver it, taking possession of his little office again. There had been phone calls, his voice rumbling behind the closed door. The rest of it she could imagine so vividly it seemed almost real. The mail would have brought an envelope from Argyle & Henderson, containing three receipts.

Because that was how his mind worked. He was fair, meticulous. She knew how much money had been stolen. She knew two men had escaped from the bank that day. His share would have been about a million dollars and he would have divided it equally between her mother, Angela and herself.

He'd have opened the envelope, glanced at the contents. Then left the room for a moment or two, perhaps going into the bathroom. Angela, curious as a cat, could have slipped into his den, looked at his desk, seen a receipt made out in her name for all that money, could have taken it.

Had taken it. Had kept it hidden all these years.

Her father would have missed the receipt almost at once. Wondered if anyone had come into the house without his knowledge, then dismissed the idea. Dora was shopping, Penny was at work, Angela at school. He would have thought the investment company had made a mistake, would have phoned asking for the third receipt.

But Angela wasn't at school. She'd been like a cat in other ways at thirteen, stealthy and secretive.

Why had he done it?

Penny put the receipt back in the secret compartment and replaced the wallet in Rob's jacket pocket.

She sat in the chair again, her thoughts roiling. Her father was a thief. He'd been living a lie all these years. Telling lies.

She didn't know him at all. Penny rubbed her hands across her eyes. But that wasn't true. She'd cuddled on his lap when she was small, walked hand in hand with him down the street or on the beach, taken her problems to him. Laughed at his imitations of Red Skelton, of Elvis Presley. Looked at the way his dark blond hair fell over his eyes and felt such a torrent of love she could hardly bear it.

He was a thief and a liar. Why? She could not take it in, could not shift her image of him. He was her father and fathers were good and kind and honest. Especially hers.

Angela had kept his secret. Why? Because she couldn't bear to hurt Dora or Penny, to blow the family apart with grief. Her own grief had been transformed into rebellion and self-destructive acts. Exactly as Rob was doing because of Greg! She hadn't failed Angela; it was her father who had done that.

He wasn't good or honest. He wasn't even kind. All their lives had been twisted because of his stupid, selfish, hypocritical acts. She'd given up drama school for a dull secretarial job so she could help with food and rent. Dora had been a slave to that wheelchair and the man in it for eleven years. Angela...had Angela married for money because of what he'd done?

The past eleven years lay before her like a city destroyed by a tornado. A city to be cleansed by burning anger, then explored and reconstructed to fit the truth.

Did her mother know? Was their romance so strong it could survive that kind of knowledge?

Rob came out of the bathroom, damp, his hair slicked back. "Are we going to eat pretty soon?"

She'd lost interest in food. But he had to be fed and life had to go on.

"Give me five minutes. Then we'll go."

In the bathroom mirror, her face looked drawn and gray. All her life she'd been living in a make-believe world. A world where the people she loved were honest and open and true. A world where she could trust her eyes and ears to give her a true picture.

A world that didn't exist.

TWENTY

Jack leaned against the back wall of the elevator, eyes closed, one hand cupped over the bandage on his side. The wound felt like it was on fire. He needed to get it looked at, but not until he'd dealt with Fredericks.

What in blazes was eating Penny? Nelson was dead, Fredericks and Moller were both in jail. She should be on top of the world. Instead, she'd ripped into him as though he'd been the one holding her hostage. It had to be because she thought he'd deserted her when Fredericks appeared and they'd jumped from the bridge.

He hailed a taxi and got in, the pain in his side stabbing at every bend and twist. Didn't she have more faith in him than that? Especially after last night?

He could see why she found it hard to trust any cop after what had happened to her father. She'd change her mind when she found out her father had been part of the bank robbery. One way or another he'd prove to her that the police were there to protect people.

Lieutenant Koyama was in his office. "Jack, your boss is on the line." Koyama pushed the phone across to him.

"Hello, Ian. I guess Koyama told you Fredericks is in custody and Nelson is dead. Get anything from Moller?"

"He won't give an inch. He's still denying everything. You question Fredericks yet?"

"We're about to start."

"Don't pull any punches. I don't think Moller's going to break so we need Fredericks to spill his guts."

On the way to the interview room, Koyama said, "I charged Fredericks with several offenses, including kidnaping. Most won't hold water, but I wanted to provide all the bargaining power possible."

"What we get will likely depend on how loyal he is to Moller," Jack said. "They go back a long way."

Fredericks was seated at the interview table, his pale eyes expressionless.

Jack introduced himself. "I'm a detective with the Vancouver police department."

That information was a shock, but Fredericks maintained his blank expression. So the whole thing's down the drain, he thought. The drug operation and the Plan. When did the kid talk—in Vancouver? Or here? Not that it mattered.

"Do you wish to call an attorney?" Koyama asked.

"No." He had no intention of spending his hard-earned money to let a shyster complicate his life.

The Vancouver detective turned on the tape machine and recorded the preliminary information for the interview, then asked routine questions about name, age and occupation.

Name, rank and serial number, Fredericks thought. Okay, do I try and bluff it out or not?

"We have reason to believe," Kinkaid said, "that you are involved with an illegal drug distribution business headed by Greg Moller. We also believe that one or both of you were instrumental in the death of Larry Wing."

"I don't know anything about drugs and I never heard of Larry Wing." It was the kid's word against his. They couldn't prove the drug charge unless Greg betrayed him.

"Rob Moller stated that he saw you and Greg Moller last Monday night in an altercation with Larry Wing, which resulted in Wing's death."

"The kid must have been dreaming," Fredericks said. "According to Greg, he's crazy about cops and cop shows. He likely thought up that story to make himself a hero."

"So you're well acquainted with Moller?"

"Sure. He operates a restaurant; I run a restaurant supply business."

"Do you know where Angela Moller is?" Kinkaid asked.

Were they on to that, too? He could feel himself beginning to sweat. "No. Greg told me she walked out on him two, three weeks ago."

The questioning went on for an hour and Fredericks fought to keep his face impassive, calmly denying every allegation. He could see Kinkaid was getting impatient.

A uniformed policeman stuck his head in the door. "Long distance telephone call for Detective Kinkaid."

Jack went out, closing the door behind him. "Thanks," he said to the young policeman, who'd joined him at the coffee machine. "I was hoping we wouldn't have to play games, but Fredericks is being difficult."

Jack drank his coffee and tried to ignore the relentless burning in his side. After ten minutes, he returned to the interview room.

"You can start telling the truth now, Fredericks," Jack said, his smile triumphant. "Moller was arrested yesterday and he's cracked. He says you killed Larry Wing."

Fredericks jerked upright, then forced himself to relax. They were bluffing. Greg was too stubborn, too avaricious, to give in that easy. On the other hand, how much faith could he have in a man who'd kill his own kid?

"You'd better reconsider your position," Kinkaid said. "We can prove the kidnaping charge and that carries heavy penalties in the States. In Canada, we intend to charge you with murder and trafficking in narcotics. Whichever way you look at it, you're going to be in prison for a long time."

Prison. The word was a dead weight in his belly. He'd never been inside, but he'd heard the horror stories from guys who had. Brute violence from the cons and neglect by the screws. His stomach heaved and he had to swallow before he spoke. "What's in it for me if I talk?"

"Talk first," Kinkaid said. "Then we'll see."

"No. I want to cut a deal now." Two could play at the bluffing game, Fredericks thought. I need to get back to Canada. I didn't kill Wing or Angela. So I was Greg's enforcer—big deal! It's the kidnaping charge that'll kill me. And they can make that one stick.

"You willing to go the whole way?" Kinkaid asked.

"I can give you everything you need," Fredericks said. "But I want the kidnaping charge dropped." Nelson was dead; there'd be no comeback there. And Moller, guilty of two murders and the drug trafficking, would be inside until he shriveled up and blew away. If Sam Denton even let him come to trial.

Jack looked at Koyama, who gave an almost imperceptible nod. "I'll do my best, but you'd better give us gold."

"It's gold."

"All right," Jack said, "let's go over the basic facts now and we'll get the details later. Did Moller send you to kill his son?"

"No. That was Nelson's job. All I did was identify the kid for him."

Yeah, right, innocent as a newborn babe, Jack thought. He twisted in his chair and bit back a groan as his wound flashed fire to his nerve ends.

"Tell us about the drug operation."

Fredericks told them. "Moller knew you guys were getting close, but he was too greedy to quit."

By the time Jack got back to the question of Angela Moller, he wanted nothing so much as to lie down and close his eyes. But Fredericks was on a roll and it was no time for intermission.

"Do you know where Angela Moller is?"

"Yeah, I know."

When Fredericks finished his story, Jack sat back, utterly drained. Poor little Rob. Poor Penny. And he was going to have to break the news.

"You ever use a weapon?"

Fredericks shook his head. "No."

"Why not?"

"I don't like violence."

He'd never forget the blood and the pain and the dark, screaming nights of horror when his old man would hammer on him and his mother. No one knew what the sight of violence did to his stomach and his bowels and his muscles. The knowledge of that weakness he would take with him to his grave. It had nothing to do with what the cops wanted.

"Doesn't seem to bother you when other people commit violent acts," Jack said. He shouldn't needle the man; Fredericks' confession would save a lot of time and money and guarantee Moller going down for life. But he was too tired to care what he said.

Fredericks looked at him without expression. "Why should I care what people do or get done to them? The whole human race is a pile of crap." The Plan was down the drain, but he might still pull together enough cash for a less ambitious version. Maybe go north into the bush where land was cheaper, instead of south. Build a fence around it. Never have to talk to anybody again except when he had to buy supplies. Yeah, he might still get there.

Thoughts of Candy took over his mind. She was the only real friend he'd ever had. He imagined her in the kennel, not eating, lying with her head between her paws, waiting for him. How long would she have to wait?

Jack left Koyama to continue the interrogation and went to the lieutenant's office to call Ian again. "It's Jack."

"I know. Who else phones me in the middle of the night? You get anything?"

"Got it all." He gave Ian the key points of Fredericks' confession and, when he was finished, heard Ian let out a long satisfied sigh.

"You done good, my son. When do I get the details?"

"Koyama's still questioning Fredericks. The tape will be transcribed when he's through and we'll fax a copy in the morning."

"I didn't think Fredericks would break so fast."

"The man's got his own agenda. Tell you about it when I get back."

"When will that be?"

"Day after tomorrow. I'm bringing Penny and Rob back with me. Then I'm on for that fishing trip."

"Maybe next weekend. Unless we get another murder before then. Which is likely to happen, with my luck."

A uniformed policeman drove him to the hospital, where a doctor stitched his wound, gave him antibiotics and sedatives and said, "Get some rest. And don't move any more than you can help." It was nearly midnight when he got back to his room at the Pacific Princess.

He was almost asleep when a fragment of memory drifting through his mind brought him wide awake.

He'd said to Penny, "I love you."

It wasn't possible. How could he be in love with a woman he hadn't known quite a week? Even if it were true, how could he have been such an idiot as to say so?

But he did love her. And he knew her; he'd seen her under the kind of pressure most people would never have to experience. There were no hidden depths to Penny. She showed what she felt and said what she thought. And he wanted, more than anything, to have her in his arms again.

He wouldn't do it, though. With her effect on him, he'd be apt to blurt out, "Will you marry me?" And if she said yes, he'd be sentencing her to a lifetime of sleepless nights while he was out on a job. Or to early widowhood. He couldn't ask her to live like that.

"She wouldn't have you, anyway," he muttered. She didn't like cops. Plus she was furious with him because he hadn't swooped in wearing his Superman cape to rescue her when the hit men had made their first move.

They wouldn't have killed her and Rob inside the Center grounds, anyway. Too many witnesses, too many people to impede their escape. That's why Koyama had posted all his available men at the entrance when he knew that the rest of the crew would be late.

Why in blazes should he care what she thought? After Monday they'd never see each other again. If she spent the rest of her life thinking he'd deserted her, so what?

No, he couldn't leave it like that. He had to make her understand what had happened, that he'd done the best he could. He deserved that much. So did all cops.

She'd refused to listen to him at the hotel but, in Koyama's office tomorrow, she couldn't stop him telling her the score. She couldn't walk away from him there.

She had to understand that cops were fallible, just like everybody else. And that no matter how well you planned, you could be zapped by an unforeseen event.

Had she come on to him because she liked him or because she'd been frightened? More likely the latter. Eventually she'd find a guy to love who'd give her a good life.

The thought of her with another man made Jack squirm and the gash in his side protested with a jab of agony. He got up and washed down two painkillers with a glass of water.

TWENTY-ONE

Penny frowned at her reflection as she swept her hair up into a knot at the back. Why bother looking elegant for a trip to the police station? Was she trying to impress Jack Kinkaid? Forget it! As for Lieutenant Koyama, he probably wouldn't blink if she walked in stark naked.

What was it Kinkaid had said yesterday? That she had more guts than brains but he loved her anyway?

"Rubbish!" she said to the mirror. He hadn't meant it, of course. It was just the way some people had of talking, saying they loved bananas or a movie.

As for having guts, she and Rob might be dead now if she hadn't taken matters into her own hands. When you were a hostage, negotiation seemed futile.

After what she'd said last night, Jack wouldn't want to talk to her again. Not that she cared. Nobody needed a man that disappeared when the going got rough.

He'd seemed strong and caring, somebody she could love and trust. It had felt like they belonged together and she'd wanted him with an intensity that surprised her. But he didn't measure up. So why did that persistent inner voice urge her to give him a chance?

Penny gave her hair one last pat and sighed. The hair style didn't mask the weariness in her face. She'd lain awake for hours, thinking about her father.

The knowledge of his crime hurt and she would be angry for a long time. He was also still the companion she'd adored as a child. He must have believed that he had a good reason for committing theft. But what could it have been?

"Aunt Penny, hurry up! Lieutenant Koyama said we were supposed to be there at ten and it's almost ten now."

Rob was funny and endearing when he nagged her like that, as though he were the adult and she the child.

"I'm coming." He'd talked of nothing this morning but seeing a real police station.

"Do you think they'd let me see the cells?"

"I don't know. Why don't you ask Lieutenant Koyama when we're finished making our statements?"

They went by taxi, Penny's mind still in the past. She'd assumed her father was perfect, which was a mistake. Nobody was perfect. She had to quit making assumptions about people because of who they were.

She didn't know how her mother would react to her father's crime. Dora had always put him first. Penny thought, I assumed she loves me because she's my mother. But maybe she doesn't. Or maybe she doesn't know how to show it. It was time she got to know Dora as a person. And accept whatever truths she found.

At the police station, they were led into an interview room by a dark, slim young officer.

"Is this where you grill prisoners?" Rob asked.

"That's right. Are you going to be grilled? What crime did you commit?" The officer was smiling.

"If jaywalking carried a jail sentence he'd probably do it for the excitement of being locked up," Penny said.

"No, I wouldn't! I don't want to be locked up; I want to put criminals inside."

Koyama and Jack joined them a few moments later. Jack looked as tired as she felt, but at ease in ordinary faded jeans and a T-shirt. Except for a brief greeting, he lounged back in a chair, his expression bland. No doubt he was angry with her for shouting at him last night.

He was still silent after she and Rob gave a detailed account of their experiences with Nelson and Fredericks. "What I'm afraid of now," she said, "is that Greg Moller will get out of prison and come after Rob again."

"That's unlikely, Miss Davis. Fredericks confessed last night, naming Moller as Larry Wing's killer and also as head of the drug operation."

The relief left her limp. "Has Angela been found?"

"I'll let Jack tell you about that. It will take some time for the transcription to be completed, Miss Davis. Can you return late this afternoon to read it over and sign it?"

She nodded.

Koyama turned to Rob. "Your aunt says you want to be a policeman when you grow up. Is that correct?"

Rob's face brightened. "Yeah. Aunt Penny said I could ask to look at the cells. Can I?"

"Certainly." Koyama looked at Penny. "May I keep him here until you return? We'll see that he's fed and given the grand tour."

"All right!" Rob said. "Wait till I get home and tell Simon about this."

She couldn't speak. It seemed obvious that what Jack had to tell her was something they didn't want Rob to hear.

Jack was still silent as he steered the car out into the traffic. He seemed to have walled himself off from her.

"I'm sorry I was awful to you last night," she said.

He gave her a quick glance. "It's all right. You were tired and upset." He lapsed into silence again.

"What is it you want to tell me?"

He didn't answer and she said, "You look as though you need to sleep for a couple of days."

"I guess. It's all part of the game, though."

Were the scar on his temple and his broken nose part of the game? Why did she want to touch him and feel his arms around her, after the way he'd betrayed her? Now her emotions were betraying her.

Jack parked the car beside Kapiolani Park, near the aquarium, and led her to a bench under a monkeypod tree. He rested his arm along the back of the bench. On the beach, breakers curled over the sand.

"I have something to tell you that's going to hurt." His eyes were shadowed. His arm moved to her shoulders.

"It's about Angela, isn't it?"

"Yes. She's dead, Penny."

She'd known that's what he was going to say. Even so, the pain gripped her heart and squeezed, spread through her body. She drew a shuddering breath, buried her face in his shoulder and let the tears come. She felt him stiffen, then relax as he put his arms around her and held her close.

Her baby sister was gone. Gone and never coming back.

She cried herself out while Jack soothed her back with his hands, resting his cheek against the top of her head. When she finally pulled away from him and reached for a tissue, she could feel her hair sliding out of its knot.

"Do you have a hairbrush in your bag?"

She handed him the brush and, while she mopped her face, he pulled the pins from her hair and brushed it with long, gentle strokes. When she felt that she could speak, she took the brush from him and put it away.

"I knew it," she said. "I knew she must be dead but I didn't want to face it. It was the only thing that would have kept her from taking Rob with her. How? When?"

"Greg beat her to death three weeks ago, according to Fredericks. He helped Moller dispose of her body. A search team went out before dawn this morning and found her."

Penny clenched her fists against Jack's chest. "Why did he do it? Why? If he wanted to get rid of her, all he had to do was get a divorce."

"Fredericks thinks it was accidental. That he must have lost control." Jack brushed his fingers over the nape of her neck. "What's going to happen to Rob?"

"I don't know. He adored her; they were never apart. How am I going to tell him he'll never see her again?"

He tightened his grip on her hand. "You'll manage. You're good with him. He may be tougher than you think."

"I'll have to do it right away. Now that Greg's in jail, Rob will be eager to get home to his mother. I can't let him build up his hopes and then smash them." She'd have to tell him about his grandfather, too. But not today. Not until she absolutely had to do it.

"Let him have his afternoon of fun first." Jack got to his feet. "What would you like to do now?"

"Walk. Along the beach."

In front of the aquarium he stopped. "Will you wait for me? I need to go in here for just a minute.

She let go his hand. "I'll be on the beach."

"I'll find you."

She watched him disappear from sight. She was cold without his arms around her.

At four, Jack drove her back to the station to sign the statement. The sight of Rob, exuberant after hours of imagining he was part of the police force, nearly brought the tears back.

"Thank you for doing this," she said to Koyama. "He'll remember it for a long time."

"He's a bright boy. He'll make a fine officer." He took her hand. "Good luck."

When there was a break in Rob's chatter about his afternoon, she said, "Jack's taking us back to the hotel to pack. We're flying home tomorrow."

"Cool!" The joy in his face was replaced by a sober thoughtfulness. Did he know? Could he sense her grief?

At the hotel, Jack said, "I'll come up with you."

"No. Thanks for the offer, though."

"See you on the plane tomorrow morning then." He walked slowly across the lobby and out the main doors.

Upstairs, she sat Rob down in the easy chair. "Jack told me some really bad news this afternoon."

He paled and went very still, looking up at her. He knows, she thought, he knows what I'm going to say, just as I knew before Jack told me.

She told him, holding nothing back. His face crumpled and he wailed into her shoulder while she held him tight, tears running down her own face. When his tears stopped, he went into the bathroom to wash his face.

She was emotionally drained, but there were suitcases to pack. She was reaching for something bunched up under a chair when Rob came out.

"That's Jack's coat," he said. "The one he was wearing yesterday."

"I'll throw it out. I'm sure he won't want it."

"Can I have it?"

She stared at him. "What on earth do you want it for? It's got Vic's blood all over it."

"That's not Vic's blood. It's Jack's."

"What are you talking about?"

"Jack got knifed yesterday."

"Who told you that?" It couldn't be true or Jack would have said something.

"Lieutenant Koyama told me all about it this afternoon. Remember when we were on the bridge and you saw Carl?"

She nodded.

"Well, Jack saw him, too, right after we jumped, and he pulled his gun and he was going to shoot Carl. But Vic stuck his knife in

Jack's side. Lieutenant Koyama said if a tourist hadn't bumped into Jack right that minute, he'd have been killed."

And she'd thought Jack had run away! She slumped into the chair, and buried her face in the jacket. She'd done it again. Been too quick to make assumptions and so sure she was right that she hadn't given him a chance to tell her the true story.

TWENTY-TWO

Six a.m. Penny's eyes burned from lack of sleep and too many tears. She'd lain awake most of the night, her mind a jumble of memories.

It would be midmorning in Vancouver. Penny dialed her parents' number.

"Hello?" Her mother's voice was faint.

"It's Penny. Rob and I are coming home today. How's Dad?"

"Not good. He's in the hospital."

Dread filled her. "What happened?"

A long pause. "He's ill, Penny. So ill he may never have to go to trial. It's multiple sclerosis."

"But..."

"I'd better tell you about the letter." Dora's voice was stronger now. "He left each of us a letter to be read after his death. When I saw him yesterday he told me where they were and I've read mine."

"When did he write the letters?" But she knew. Eleven years ago, after the bank robbery.

"He says he was diagnosed almost twelve years ago and decided to keep it a secret. He helped rob the bank as a way of providing for Angela and you and me." Dora's voice broke. "He asked us to forgive him."

"I knew there had to be a reason for what he did." She remembered how tired he used to be after work, remembered his words being slurred sometimes and thinking he'd had too much wine to drink at dinner. "I don't think I'll ever forgive him, though."

"I have," her mother said, "but it wasn't easy. I trusted him to share everything with me and he didn't."

"Is he still going to be charged for the robbery?"

"Of course. They have to do that, Penny."

"Even though the bank will get back all of his share of the money?"

"He committed a crime. It doesn't matter whether he gained anything by it. That's what the lawyer says."

He'd lost everything and spent eleven years putting on a front, manipulating three women who loved him. Dora would go on loving him. Penny wasn't sure she could. He'd used her, lied to her. He was a stranger.

"Mom? You know about Angela?"

"A policewoman came and told me. I can't believe Greg did that to her. I guess I can't believe any of it yet. There have been too many shocks in the last few days."

Did anyone tell her mother about Greg trying to kill her grandson? If not, she'd do it herself. Not now, though.

"Your father and I must decide what to do about Rob."

"Yes," Penny said. But she had already decided.

At seven, room service delivered a thermos of coffee and a glass of milk. Penny took her coffee out on the lanai where Rob was talking to the white pigeons.

"Would you like some milk?"

"I'm not thirsty. When can we go?"

"The limo's due at eight. Not long now."

He walked back and forth, running his hand along the top of the railing. "I wish eight o'clock would hurry up. I want to go home and see Simon and tell him about those guys and how we got away."

His friend Simon was the only security blanket he had now, except for her and his grandparents. She wondered if 'home' meant Greg's big house.

"Where am I going to live, Aunt Penny?"

"With me. Unless you'd rather stay with Gramma."

He shook his head and said firmly, "With you."

"Well, that's settled, then."

She looked at the surf frothing over Waikiki beach and the palm trees at its edge. Paradise of the Pacific, some people called this island. Someday she might be able to think of it that way.

Would Rob be happy living with her? The decision to adopt him had arrived, without conscious volition, sometime during the night. Surprised, she'd argued with herself. She knew nothing about raising kids. She didn't have a job. There were dozens of reasons why it wouldn't work.

The decision had remained firm. There'd be some bad times ahead, for both of them, but she loved him. It would take some time for him to feel secure again, to finish grieving for his mother. She had her own grieving to do. But they'd make it, one way or another.

The airport limo was nearly full. Penny led Rob to the back. It didn't matter anymore if they were first or last off the bus; no one was stalking them now.

At the next stop, the last seat was taken by a slender, stunning woman wearing an exquisite cream linen suit. Her eyelashes were long and thick, her nails long and scarlet. An actress or a model, Penny thought.

Darn! She was doing it again.

"Rob, see the woman who just sat down?" Penny said in a low voice. "What do you think she does for a living?"

He gazed at the woman's feet and ankles, poised gracefully in the aisle. "I bet she raises cats. You know, those skinny ones. Siamese."

"What makes you think so?"

"Well, she's got scratches on her ankles."

Penny squinted. Sure enough, scratches. This could turn out to be fun.

"Good! What about that dark man with the navy blue suit and the briefcase? A salesman?"

"He looks like Godzilla. That's the kind of suit he wears." Rob's thumb went to his mouth. He looked at it, then put his hand back in his lap.

"That doesn't mean he's like Greg, though."

"No, but I'd want to find out before I talked to him. Aunt Penny, what about the fat lady near the front? The one with the print dress and the shopping bag."

"I'd say she was a housewife. What do you say?"

"An actress. I saw somebody just like her in a TV movie. Or maybe she's a chef in a big hotel."

"She might be a writer," Penny said. "She's got a notebook on her lap and she's writing in it."

"Okay, what about the bus driver? Is he really a bus driver or is he a cop working undercover?"

Denton put the phone down and went to the window to look at his favorite view of Seattle. Elliot Bay and the high rises gleamed misty gray in the teeming rain.

So Moller had got himself arrested. Not surprising. He was a fool. Too much of a fool to be trusted to keep his mouth shut.

Denton went to the phone. "Len, I want you to take care of someone for me. Come to my office now."

Too bad Nelson was dead. But Len was a better man for this job. Moller would be found hanging in his cell. A suicide, of course.

The runway fell away beneath and the jet climbed steadily into the morning sun. Rob sat by the window, Penny in the middle, Jack beside her on the aisle seat.

Penny glanced at Jack. She had to apologize for insulting him. She'd never given him a chance to explain what had happened at the Polynesian Cultural Center.

The flight attendant arrived with a smile and three glasses of orange juice. "I don't want any," Rob said. He'd become quiet the moment they were on the plane and heading home. The next few months would be rough for him, learning that home no longer meant Angela.

"I'd like coffee as fast as it's humanly possible," Jack said. No silly costumes today; he was wearing slacks and a polo shirt and looked rested but somber.

The plane leveled out, flying into a clear sky. Rob touched Penny's hand. "Do I have to go back to our house?"

"Not if you don't want to. I can collect your things and bring them to the apartment."

He considered this. "Is that other bedroom in your place going to be mine?"

"Of course. We'll do it up however you want."

"Okay. Maybe I will go to the house with you. There's a picture of Mom I want."

"Whatever you decide, Rob."

Breakfast came. Penny arranged seat trays, opened packets and tried not to bump anyone with her elbows.

"How's your knife wound?" she said to Jack.

He raised his eyebrows. "How did you know about that?"

"Rob told me. You risked your life for us and I want you to know how grateful I am. And how rotten I feel for thinking that you deserted us."

"All part of the game, like I said yesterday." He stirred sugar into his coffee. "If I hadn't been delayed by the crowds, the story would have been different."

"Did you see the whole scene in the lobby?"

"I was there—behind a pillar with my weapon aimed at Nelson's head. I'd have got him, but you were in the way."

"Why didn't you tell me you'd been hurt?"

He shrugged. "When Ian told me yesterday about your sister, I figured my scars weren't too important."

When the remains of the meal had been removed, Rob said, "Jack? Will Greg get out on bail?"

"I don't think it's likely. Not with such serious charges against him."

"What about parole?"

"Not for many years," Jack said. "By the time he sees light of day again, you'll be grown up."

"I'm gonna be a policeman for sure," Rob said. "Then Godzilla will be afraid of me."

"We'll start saving for police college when I get a job," Penny said.

"I thought you didn't like policemen, Aunt Penny."

"I didn't. But I've changed my mind."

"That's good." Rob turned back to the window.

"I think so, too," Jack said softly. He rummaged inside his camera bag, producing a box wrapped in shiny silver paper. "A present for you."

She took it, surprised and pleased. "Why?"

"Just because."

Puzzled, she ripped off the wrapping, opened the lid and reached into the crumpled tissue paper.

It was the monkeypod dolphin from the aquarium gift shop. She held the smooth, satiny wood against her skin, rejoicing in the graceful curves, the freedom and confidence of the leaping animal.

"How did you know how much I loved this carving?"

"I was watching you, remember? Your face said it all."

She kissed him on the cheek. "Thank you."

"You're welcome. Regard it as a memento of a very exciting tour of Hawaii. A wild and crazy adventure."

"Exciting, no; terrifying, yes." She'd been looking for adventure when she set off to Toronto. This past week had given her more than enough for a lifetime. And something else, too.

"Jack, why did you say you loved me?"

He glanced at her, then turned his head away. "Because it's true."

"Will you say it to me again?"

"No. The last thing you need is to be involved with a cop. A woman shouldn't have to accept that kind of risk."

"Don't you think I'm qualified to decide what risks I want to take? I'm not afraid."

"I know you're not," he said. "You can handle anything that comes down the pike; you proved that this week. But this is different."

"No, it's not. Look, I didn't have to accept the risk of being bait for Nelson and Fredericks, did I? I could have backed out; you said you'd provide a new identity for me. Isn't that right?"

"Right," he said cautiously.

"You can't keep people safe by making their decisions for them. It's my right to choose what risks I take. Hang loose, Jack. You just told me I can handle anything."

He sat silent for so long she was afraid he was going to sidestep the issue completely. How could she convince him that sharing his life even for just a short time was worth any risk involved? That having some happiness to remember was better than having none at all?

At last he turned to her with a smile that made her feel warm all over. "I think we could give it a try."

"Are you asking me to marry you?"

"I'm asking you for a date. I'm a pretty cautious guy, you know. I'd like a chance to enjoy the usual rituals. And a chance to find out if you really mean what you say about taking risks."

And she needed time to find out if what she saw in Jack was real—or if there were hidden shoals.

"Have anything in mind?"

"Want to go fishing next weekend?"

"Do I have to cook bacon and eggs over a campfire? Learn to clean fish?"

"Yep."

"Okay."

Jack reached over and nudged Rob. "Want to go fishing next weekend with your aunt and me?"

"For real?" Rob's face lit up.

"For real."

"All right! I've never been fishing."

Penny leaned her head against Jack's shoulder and felt contentment as his arm circled her waist.

"Jack, I have to ask you an important question."

She could feel his arm tense. His expression was apprehensive.

"Do you like your eggs over easy or sunny side up?"

His arm relaxed. "Over easy. And no smart remarks until I've had at least one cup of coffee."

Other Titles from Electric eBook Publishing:

* Lady Blue by Judy Bagshaw (Romantic Suspense); $13.95 USA / $18.95 Canada
* Strangers Call in Moonlight by George WJ Laidlaw (Romantic Suspense); $13.95 USA / $18.95 Canada
* Ms. Magenta by Carla Mobley (Poetry Anthology); $12.95 USA / $17.95 Canada
* More Baseball Trivia: A Triple Play by Bob Alley (Sports Trivia); $12.95 USA / $17.95 Canada
* Paranoid Schizophrenic by Daniel Martinez (Psychological Thriller); $13.95 USA / $18.95 Canada
* Tour Into Danger by Lea Tassie (Romantic Suspense); $13.95 USA / $18.95 Canada
* Rescued Heart by Vanessa Kay (Historical Romance); $13.95 USA / $18.95 Canada
* The Willow Tree Girl by Joanna M. Weston (Middle Reader); $12.95 USA / $17.95 Canada
* Shannon Holmes, Private Detective by Barbara Saffer (Middle Reader); $12.95 USA / $17.95 Canada
* The Face Behind the Window by Adriana deRoos (Young Adult Historical Fiction); $13.95 USA / $18.95 Canada
* Escape by Brian T. Seifrit (Action / Adventure); $13.95 USA / $18.95 Canada
* Mr. Hate by Terry Vinson (Thriller); $14.95 USA / $19.95 Canada
* Indigo Dreams by Shannon Mobley (Young Adult Fiction); $12.95 USA / $17.95 Canada

Order Form

Title	Qty.	Price

Name _____

Address _____

_____

Phone _____

Method of Payment   ☐ Check   ☐ Money Order

Order _____

Tax: _____

All prices include shipping; Canadian residents required to pay applicable taxes.

Total: _____

Electric eBook Publishing
PO Box 211
4812 Joyce Avenue
Powell River, BC CANADA V8A 4R0
Phone: 1-877-483-9614 Fax: 1-877-483-9615
Email: sales@electricebookpublishing.com
Order online at: http://www.electricebookpublishing.com